# IN THE LONDON LION'S DEN

Though still young in years, Lady Lucinda Mays thought that her status as a widow would grant her safety from the London marriage mart.

But she did not reckon with the web woven ever more tightly by her wickedly worldly cousin, who needed her fortune to save his skin . . . or with the insidiously irresistible aid offered to her by a smiling stranger who refused to tell her why . . . or with the dazzling attentions of an elegant lord who reminded her all too much of the man who had so grievously betrayed her . . . or with the power that the gentleman, in whose mansion she now lived, began to exercise over her.

In a London where words of love so easily could be lies and men could mock the most sacred vows, Lucinda had to learn to use not only her wits but her teeth and claws if she did not want to be a lamb waiting to be devoured. . . .

# Love
# for
# Lucinda

by

## Gayle Buck

A SIGNET BOOK

SIGNET
Published by the Penguin Group
Penguin Books USA Inc., 375 Hudson Street,
New York, New York 10014, U.S.A.
Penguin Books Ltd, 27 Wrights Lane,
London W8 5TZ, England
Penguin Books Australia Ltd, Ringwood,
Victoria, Australia
Penguin Books Canada Ltd, 10 Alcorn Avenue,
Toronto, Ontario, Canada M4V 3B2
Penguin Books (N.Z.) Ltd, 182–190 Wairau Road,
Auckland 10, New Zealand

Penguin Books Ltd, Registered Offices:
Harmondsworth, Middlesex, England

First published by Signet, an imprint of Dutton Signet,
a division of Penguin Books USA Inc.

First Printing, January, 1996
10  9  8  7  6  5  4  3  2  1

# Chapter One

It was early morning. The winter sun slanted through the chilled panes of the windows. The gloom was not entirely dispelled in the bedroom, and a bunch of candles burned for additional illumination. The fire crackled on the hearth and kept the chill at bay.

A maid fussed briefly over the day dress that was laid carefully on top of the bed coverlet. She kept one eye upon her mistress, watching her pace slowly back and forth across the carpet. There was only the soft rustle of her lady's heavy skirt to break the expectant silence.

The mantle clock struck the hour. It was the sound for which her lady had been waiting.

Lady Lucinda Mays turned and looked into the cheval glass. Her examination of herself was critical. She saw the same lovely countenance, set with the same wide blue eyes and the full, rather sensuous mouth. She looked much as she had at eighteen. But instead of a gay riband threaded through her hair, her head was covered with a delicate lace cap tied with gray ribbons. Instead of being attired in a pale elegant muslin, her neat figure was arrayed in a subdued dove-gray day dress. The gown was cut close to the throat and had full-length sleeves. A black-edged handkerchief was tucked inside one laced cuff.

With a deliberate movement, Lucinda reached up to remove the confining lace that covered her wavy dark hair. She flung down the hated cap and turned away from the mirror.

Madison, her dresser, stood waiting with her hands clasped in quiet anticipation. The woman stood beside the bed, upon which was lying a day dress of bright robin's egg blue.

"One year to the day, Madison," said Lucinda quietly. A smile quivered upon her lips. "Pray get me out of this ugly gown. I hope never to wear mourning again!"

"Yes, my lady, and with pleasure," said the maid.

Within minutes Lucinda had been divested of the despised mourning gown and was reattired in the blue day dress. She turned again to look at herself in the cheval glass. A smile curved her lips. The transformation was complete. A bubble of joy swelled up inside her. She laughed for the sheer pleasure of the moment.

Lucinda turned to her dresser. Her brilliant blue eyes were dancing. "I am free at last. Give the orders, Madison. We are going to London. I wish to leave first thing after breakfast tomorrow." She picked up a paisley shawl and arranged it about her shoulders before she swept across the room to the door.

"Yes, my lady!" Madison hurried to open the bedroom door for her mistress. As Lady Mays exited, the dresser stood to watch her stepping briskly down the hallway. The dresser smiled and softly closed the door.

Lucinda came to the head of the stairway and started down. Halfway down the stairs she paused. She took a fortifying breath.

Her father would be in the breakfast room, waiting for her. He had arrived unexpectedly three days before. Lucinda had been dismayed that he had chosen this particular time to pay her one of his paternal visits, but it could not be helped.

Lucinda had said nothing to Sir Thomas of her plans. It was perhaps unfortunate that he had delayed in his departure from her home. She had given only a passing thought to setting aside those same plans until her father had left. It would have been cowardly to wait, only to spare herself what could possibly be a distressing scene. Yet now, on the verge of the telling moment, she felt a flutter of trepidation.

Lucinda straightened her shoulders. She had vowed to herself that when this day dawned, she would claim back her life and so she would. She had already begun by putting off the detested mourning, thus symbolically cutting once and for all the bonds that had been placed upon her when she had wed three years before. Answering her father's inevitable questions would be a good test of her fortitude.

Lucinda traversed the remainder of the stairs and crossed the hall. She entered the breakfast room. No matter what time her father arose, it was Sir Thomas's unchanging custom to delay his own meal until there was someone to share the breakfast table with him. He disliked being left to his own company at any time, but especially in the quiet of the morning. Lucinda had often wondered about that particular quirk of her father's. He had always seemed to have a distaste for solitude, and it was incomprehensible to him that others should feel otherwise.

Sir Thomas was already seated at the table when Lucinda entered. She advanced with outstretched hands. "Papa."

Sir Thomas Stassart looked up, smiling, as he rose from the table. But his genial expression swiftly faded upon catching sight of his daughter. He received Lucinda's filial salute upon his cheek with total disregard. "Daughter! What is this? You have put off your mourning!"

"Yes; do you not agree that this blue suits me, Papa?" asked Lucinda calmly, disengaging herself and moving away to seat herself opposite her father at the table.

The footman in attendance seated her. She thanked him with a brief nod and a smile before she turned again to her stunned parent. "Did you sleep well, Papa? I do trust that Pottsby has served your morning coffee just as you like it?"

"Never mind my coffee or how I spent the night, Lucinda," said Sir Thomas testily, returning to his chair. He was a short, portly gentleman, and just then he resembled nothing so much as a ruffled pheasant in his brown coat and striped waistcoat. "I wish to know what maggot you have gotten into your brain."

Lucinda arched perfectly formed brows. A lift of amusement marked her lips. She chose to be deliberately obtuse. "I fail to understand you, Papa." She nodded to the footman to serve her a portion of eggs and kidneys. "Yes, please. And the toast and marmalade. Thank you."

Sir Thomas waited only until the footman had stepped back from the table before he exclaimed, "This gown, Lucinda! What means it?" He waved a comprehensive hand at his daughter's elegant attire.

"You do not care for it, Papa? I am disappointed. I was certain that it was all the crack. I think it rather becoming, actually," said Lucinda, putting marmalade on her toast.

"You well know that it is not your fashion sense that I question," said Sir Thomas, feeling goaded. "Do not play the clothhead with me, Lucinda. I am referring to the putting off of your mourning. Why, Lord Mays was laid in his tomb scarcely a year ago and—"

"I beg your pardon, Papa, but I must correct you. Lord Mays expired on this day one year and"—Lucinda glanced at the mantle clock and continued—"a half hour past. Or so I was informed."

There was a muffled choke at the sideboard, quickly covered by a rattle of cutlery. The butler bent a censorious glance upon his subordinate. However, he, too, was suddenly smitten with a sudden industriousness with the side dishes so that he could bend his ear. The conversation at the table had taken an interesting turn.

Lucinda and Sir Thomas took no notice of the servants. She did not care what was overheard, for her position was no secret. As for her father, he was at that moment so overcome that he scarcely recalled his surroundings. All of his startled attention was riveted upon his daughter.

"Lucinda, your attitude is preposterous!" said Sir Thomas.

Lucinda said coolly, "On the contrary. My obligatory period of mourning was ended some minutes ago. I have therefore put off my widow's weeds."

"Lucinda! Of all the outrageous—"

She held up her hand at the expression upon her parent's face. Very quietly, she warned, "I will brook no censor, Papa, even from you."

Sir Thomas was taken aback. He looked narrowly at his daughter. As he recollected that she was no longer a young miss dependent upon him, he thought better of what he had been about to say. He cleared his throat. "No one knows better than I, unless it is perhaps your mother, how difficult has been your position, Lucinda. You have borne your exile here at Carbarry with admirable fortitude. It was very bad of Mays to banish you in the manner that he did, especially in light of his . . ." Sir Thomas stumbled, a dull flush coming into his

face. One did not discuss such things with one's daughter even
though she had been a married woman. "But I shall say nothing of that, for I would spare you pain."

Sir Thomas's daughter was not so nice in her sensibilities.
"You are referring to my husband's paramours," said Lucinda
flatly.

There was another rattling as the footman dropped a lid.
The butler shot such a sulfurous look at the man that he
blanched. This time, just as the butler had feared, the noise
was noticed. Sir Thomas suddenly became aware of their audi-
ence. "Daughter!" Sir Thomas rolled his eyes in the direction
of the servants. Repressively, he said, "Perhaps we should discuss this between us at a more opportune time."

At her father's unmistakable signal, Lucinda shrugged with
indifference. "It is scarcely a secret, Papa. How could it be?
Lord Mays had his train of mistresses before he ever acquired
me. He retained them instead of me when the novelty of
parading a wife palled."

Sir Thomas forgot the presence of the servants. "Lucinda,
surely you exaggerate. No man in his right mind rids himself
of a wife because he is bored!" he exclaimed.

"Believe me, I was not long in stumbling onto the realization that my sole value to Lord Mays was founded upon my
reputation as a touted beauty," said Lucinda with a tiny smile.
She gestured expressively. "It was considered the coup of the
Season when Lord Mays carried me off to the altar. Once the
acquisition was made, of course, the other contenders took
only a waning interest in the prize. Lord Mays soon found
himself possessed of a beautiful, well-bred wife, and no one
cared anymore."

"This bitterness ill becomes you, Lucinda," reproved Sir
Thomas, though feeling a stir of distress. She was his daughter, after all. It disturbed him that she had suffered such an in-
dignity as she was declaring.

"Am I bitter?" Lucinda thought about it a moment. She
shrugged a little. "Perhaps I am. Yet I am grateful for one
thing. I am grateful that Lord Mays did banish me just seven
months after we were wed, for I found it increasingly intolera-
ble to put up a smiling front. It saved my sanity, I think, to

come to Carbarry. And though I was naturally sorry to hear that Lord Mays was dead, I will freely admit to you, Papa, that I was also rather relieved. The farce was at last played out after three long years."

"Lucinda!" Sir Thomas smashed his fist down onto the table. The cutlery jumped. His distress had given way to horror at his daughter's seeming callousness. There was obviously much more that he wished to say, but his feelings overcame him. He seemed at a loss for words, his mouth opening and closing.

In the excess of his emotion, Sir Thomas had forgotten that they were not alone in the breakfast room. Lucinda had not, however, and she realized that the butler and footman were now unashamedly listening. Lucinda saw how overwrought was her parent, and she thought it prudent to draw a measure of privacy over the rest of the conversation. She dismissed the servants with a gesture, and with visible reluctance they exited.

Scarcely before the serving door had closed, Sir Thomas burst out, "I forbid you to speak anymore in this disrespectful and erratic vein. When I recall how Lord Mays provided everything—everything!—that you could possibly desire!"

"Jewels and gowns and fripperies to make the envious stare and the rest of society to convey their compliments on how well I reflected honor upon his lordship. My portrait painted by the most expensive artist that one could afford. Oh yes, and let us not forget the loneliness and tears and the daunting prospect of living out the remainder of my life in such a sad fashion," said Lucinda. She sighed and shook her head. "You are quite wrong, Papa."

"How can you talk so? Why, any woman alive would have been eager to have had all that you were given," protested Sir Thomas.

Summoning up a little smile, she said quietly, "No, Papa, I do not believe so. I was given nothing that I desired. With the marriage settlements, Lord Mays gave you and Mama everything that *you* desired."

At this home shot, Sir Thomas's florid face reddened. "You were not unwilling to wed Lord Mays, as I recall. Your mother and I—we would not ever have forced you into a marriage that you found repugnant. Why, Lord Mays embodied all that one could hope for one's daughter—wealth and position and birth. His . . . his predilection for sordid feminine company was unfortunate, of course, but we were confident that once you were wed that *that* would be a thing of the past."

"Yes, so Mama explained to me. But it did not prove to be so."

"No, it did not." Sir Thomas sighed heavily. His daughter's expression became amused, and he realized suddenly that he was beginning to tread dangerous ground. He instantly reiterated his strongest point. "You were not an unwilling bride, Lucinda. You, too, saw all the advantages of the match!"

"I was a dutiful daughter," Lucinda agreed. She smiled at her afflicted father. "Pray do not misunderstand me, Papa. I do not blame you or Mama. I had every expectation of finding happiness with Lord Mays. I meant to be a good wife to him so that in time he would come to have affection for me. However, it was simply not to be. Now I am free of my unhappy state. Pray do not grudge me my happy content that it is so."

Sir Thomas could not withstand his daughter's sincere plea. Indeed, there was much truth in all that she had said. He sighed again very heavily. "I regret that you were made so unhappy, Lucinda. Lord Mays was a cad to use you so. However, as you say, he is dead, and that should be the end of it. At least you have been well provided for. I am glad now that I insisted that some provision was to be made for you in the settlements. Lord Mays was generous in deeding over to you and your heirs Carbarry and its income. It is a minor estate, true, but nevertheless one of some substance. There is also the annuity."

"I have no cause for complaint. Certainly I am more fortunate than many who are left widowed and have nothing but a widow's portion," said Lucinda, glad to be able to agree with her father on this one point. "You were farsighted in that, Papa."

Sir Thomas became visibly more cheerful. He nodded in satisfaction. "You are right, daughter. So, you are out of black gloves. Very well then! It is time that we think of the future."

"That is precisely what I have been doing this whole twelvemonth, Papa." Lucinda smiled, anticipating her father's inevitable reaction to her announcement. "I have decided to go to London."

"London!" Sir Thomas stared at her, once more visibly shaken. "But why? What do you mean to do?"

"Why, I mean to amuse myself a bit," said Lucinda on the quiver of a laugh.

"Well, naturally you shall do so. But I mean to say, what plans have you?" asked Sir Thomas.

Lucinda took pity on her faltering parent. "I am going up to town for the Season, Papa. My husband's heir and cousin, Wilfred Mays, is unmarried, as you know, and prefers to keep lodgings in town rather than live in the town house. Wilfred has graciously consented to my opening up the town house for an indefinite period, which I have already undertaken. As for my plans, they are quite simple, really. I shall shop and go to routs and dance every night if I wish. I shall fling myself into every amusement and dissipation imaginable until my head is in a dizzy whirl. In short, I intend to purge the taint of my wretched marriage from my life."

Sir Thomas was profoundly shocked. He had a sudden vision of his beautiful daughter painted and bejeweled and immodestly gowned, laughing from under her lashes at every male within her sight and whirling away in their arms. He spluttered, "Why, you cannot mean what you are saying, Lucinda!"

"I have never been more sober in my life, Papa," said Lucinda.

"But only think how you will look. You are so young, scarcely fledged when all is said. You will be the object of every eye and tongue, and there will be none to protect you from slight and slander." In his agitation Sir Thomas rose from the table and took a short turn, his hands clasped tightly behind his broad back.

"I am no longer a dreamy-eyed schoolgirl with little more than her face and figure to recommend her, Papa," said Lucinda on a tart note.

"No, of course not. You were never that. You were always a

girl of uncommon sense," said Sir Thomas, coming back to press her slim shoulder.

## Chapter Two

Lucinda had the inspiration to freshen his coffee cup. After she poured, Sir Thomas returned to his chair and picked up the cup. Encouragingly, Lucinda said, "There is nothing to make you anxious, Papa. I only wish for a little gaiety."

With a bothered expression, he said, "That is all very well for you to say. However, I will not conceal from you that I think this a very odd start, Lucinda! I cannot foresee anything for you but disaster. You will be alone and unprotected. Indeed, I fear greatly for your reputation."

"I am Lady Mays and a very rich widow. I do not think I shall lack for respectability," said Lucinda dryly.

"Respectability!" Sir Thomas fairly pounced upon the word. "You cannot go up to London alone and unchaperoned, Lucinda. You must have a respectable female with you in order to protect your reputation. Your mother cannot be expected to do it, for she has promised to go for Letty's lying-in next month. It would be selfish to request either of your other sisters to abandon their husbands and families for several months only to afford you pleasure."

"Pray do not fret, Papa. I have already invited Miss Tibby Blythe to join me." Lucinda was surprised by her father's sudden frown. "Surely you recall my former governess, Papa?"

Sir Thomas nodded. His heavy brows were still drawn. "Of course I do. Miss Blythe was an exceptionally stern preceptress. Your mother and I much admired the fashion in which she molded you and your sisters' characters."

"Then I do not understand. What possible objection could you have to her?" asked Lucinda, now made curious.

Sir Thomas pulled momentarily at his underlip. "I approve of your rare good sense in retaining Miss Blythe as your companion, Lucinda, but I do wonder that you thought of her at all when your announced intention is to cut a dash." Meeting his daughter's astonished gaze, he shrugged uncomfortably. "I was always secretly of the opinion that Miss Blythe's long face threw rather a damper over things. She had all the appeal of a crusty dragon."

Lucinda with difficulty suppressed a smile at her father's revelation. She and her sisters had been aware for many years that beneath Miss Blythe's uncompromisingly respectable exterior had beat a heart that thrilled to the nonsense in romance novels. However, this was certainly not the time to disabuse her father of his mistaken estimation of her former governess. "It is true that Miss Blythe has always possessed a formidable air. However, I felt that it was only proper to provide myself with a chaperone of stern countenance, one who would keep a close watch and ward off the wolves. A chaperone, moreover, who knew what was due to my name."

Sir Thomas pursed his mouth thoughtfully. "You do not want for all sense, in any event." He looked closely at his daughter, and his expression softened. "Aye, Lucinda, I can well understand how you must crave a bit of excitement after leading such a quiet life as you have. I have often pitied you living here with no company but your own to enliven the days. It is no wonder at all that you should want a change. I do not begrudge you that, my dear!"

"Papa, you speak as though I had been shut up these past three years," said Lucinda with a laugh.

"And so you have! How could you have remained in London when Lord Mays disgraced you so? He did not even have the decency to provide a separate household for you somewhere else, such as in Bath, where you could have still enjoyed society! Instead, he buried you alive at Carbarry!" said Sir Thomas with unwonted forcefulness.

As his daughter stared, he managed to bring his deep-held emotion under control. He reached over to pat her hand in a reassuring fashion. "It will do you good to buy yourself a few fripperies and call upon your old acquaintances. You have lived too quietly by half. Indeed, I even begin to approve of this scheme of yours if you do mean to have Miss Blythe to you, and so I shall tell your mother. Mind, I still do not care for the notion of your spending the whole Season in London. But I shall say no more against it."

Lucinda looked at her father a little curiously. "You do not think that Mama would approve even when I have retained Miss Blythe as my companion?"

Sir Thomas shrugged with exaggerated indifference, but his eyes were suddenly sharp on his daughter's face. "Lord Potherby, you know."

"Oh, I see," said Lucinda, and she did.

Lord Potherby was the owner of a property adjoining Carbarry and had thus been her closest neighbor since she had taken up residence three years previously. The gentleman had met her parents on the occasions of their rare visits, and he had impressed both of them with his undeniable worthiness.

Lord Potherby was wealthy and of extremely good birth. He had always quite openly admired his beauteous neighbor, Lady Mays. If he had been of a different kidney, he might have tried to figure in her affections despite her marital status. But Lord Potherby was a true gentleman.

Over the years Lord Potherby had become disgusted by Lord Mays's well-known progress as a womanizer and a ruthless collector of objets d'art. When Lord Potherby met Lady Mays, and learned through the grapevine both the circumstances of her marriage and the cause of her sudden appearance at Carbarry, he had at once set out to establish himself as her supporter and admirer.

Since Lord Mays's untimely death, Lord Potherby had gone a step further. He openly engaged himself to become indispensable to the beautiful unbereaved widow. Lady Mays's correct observance of a period of mourning was all that had hindered Lord Potherby from making a formal declaration for her hand. He deemed that it would not have been in good taste to urge the widow to remarry before her mourning was completed.

There was nothing in Lady Mays's demeanor that had ever encouraged his lordship to believe that she looked with favor upon his suit. However, Lord Potherby was confident that once the onerous social obligation of her mourning was met and Lady Mays was free to express herself at last, then she would gratefully accept his courtship.

Sir Thomas and his good wife approved of Lord Potherby's obvious suit for their daughter's hand. They encouraged his lordship's pursuit whenever they were at Carbarry, inevitably requesting that Lord Potherby be included in all their amusements.

Lucinda could only be glad that her parents did not live close enough to really promote the match through social gatherings. She esteemed Lord Potherby as a neighbor, certainly. But that did not mean that one wished to marry the gentleman. She and Lord Potherby were completely unsuited to one another, if for no other reason than that she was several years his junior. She had just emerged from a disastrous marriage with an older gentleman, and she had no desire to enter into another such unbalanced union.

However, even Lucinda had to admit that Lord Potherby appeared to be a veritable cherub after her late husband, Lord Mays. It was really no wonder that her parents deemed the match to be a good one. Besides his other advantageous worldly attributes, Lord Potherby was eminently steady of character. Not a breath of scandal attached to his name. He would indeed make a welcome change when one compared his lordship to Lucinda's unlamented departed husband, Sir Thomas and his good wife agreed.

It was a pity that Lucinda did not this time agree meekly to her parents' judgment.

"Papa, I have no intention of marrying Lord Potherby," said Lucinda. "You and Mama might as well give up this unfounded hope that I shall, for my mind is quite made up. We simply would not suit."

"You are not getting any younger, Lucinda," said Sir Thomas. He quite conveniently forgot that he had stated not many minutes before that she was too young to be let go to London by herself. "You are practically on the shelf. You cannot hope to compete with the fresh crop of young misses that are coming out each year."

"Really, Papa! You are too absurd," said Lucinda, laughing. "Why, I would be a nodcock indeed if I thought to make myself out to be an ingenue. No, the young misses may have free rein of the marriage mart and with my goodwill. I am too experienced in the ways of the world to desire to go that route again!"

An unwelcome thought occurred to Sir Thomas. With a lamentable lack of tact, he said, "I hope you have not taken a silly notion in mind to set your cap at some experienced buck this Season, Lucinda. I fear that you will be rolled up at that game. A widow cannot command the same pristine reputation as an unmarried girl, and that is what these gentlemen are looking for."

"I am not going up to London to find myself a husband!" said Lucinda, pardonably ruffled. "It is just as I have told you. I intend to indulge in a little gaiety. That is all! How could you think that I would behave with such . . . such desperation?"

Sir Thomas appeared not to be convinced. He was frowning. "Every woman wishes to wed, Lucinda. It is ingrained in them."

"That is absurd. Why, I know of any number of women who have not wed," said Lucinda.

"No doubt you are speaking of the lower orders, Lucinda. One of your quality always wishes to wed. It is bred into your very bones," said Sir Thomas solemnly.

"Papa, I did not think you were so gothic in your notions," said Lucinda, staring at her parent in disbelief.

Sir Thomas drew himself up. "Not at all, daughter. I know whereof I speak. No, the more I think about it, the more I see that this scheme of yours will not do after all."

"Papa!"

"Enough, Lucinda. You must be guided by me in this. I would spare you the mortification of being left at the altar. That is, even if you *were* able to bring some buck up to scratch," said Sir Thomas. As a clincher, he added, "Best to marry Lord Potherby right away and then go up to London for amusement."

Lucinda was torn between exasperation and laughter at her

father's idiotic notion that she was planning to entrap a husband over the Season. However, she knew it would do little good to try to reason her father out of an idea once it had taken hold of his intellect. She was forced to be satisfied with a skirmishing hit. "I could scarcely expect to find amusement as Lady Potherby!"

Sir Thomas took her point at once. He nodded reluctantly. "Lord Potherby can be a bit of a slowtop on occasion," he admitted. "But that should scarcely weigh against the many advantages of the match."

"Lord Potherby is a crashing bore," said Lucinda, not mincing the matter.

"His lordship is a very worthy man. He would make you an excellent husband," said Sir Thomas reprovingly.

Lucinda threw up her hands. "Papa, I think that we should leave off this conversation if I am not to come to cuffs with you. And I do not in the least wish to quarrel when we are shortly to part from one another." Dropping her napkin beside her plate and rising from her chair, she went around the end of the table to place a kiss on the top of her father's head.

Sir Thomas was mollified by her loving salute. He patted her hand where it rested upon his shoulder. "Very well, Lucinda. I shall say nothing more for now. You have always been a good, dutiful daughter. I know that in the end I may rely upon your good sense."

Lucinda chose to ignore the implication inherent in her father's words. But she did not repeat her declaration that she would not wed Lord Potherby. Instead, she pretended that he was referring to her plans for the Season. "You may also rely upon Miss Blythe," she said, smiling.

Sir Thomas laughed. "Oh aye, and in that good lady, too."

He stood up and gathered his daughter in a brief fond embrace. When he put her from him, he said, "I shall tell your mother not to be anxious on your behalf. We must trust you to know your own mind, even though you are still too young to know much about the ways of the world. I do not scruple to tell you that Miss Blythe shall be of immeasurable value to you in that regard. You must allow yourself to be guided by her, for she does not want for sense."

"I know it," said Lucinda, tucking her hand into her father's arm as she walked with him toward the door. Outside the breakfast room, she turned to smile up at her father. "I am seeing my estate agent this morning, but afterward I shall be free. Shall I see you at luncheon?"

Sir Thomas shook his head. "I believe that I shall take my leave of you now." He gestured to the waiting footman. The servant came forward with his greatcoat, hat, and gloves.

Lucinda's surprise at his readiness to be off made her utter, "Are you leaving this instant? I did not realize that you had already made your preparations."

"I had decided to do so when I wakened this morning. I have tarried longer than I informed your mother that I would," said Sir Thomas. He winked broadly at his daughter. "Besides, I know something of females, having lived in a houseful these many years. You will be wanting to see to the packing of half the house for this jaunt of yours. I would be very much in the way."

"Indeed you would," agreed Lucinda. "But surely it is too early to think of leaving. Why, you have scarcely left the breakfast table!"

"I meant to stay only long enough to have a few minutes with you this morning after I realized that your mother would be fretting that she has not heard from me before this," said Sir Thomas, shrugging into his greatcoat. He took his hat and gloves from the footman and put them on. Then he turned to kiss his daughter upon her upturned cheek. "I have the carriage waiting at the front steps, so I shall be on my way."

"Very well, Papa." Lucinda did not urge Sir Thomas to change his mind, and she saw him out. She was glad of her shawl when she emerged from the warmth of the house into the winter cold. She waved from the top of the front steps as her father climbed into the carriage. "Give my love to Mama," she called.

Sir Thomas waved acknowledgement from the carriage window. "You may depend upon me to relate all the news!" he promised. He put up the glass as the carriage started forward.

Lucinda shook her head, but she also smiled with affection. It was inevitable that Sir Thomas would confide the particulars of Lucinda's amazing scheme to his wife. Lucinda knew that she would then receive a letter from her mother requesting a more comprehensive explanation and offering a catechism of advice.

The vehicle rolled away down the drive. Lucinda waved again, but she did not tarry to watch her father's carriage round the bend in the gravel drive. She retreated into the house immediately.

The footman thought it was the cold of the bleak January morning that had driven her ladyship inside so soon. But Lucinda's thoughts were not dwelling on the frigid air.

Instead, she was already occupied with all of the matters that still had to be settled and accomplished before she could set out for London the following morning. The culmination of a year's careful planning was almost at hand.

"Pray have Mr. Latham sent to me in the study," she said to the footman.

"Yes, m'lady."

Lucinda was still smiling as she entered the study. She sat down at the huge mahogany desk where she had routinely attended to the many demands of the estate. Glancing slowly about the well-appointed room, she sighed softly. It was a pleasure to reflect that this would be the last decision that she would need to make about the workings of Carbarry.

She was positively looking forward to the formal task of handing over the working of the estate into Mr. Latham's capable hands for an indefinite time. Once that was done, she would be released from the last obligation that tied her to Carbarry.

## Chapter Three

The transition to London was accomplished smoothly and without mishap. Those servants who accompanied Lady Mays from Carbarry to the town house settled quickly into their new surroundings. With scarcely an hour lost, the running of the household was established.

Lucinda had written Miss Blythe some months previously when the lady was to meet her in London and had sent the necessary traveling funds. Within a fortnight of Lucinda's own arrival, she had been joined by her companion, the esteemable Miss Blythe.

The household took swift measure of her ladyship's companion and concluded that Miss Blythe was a female of superior qualities. The lady was soft-spoken enough, but there was about her speech a quiet steel that commanded respect.

Miss Blythe's appearance added to the impression. She was a lady of spare proportions and was always dressed with propriety. Her dark hair had softened with gray, but it was ruthlessly swept back in a tight coronet. A pair of spectacles perched upon the bridge of her proud, prominent nose, emphasizing her piercing gaze. It was known that Miss Blythe had formerly been a governess, and the general verdict was that no pupil of hers would have dared to take advantage of such a stern individual.

However, beneath the austere exterior that Miss Blythe presented to the world was a woman of imagination and with a penchant for the romantic. It was perhaps to her benefit that she had never had a great deal of beauty, for then she could not have played the role that she had so successfully managed through her career as the governess par excellence. For a young woman of respectable family who had had no means and no offers, becoming a governess had been the only logical choice.

Through the years there had been times when Miss Blythe had wondered what turn her life might have taken if circumstances had been different, but on the whole she had no regrets. That had become doubly true since she had agreed to become her dear Lucinda's companion.

Miss Tibby Blythe gazed with appreciative eyes around the well-proportioned sitting room. It never failed to please her. With a bony forefinger she touched a delicate figurine that rested on the polished mantel.

Miss Blythe sighed with contentment. Wherever she looked,

in whatever room she found herself, there was great beauty. Magnificent pieces of art and sculpture, priceless vases and gilt mirrors, luxurious oriental carpets and beautifully carven furniture made abiding at Mays House an experience in delicious decadence.

Miss Blythe still had difficulty in believing the good fortune that had led her former and best-loved pupil to request her companionship and to install her in such wonderfully sybaritic surroundings. It was close to living in a sumptuous palace, she thought.

"Tibby? Oh, there you are." Lucinda came into the sitting room, pulling on her pale kid gloves. She glanced around and then looked at her former governess, smiling. "Well, Tibby? Has it come up to your expectations?"

Miss Blythe had turned. At Lucinda's inquiry, she clasped her hands in front of her spare bosom in an expression of bliss. "Everything more than exceeds any puny expectations of mine, my dear. The comfort of my room. This delightful town house. London itself. Why, it is all more than I can yet comprehend." She shook her head in self-amusement. "When you wrote to me and begged me to come to you as your companion, I never dreamed that I should step into a fantasy existence."

"A fantasy indeed," said Lucinda thoughtfully, smoothing her gloves over her wrists. She looked up and laughed. "I am glad that you are not disappointed. I own, I was not certain what we might expect since the house had been shut up for the past year. But my cousin-in-law, Lord Wilfred Mays, was extremely gracious in allowing me to order the house as I wished and the caretakers kept it up nicely."

"I do not know how you were ever able to bear leaving it," said Miss Blythe, once more gazing about her appreciatively.

Lucinda also looked around, but more subjectively. The sitting room was beautifully appointed, as was every other room in the town house. The uninitiated saw only the magnificence, the opulence, the luxury. However, she knew better than most that beauty was not always a reflection of what was good or best. Surrounded by such outward trappings of wealth, she had learned the poverty of bitter disillusionment and inconceivable loneliness.

It had been in this very room that the impassive butler had brought to her the verbal message that her husband had arranged for her to leave London within the hour. She would not be returning. His lordship had not bothered to convey his wishes in private, but had sent them by a servant.

This final humiliation had been a devastating blow, and it had all but broken her pride completely. The weight of her distress had nearly shattered her composure. But she had managed not to make a spectacle of herself. In a voice that she had not recognized as her own, she had requested that her maid be sent down to her. It had only been through Madison's offices that she had been able to walk upstairs to her dressing room and attire herself for the journey.

Strange, Lucinda reflected, as she looked around the sitting room. There should be ghostly emotions vibrating forever in these surroundings, but she had felt nothing.

She had actually dreaded reentering the portals of this house and steeled herself against it. She had even wondered whether she could live at Mays House for an entire Season. The memories had come, of course, but she remained oddly unmoved. Simply, the town house was not home to her. She moved within its walls and enjoyed its luxuries, but it was as though she was merely a guest to whom polite hospitality had been extended. It had actually come as something of a relief to discover that the place had so little hold upon her.

Lucinda saw that her companion was looking at her rather strangely. She realized that she had been silent too long and at once volunteered an explanation. "Mrs. Beeseley has promised us a fine roast for our dinner, by the by. I was thinking just now that we must take care to return from our outing in good time so that we do not offend the cook's sensibilities." She gestured toward the door, lifting a brow inquiringly. "Shall we go? Are you ready?"

"Oh, I am quite ready." Miss Blythe smoothed her own gloves and adjusted the reticule strings over her wrist as she moved after Lucinda to the door. Her thoughts were still revolving pleasurably on the promised treat that Lucinda had revealed was in store for them. She voiced her approval of the housekeeper's diligence. "An excellent woman altogether. She knows how to keep the household well in hand, and she is never behind in the least courtesy. Did you know that Mrs. Beeseley has given orders that my sheets are to be properly warmed each night? That is the mark of the superior house-keeper." Miss Blythe laughed a little self-consciously at how contented that she had sounded. "Oh, my dear! I am persuaded that I shall very much enjoy my position as your companion."

"You are to be my chaperone as well, Tibby," reminded Lucinda as they left the sitting room and traversed the entry hall. "You will be constrained to accompany me to every function that I take a fancy to attend. I only hope that you do not become jaded by all the amusements that we are certain to be offered."

"Jaded! Oh, I should think not indeed, my lady," said Miss Blythe. She was mindful of the footmen in the hall and took care to address her former pupil respectfully. "What an ingrate I would be to prefer my last post with the most obnoxious charge of my career to accompanying my dear Lady Mays to any diversion she chose."

Lucinda laughed, but she shook her head as well. Pausing on the doorstep, she said, "Pray do not call me that when we are private."

"But the servants, my dear. I must keep a proper distance between us before them," said Miss Blythe.

"You are my friend, Tibby. Surely that gives you leave enough to disregard what anyone else may say! It is bad enough that you insist upon such formality between us when we are in company," said Lucinda.

"I own, it does come awkwardly to my tongue," said Miss Blythe. "I had grown too used to thinking of you as Lucinda Stassart over the years, and old habits die hard."

While they spoke, the ladies had descended the outside steps to the curb where the carriage was waiting. A footman handed them inside, and they made themselves comfortable. As the carriage started off, Lucinda said, "You never did approve of my marriage to Lord Mays, did you, Tibby?"

Miss Blythe looked at her former charge. Her rather plain face reflected her dismay. "My dear."

Lucinda gave a slight smile. "You said not a word. But I knew that you did not approve. It was why I did not discuss the matter with you. Perhaps I should have done so."

Miss Blythe covered Lucinda's gloved hand with her own. "My dear Lucinda, it was not for me to voice my opinion. It would have been quite improper of me to have done so. It is quite true that I harbored strong reservations. You were so young and I had heard something of Lord Mays's unsavory reputation. But I knew also of your family's difficulties. Such terrible mortgages and debts and that wretched boy scarcely helped matters!"

Lucinda gave a gurgle of laughter. "My cousin Ferdie. What a coil he always made of things. But he is Papa's heir, and he could not be left dangling, after all."

"The experience might have done his character a great deal of good," said Miss Blythe austerely.

"I suspect that Ferdie is quite past redemption," said Lucinda candidly. "He never seemed able to stop himself from gambling even when his pockets were all to let. It is why my uncle finally refused to cover his debts any longer."

"It is a pity that Sir Thomas was not of the same strength of mind," said Miss Blythe. "Then perhaps you would not have been thrust into such an unequal marriage. Forgive me, my dear! I had not meant to speak so bluntly. It was just that the thought of your cousin, and your own questions, have roused me from my silence."

"Ferdie's embarrassments were not altogether to blame for the desperate straits in which we stood," said Lucinda quietly. "The estate had been mortgaged before ever Papa came into his inheritance. And there were the rest of the debts and the expenses that had accrued over the years. The future of our family fortune would have been staked upon my face in any event. Lord Mays took upon himself the light of a savior when he offered for me. I was willing enough to wed him. You must not think that I was forced to accept his suit."

Miss Blythe folded her thin lips, considering it best that she did not voice her opinion of that. "I did not think it a good match. But I did hope that you would come to be happy," she said.

Lucinda smiled. However, there was a quality about her smile that startled her companion. Miss Blythe stared at Lucinda, wondering what possible thoughts could be behind such an expression. She was soon enlightened.

"That is precisely what I intend to be now that I am a widow," said Lucinda quietly. "I am free at last of my shackles."

Miss Blythe was unutterably shocked. "Lucinda!"

The hard look settled in Lucinda's eyes. She glanced at her companion, her mouth forming a tight smile. "I am sorry that my irreverence shocks you, Tibby. However, I will not play the hypocrite. I had no cause to mourn my husband's death. There was a fleeting regret, certainly, but it was followed almost instantly by a feeling of release."

Miss Blythe's lips parted, but she did not utter a sound.

Lucinda cast an anxious look at Miss Blythe. She knew that she had horrified her former preceptress. "Can you possibly understand that, Tibby? Do I sound like an unfeeling monster?"

"No, my dear. I do not see you as an unfeeling monster," said Miss Blythe slowly. Her soft heart positively bled for the younger woman. "And I believe that I can enter into your feelings up to a point. You were undoubtedly greatly hurt by his lordship, especially when he banished you completely out of his life. It is not at all difficult to understand why you did not hold him in affection."

"Thank you, Tibby," said Lucinda gratefully. She gave her companion's hand a squeeze. "I had hoped that you would understand. It is a comfort to me."

The carriage had stopped in front of a fashionable modiste's shop. The carriage door was opened, the step let down, and the ladies descended.

Whatever further thoughts that Miss Blythe might have voiced on the matter she kept to herself, but she could not banish a strong feeling of distress for her former charge. It greatly disturbed her to discover how much the innocent and dutiful young Stassart daughter had changed. She had never guessed it, for up until this moment Lucinda had appeared to her very like her former self.

It was something requiring deep contemplation, for Miss Blythe foresaw that her duties as chaperone and companion might be a little more complicated than she had anticipated. As she followed Lucinda, she wondered just what other facets of the young woman's character had undergone unwelcome change.

Upon entering the modiste's shop, Miss Blythe swiftly discovered that her position was also to be much more prominent than she had assumed. She was pleasurably appalled when she realized that Lucinda meant to trick her out in an entire new wardrobe.

"Lady Mays! I must protest. I cannot allow you to spend a king's ransom on *my* back," exclaimed Miss Blythe.

"Nonsense, you will be sensible and accept your good fortune," said Lucinda, laughing. She spied a bright splash of silk and indicated the roll to the woman waiting upon them. "What of that watered green, pray?"

Miss Blythe waited for the saleswoman to move off after the silk before she spoke, but she also lowered her voice so that she could more easily fashion her plea. "Lucinda, you simply cannot order all these gowns and dresses for me. Why, whatever would I do with the half of them? I am a governess. I have never worn such stuff as this. Indeed, I would be very shortly turned off if I were to be so presumptuous as to dress better than my employer!"

"You are no longer a governess, Tibby. You are my companion, and you must be suitably attired if you are to chaperone me to fashionable soirees and balls and such," said Lucinda. She fingered the watered green that the saleswoman was holding out for her inspection, and she nodded. "Yes, we must have this as well."

"But my dear!" Miss Blythe looked helplessly at the mountain of bolts of cloth that represented day dresses and walking dresses and evening gowns.

Lucinda squeezed her companion's arm affectionately. "Never mind, Tibby. I can stand the nonsense if that is what so concerns you. As for what is proper—yes, I can see it in your eyes! That is your next objection."

"Of course it is," retorted Miss Blythe. "Why, it would be most *improper* in me to allow you to give me even a fraction of what you have outlined."

"It was you who taught me that one must be gracious in accepting gifts in order not to wound the giver," said Lucinda, smiling. She saw that her companion was still troubled, and she entreated, "Please, Tibby. I have never had anyone upon whom to lavish my ill-gotten wealth. Pray do not deny me this pleasure."

"Oh, my dear," said Miss Blythe, shaking her head. She drew her gloved finger over a particularly attractive velvet, daring to visualize the lovely garment that would be made out of it. She wavered and was lost at last.

Lucinda knew that she had successfully carried her point. She smiled, and her brilliant blue eyes began to dance. "We shall have such an amusing time, Tibby, I promise you! You will be quite the grand dame in your new finery."

"I only hope that you intend to outfit yourself as well," retorted Miss Blythe.

"Oh!" Lucinda's expression held astonished realization. "I was taking such pleasure in ordering for you that it completely slipped my mind to order anything for myself."

"Then you must at once rectify your mistake and give the proprietress pleasant daydreams of being able to retire upon the huge sums you shall be dropping in her shop!" said Miss Blythe tartly.

Lucinda laughed and called the proprietress to her. When the ladies left the modiste's shop, they had fervent promises that what they had ordered would be given the very strictest priority. Madame the proprietress herself promised to deliver at least two gowns for each of the ladies within the week.

Lucinda was well-pleased with their first foray. "We have made a fair beginning, Tibby. Now all we require are visits to the milliner, the boot maker, the glover, the—"

"Surely, surely you do not intend to make further purchases on my behalf?" asked Miss Blythe, dismayed but hoping that her suspicions were not correct.

"Tibby, you cannot put on last year's gloves with that ravishingly elegant evening gown we have ordered for you. Nor can you wear sensible boots in the drawing room; you must have some slippers! Then there are bonnets to be thought of and shawls and—"

"Stop, I pray you!" cried Miss Blythe. "I am already overcome. Indeed, I shall require a strong sedative if you go on in this vein, Lucinda!"

Lucinda gave her companion's arm a little shake and said coaxingly, "Give over, do, Tibby. I promise that I shall not *force* anything upon you should you dislike it. But you must confess that it is imperative that you appear to advantage if you are to be an effective chaperone for me."

"Yes, I suppose that is true," agreed Miss Blythe with visible reluctance.

"Then let us be off, for the morning is quickly slipping away from us, and I wish to put behind us the major purchases," said Lucinda. "Come on, Tibby, into the carriage!"

Thus Miss Blythe succumbed and allowed herself to be borne off upon a shopping spree of proportions that she had never dreamed possible.

# Chapter Four

The arrival in London of Lady Lucinda Mays did not go unnoticed. Indeed, curiosity was rife throughout society among those who recalled her come-out. Since she had emerged directly from the schoolroom and had been wed before her first Season was out, there was no one who could claim to have been her intimate friend, and that only added to the speculation.

Miss Lucinda Stassart had been a brief shining star for society to sigh over. She was exceedingly lovely, modest, and of unexceptional birth. She had had no portion, it was true, and the family's circumstances were well known. Yet she had been assiduously courted and admired.

Those gentlemen too old or too impecunious to wed her had still paid her homage for the sake of her beauty, with the tacit understanding that they did so because it was all the rage. That handful of gentlemen both eligible and wealthy enough to overlook Miss Stassart's lack of portion had vied hotly with one another over whom would claim the prize.

Lord Mays had thrived on the envy of others who could do no more than wish to possess what he could acquire. As Miss Stassart's star scaled ever higher in the social stratosphere, she became ever more valuable in his lordship's eyes. It became almost an obsession with Lord Mays to possess her.

Never before had Lord Mays deigned to look at any of the misses that were entered so hopefully into the marriage mart. He had his houses, his horses, his collections of art, his mistresses. He was the envy of his peers. What need had he of a wife? But a lady of Miss Stassart's unimpeachable birth could not be acquired and paraded without a license and marriage settlements.

Coldly, calculatedly, Lord Mays put a price tag upon Miss Stassart that he was willing to pay. Without emotion he conveyed to his prospective father-in-law his willingness to relinquish the monies required to settle the Stassart mortgages and all of the family debts, as well as those debts incurred by the heir.

Sir Thomas had been utterly confounded. His wildest dreams had never led him to imagine such good fortune. He was not a stupid man, however, and he recovered sufficiently to demand something for his daughter. So it was that Lord Mays agreed to make over one of his minor estates to his intended wife with an annuity that was to be hers and for her descendents.

Then Lord Mays had unemotionally pledged himself to honor and cherish a girl who meant nothing to him. She was a possession, acquired through his wealth to excite the envy of his peers.

Lucinda had known that it was her duty as the beauty of the family to accept the most obliging offer made for her hand. An advantageous marriage was the only way to bring solvency back to a family that for generations had been plagued with debt.

Lord Mays was polished in his manners and possessed considerable charm of address. His person was set off to advantage by an excellent tailor. Jewels winked and glittered in his snowy cravat and on his fingers. There was nothing about his lordship that was repelling to a young, inexperienced schoolroom miss.

The lines of dissipation in his lordship's face certainly emphasized the difference in age between him and his intended wife, but Lucinda put away her romantic yearnings and dutifully accepted the future that her parents had been ever so happy to accept upon her behalf.

Lucinda meant to be a good wife and had hoped that one day Lord Mays's heart would become captive to her own. She had been told a little about Lord Mays's reputation, but with the optimism of youth she had anticipated that once she became his lordship's wife the paramours would no longer be part of his life.

She had had no reason to suspect that it would be otherwise, for Lord Mays was flatteringly attentive. He even seemed jealous when her other admirers had paid her fulsome compliments or had partnered her onto the dance floor. Lord Mays always spoke charming things to her, and his eyes lit up whenever she chanced to come into his view.

And so with the exchange of vows, and the consideration of a princely sum to her parents, Lucinda had embarked upon her new life as Lady Mays, full of optimism and confidence and hope.

By the world's measurement, Miss Stassart had made a spectacular marriage. Lord Mays was considerably older, and certainly his reputation was regrettable. However, one felt only envy for the young woman's good fortune. She resided at one of the most prestigious addresses in London. She was coifed and gowned by the most expensive and exclusive dressers in town. Her jewels were spectacular and always in abundance. Her matched team and custom-made carriage were perfection in motion. She played hostess to the most opulent dinners and balls that one could possibly attend.

It was naturally the match of the Season, and it was generally agreed that Lord Mays had pulled off a major coup in winning the loveliest young lady that had graced London in many years.

Lord Mays paraded his new wife about everywhere, deriving much enjoyment from the envious comments. He laughed good-naturedly at the witticisms and innuendoes that touched upon his wife's desirability. He at once commissioned a well-known artist to do his wife's portrait, and when it was completed, had it hung in a prominent place in the dining room.

The portrait was much admired. Lucinda responded to the compliments with a forced graciousness that hid well the true state of her emotions. She had inevitably discovered that beneath her husband's charm and smooth address beat a most selfish heart. His lordship's eyes still lit up when she entered the room, but now she knew it was not due to affection, but rather, a clinical appreciation of her beauty.

Lord Mays liked for his wife to appear to advantage. She was always beautifully turned out. Precious gems glittered in her hair, from her ears, about her throat and wrists, and on her fingers. Lucinda was truly the envy of many ladies, but she herself regarded the diamonds, emeralds, rubies, and pearls as so many links of an intolerably heavy chain.

She was a possession. The only difference between herself and the Dresdens on the mantle or the priceless artwork in the gallery was that she drew breath.

Interest eventually waned in the most touted match of the Season. Lord Mays did not hear quite as many compliments for having snatched the prize from all other competitors. The war had ended with a spectacular, riveting battle. There were other things to exclaim over.

Lady Mays was still admired, of course, but she was no longer a cause célèbre. Her jewels and her gowns did not excite society as they once had. Other, newer, sources of interesting gossip sprang up. Lord Mays became increasingly disgruntled and bored with the task of escorting his wife to various functions.

His lordship had not given up his latest mistress upon his marriage. However, he had almost decided to look for another ladylove because the woman had begun to pall on him. The lady was shrewd enough to read the signs. She had every intention of being able to retire from her present occupation, using Lord Mays's largesse as the foundation of her fortune. She staked herself to win a carriage race against another lady of dubious virtue and won. Her timely escapade brought to his lordship flattering attentions. Lord Mays received the sly congratulations of his acquaintances with renewed good humor. He decided to keep his mistress a while longer.

His lordship's wife, who would never do anything outrageous to spur such vulgar interest in herself, had become something of a liability. Lady Mays was perfunctorily banished to her country estate. Her portrait continued to hang in the dining room. The likeness of a beautiful young woman, flat and undemanding, was a polished jewel of the portraiture art. It was a fitting addition to Lord May's collection.

At the time of Lady Mays's disappearance from society, there had been mild speculation as to the reason. Some thought that she had lost enough of her looks so that Lord Mays could not bear the sight of her. There was even talk of a horrible accident that had left her hideously scarred. Others opined that she had become unwisely tiresome over his mistress. None would have believed that she was put away simply because she no longer brought to him the envy of his peers.

In any event, word got swiftly round that Lady Mays had returned to London. Aware that she would be the object of interest, Lucinda had taken care to write short notes to old acquaintances, reintroducing herself to them so that their curiosity would be piqued. When the brass knocker was hung on the door of the town house, indicating that the occupants were in residence, callers began to leave their cards.

Most of the ladies came out to see for themselves whether Lady Mays had lost her looks. They were disappointed. It was obvious that Lady Mays had not only retained her beauty, but she had also acquired an assurance that she had lacked as a miss just out of the schoolroom.

There were several oblique references made to Lady Mays regarding her stay away from London. One lady went so far as to voice the majority opinion. "His lordship was a scandalous rake, of course. You must have suffered terribly, my dear Lady Mays. It is a pity that Lord Mays did not honor you as he should have. I am sure I do not know what I would have done in your place."

Lucinda merely smiled and ignored the latest attempt to fish into her past. "May I freshen your tea, Mrs. Grisham? I find that hot, sweet tea does wonders on a chilly day. I believe you mentioned that your daughter is coming out this Season. How very exciting for you!"

The lady was sufficiently diverted that she did not allude again to Lucinda's relationship with her late lord. When Mrs. Grisham had at last taken leave of her hostess, Miss Blythe exclaimed, "The effrontery of that woman! I could scarcely contain myself. I wonder that you did not give her a blistering setdown, Lucinda, for it would have been well deserved."

"I was tempted," admitted Lucinda. She grimaced. "However, what would I have gained, Tibby? They will talk about me in any event, and I would have set up her back without gaining a thing. No, I think it better simply to present an unassailable civility."

"I do hope that we have seen the last of the nosy bodies. I cannot conceive that these women do not have something better to do than to pry into what does not concern them," snapped Miss Blythe.

However much Miss Blythe wished for it, Mrs. Grisham was not the last inquisitive visitor that visited Mays House that first week. It was a trial to Lucinda to be examined in such a rude fashion, but in the end she felt it to have been worth it. All the ladies who called urged upon her several invitations in the upcoming days and weeks. That circumstance alone was of immense satisfaction to her, for it meant that she would shortly be able to realize her purpose in coming to London.

The one invitation that Lucinda most treasured was extended to her by Lady Maria Sefton. Her ladyship was one of the patronesses of Almack's and had sponsored Lucinda into that exclusive club upon her come-out. Lady Sefton was the kindest of the exalted ladies who arbitrated Almack's membership, and she was not behind in reacting to Lucinda's short note.

Lady Sefton was shown into the drawing room and came in with her gloved hand extended. "My dear Lucinda. I hope that I may still call you that?"

Smiling, Lucinda shook hands with her ladyship. "Of course you may, ma'am. I am grateful that you honor me with such condescension."

"Why should I not? You were a charming girl. I always considered it to be a pity that you were not wed to someone of more sterling character," said Lady Sefton. She nodded to the lady seated with Lucinda. "I do not believe that I have had the pleasure."

"My friend and companion, Miss Tibby Blythe," said Lucinda. "Miss Blythe was governess to me and to my sisters."

"It is an honor, my lady," said Miss Blythe.

Lady Sefton nodded. Her gaze was assessing. "You will do very well, Miss Blythe. Some are already spreading tales of the beauteous widow. You grow notorious without cause, Lucinda. However, there will be none who will be able to point the finger of censor at Lady Mays whilst you reside with her, Miss Blythe."

"I hope not indeed, my lady," said Miss Blythe quietly.

Lady Sefton nodded again and turned to Lucinda. "I have come to invite you to a small soiree a month hence, my dear, you and Miss Blythe. My credit and approval will do much to aid you in reentering society. I always disapproved of Mays's treatment of you. It was unfortunate in the extreme that he was that cold sort. Perhaps now that you are at liberty again, you will be able to find a gentleman who is more worthy of you."

Miss Blythe arched her brows as she glanced at her erstwhile pupil.

Lucinda ignored the interested look. She shook her head, smiling. "I have no thoughts of remarrying, my lady. I have returned to London simply to amuse myself a little. I have been too long away, and I have missed the round of social functions."

"Well, there is time enough to think of the other," said Lady Sefton. She rose and held out her hand. "I know that it has been a short visit, but I shall nevertheless leave you now. I will send the invitations for the soiree at once. Miss Blythe, I shall look forward to seeing you again."

"Thank you, my lady," said Miss Blythe, overcome by the lady's kindness in giving notice to her.

Lucinda thanked Lady Sefton and saw her ladyship out.

When she returned to the drawing room, Miss Blythe said, "I thought her ladyship to be an eminently kind and sensible sort."

"Yes, Lady Sefton was always kind to me. I am glad that she recalled me with such affection," said Lucinda.

"I took particular note that Lady Sefton assumed you had thought of remarriage," said Miss Blythe. "It would be wonderful indeed were she to take an interest on your behalf. I have no doubt that her ladyship would make quite a successful match for you, for civility would not allow you to refuse her good offices!"

"No, indeed," said Lucinda, laughing. "But truly, Tibby, whatever anyone may think to the contrary, I do not at all find the idea of giving my hand away again appealing."

Miss Blythe returned to her embroidery with a thoughtful air.

# Chapter Five

Few of those who called at Mays House were as disinterested or as cordial as Lady Sefton. Lucinda had not had the time during her short come-out to forge any deep friendships. Indeed, it would have been difficult to do so in any event. The jealousy of her peers who had been less blessed in their appearances and the envy of their mothers had crippled all of Lucinda's efforts to prove herself friendly.

Her brief sojourn as Lord Mays's hostess had been equally distancing for her. Her exalted position as the wife of one of the richest lords in England had guaranteed that she remain the object of jealousy and envy, and it had served to isolate her from other women who might otherwise have made overtures of friendship.

However, there was one caller who was more than an acquaintance.

Lord Wilfred Mays had succeeded to a title that he had never expected. He was a kindhearted young gentleman of considerably simpler tastes than had been his predecessor. He spoke precisely what was on his mind at any given moment, sometimes to his subsequent embarrassment.

Lucinda had come to regard his lordship with a mild affection, even though they had not come in one another's way much while her husband had been alive. Since her widowhood, however, a friendship had quickly sprung up between them, and Lord Mays wasted little time in waiting upon her.

Miss Blythe had left the drawing room for a few moments, but upon Lord Mays's card being sent up to her, Lucinda at once received his lordship. She went to him with both hands outstretched. "Wilfred! This is an unlooked-for pleasure. I had not anticipated that you would call on me so soon, but I am happy that you have."

Lord Mays bowed over her hands. When he straightened, he smiled crookedly at her. "I am glad to have found you at home. I was half expecting you to be out already, gadding about the town."

There was not an ounce of guile in him, nor did he go out of his way to attach her attention. He knew himself to be merely a passable fellow in physical appearance, and he was therefore not burdened with a false vanity. He had thinning sandy hair, and there was a glint of red in his brows and stubby lashes. His gold-brown eyes were his most notable feature, while his expression was unceasingly amiable. His attire was never gaudy and was always of an excellent cut. He carried himself well, being an active pursuer of the manly arts of boxing and fencing. Yet he was not above average height, and so when he smiled at Lucinda, he was looking almost directly into her eyes.

"I shall be in a week or more," said Lucinda on a laugh. "You can have no notion how many callers I have had, nor

what invitations have already come my way. I am persuaded
that I shall enjoy the Season very much."

Lord Mays glanced approvingly at Lucinda's fashionable
day dress with its knots of dark green satin ribbons and the expensive silk shawl that dipped gracefully from her elbows. He
had an instinctive eye for what looked well on man or woman.
"You look marvelous, Lucinda. I particularly like that shade of
rose on you. You appear for all the world to be the most delicate bloom in the garden."

"You are a flatterer, indeed, sir! But come, sit down beside
me and tell me how you come to be here this afternoon," said
Lucinda, drawing him over to a settee.

Lord Mays sat down, casting a disparaging glance about the
room as he did so. He put a finger up to the top of his starched
white cravat as though it had grown tight, and observed, "I
have never liked Mays House. It is not anything in my style."

Lucinda glanced around. A peculiar smile played about her
mouth. "Yes, it is sinfully ostentatious, is it not?" A thought
occurred to her. She turned back to Lord Mays and eyed him
curiously. "What will you do with it? Do you ever intend to
live here?"

"Not as long as I have a choice," said Lord Mays bluntly. "I
prefer my own lodgings, as you know. I suppose one day
when I marry I shall be forced to take on the place, though.
The ladies all seem to like this sort of house." The despondent
observation roused him to confide, "I'll tell you one thing,
though! I would have my bride get rid of all these objets d'art
and knackery. As it is, a fellow can scarcely relax at his ease
for fear of breaking some vase or other!"

Lucinda laughed. "I shan't regard it if you do not. They are
all yours, after all!"

"No, they ain't," said Lord Mays with devastating accuracy.
"They belonged to my cousin, and they all have his stamp on
them. Everything my cousin bought was of the same sort—
beautiful, expensive, and useless!"

As Lucinda's expression altered, he realized that he had in
an oblique fashion insulted her. Quickly, he said, "I don't
mean you, Lucinda! Of course I don't. Why, you are the one

good thing that my cousin brought into this house. I shouldn't set foot in it at all if it weren't for you."

Lucinda inclined her head with a flickering smile. "You are kind to say so, Wilfred. However, I hope that you will not hesitate to tell me when I am become *de trop*. I should not wish to stand in the way of your taking possession."

"Have no fear of that. You may call this roof your own as long as you wish. *I* have no desire to live here, but someone must if only to be certain that the place is properly cared for," said Lord Mays. He grinned at her. "You are doing me a great favor, actually. Otherwise I would have had to continue to pay a caretaker a fortune, probably for years."

Lucinda laughed, her countenance alight with amusement. "I am happy to have spared you that, at least! You make me feel quite helpful, Wilfred."

"I should think so! It's a pity that you cannot help me with that sprawling barrack that my cousin called a hunting box. Hunting box!" Lord Mays snorted disparagingly. "I am hoping to sell it. I have my man looking into it now. Did you ever see that old abbey that my cousin filled with precious Greek statues and other such claptrap as that? The gloomy place gave me the shivers, let me tell you. I was never more glad than when old Crowley approached me and offered to buy it from me."

"Are you divesting yourself of everything, then?" asked Lucinda, fascinated.

"Oh, no. Just those things that don't please me," said Lord Mays cheerfully. "You have no notion how busy I have become. It is a plaguey nuisance at times. At least my cousin had excellent taste in horses. I shall keep most of them."

The door opened and Miss Blythe came in. She looked curiously at the well-dressed visitor, who had automatically risen to his feet upon her entrance. "I am sorry, my dear. I did not realize that you had a caller."

"Tibby, this is Lord Wilfred Mays. You will recall my relating to you his kindness in letting me use this house for the Season. Lord Mays, my companion, Miss Blythe," said Lucinda.

Miss Blythe went forward with a smile, her hand outstretched. "My lord, it is indeed a pleasure. I am certain that

Lady Mays has already expressed her gratitude to you, but pray allow me to add my own. We are enjoying London."

Lord Mays shook hands with Miss Blythe. He cleared his throat self-consciously. The companion was just the sort of lean, grim-faced female that he was made most nervous around. Despite her pleasant words, this Miss Blythe reminded him forcibly of a rather strict nanny that he had had as a young boy. "Not at all, ma'am! The pleasure is mine entirely. As I was just telling Lady Mays a moment ago, the house is hers as long as she wants it."

"You are indeed kind," said Miss Blythe, her expression mellowing yet further.

Lord Mays looked faintly alarmed at being the object of such patent approval by the starched-up companion. It would have made more sense to him if she had displayed a stiff politeness that bordered on coldness and had sent him on his way. He had been found sitting alone with Lady Mays, after all.

Lucinda understood with some amusement the source of Lord Mays's obvious discomfort. She set out to rescue him.

"I am giving a supper and ball in about a fortnight. Shall you honor me with your presence, my lord?" asked Lucinda.

"Of a certainty, Lady Mays. I will be delighted," said Lord Mays. He saw by the mantle clock that a quarter hour had already passed. Reluctantly, he adhered to the convention that dictated the correct length of a visit. "I should be going. I shall be looking forward to receiving an invitation, my lady."

Lucinda rose, giving her hand into his. "Good! I trust that it will not disappoint you. I hope for a wonderful success."

Lord Mays smiled at her. "Oh, I am certain of that! I am sure you are a rare hostess."

He glanced once more around the drawing room, but without admiration. He grimaced slightly. "I recall the affairs that you hostessed while married to my cousin. There was never anything more grand. But that was my cousin all over, wasn't it? Grand. Abbeys, yet!"

"Quite," agreed Lucinda dryly. "I hope that my entertainments will not be stigmatized as 'grand.' I would rather hear them raved about as insufferable squeezes!"

"That's the ticket! I shall be certain to tell everyone I know that you mean to throw a bang-up affair," said Lord Mays, grinning. He bowed over her fingers, nodded politely to Miss Blythe, and then took himself off.

Miss Blythe looked after the departing peer with interest. She turned a speculative gaze on Lucinda. "That was an exceedingly presentable young buck, I thought. And you stand on such excellent terms with him. It is quite obvious that he admires you. Is he already married?"

Astonished, Lucinda looked quickly at her companion. Miss Blythe's expression reflected only a mild curiosity, but her former pupil knew her far too well to believe that it had been an idle question.

Lucinda shook her head, laughing. "Do not even think it, Tibby! Wilfred and I have become friends. Neither of us is the least attracted to the other, nor do either of us wish to become riveted. Indeed, I suspect that Wilfred would be horrified at the very notion of wedding anyone just yet. He is enjoying all the advantages of his new position. It would be too much to expect him to take up the responsibilities of a wife and the inevitable growing nursery!"

"A pity, indeed," said Miss Blythe. She sat down in the wing chair that she favored, which was situated in front of the warm fire. She drew her embroidery out of the basket that had been left close to hand. Serenely she began plying her needle. "I should so like to see you settled and happy, Lucinda. The regard of a worthy gentleman goes far in guaranteeing a female's content."

"I do not necessarily need to enter wedlock to acquire contentment in my life, Tibby," said Lucinda, amused.

"No, my dear, I suppose not," said Miss Blythe. Her voice held a faintly dubious note.

"I can be very happy by myself. The Season is before me, and I shall dissipate myself until I am utterly worn away by diversions," said Lucinda, mildly stung by her companion's obvious lack of conviction.

"What shall you do then?" asked Miss Blythe mildly.

"What?" Lucinda was taken aback. "How do you mean?"

"What shall you do when the Season's amusements come to an end?" asked Miss Blythe.

Lucinda stared at her companion, not at all certain how to

respond. She had not thought beyond the Season. For several months she had thought of nothing but her plans for her own enjoyment. It had never once occurred to her that she would find herself at loose ends when the Season drew to a close. Of course, Carbarry waited for her, but it seemed somehow tame to simply leave London and return to her quiet life.

Lucinda airily waved a dismissive hand. "Oh, there will be any number of things to do. Perhaps I shall travel. I should like that, I think. The war is over, and it will be possible now to see all the sights."

"The sights always appear at their best when they are shared with someone else," suggested Miss Blythe. "And I do not refer to the company of a paid traveling companion, my dear!" She looked pointedly at her former pupil over the rims of her spectacles.

"You are an incorrigible romantic," accused Lucinda.

Miss Blythe considered the matter for a moment, then nodded. "I do believe that I am," she agreed. "It was through my offices, really, that your sister Letty was finally able to attract dear Reverend Birchfield's attention. It was a very pretty wedding and vastly touching. I believe that I had to resort to my handkerchief up to a dozen different times."

Lucinda groaned. "Pray do not attempt to play the matchmaker for me this Season, Tibby, I beg of you! I do not wish to attract particular attentions from any gentleman."

"How odd of you, to be sure. I had quite made up my mind that that was what you truly hoped to gain from the Season," said Miss Blythe.

"I did not come up to London to find myself a second husband," said Lucinda, throwing up her hands. "Why everyone must instantly leap to that conclusion, I fail to understand!"

"Oh, has someone else besides Lady Sefton mentioned the possibility?" asked Miss Blythe interestedly.

"My father," admitted Lucinda. "He was so gothic as to warn me against *competing* with the misses who are making their debuts. I would not show to advantage because I am too long in the tooth, if you please!"

"Quite sound advice," observed Miss Blythe. "I have always known Sir Thomas to be a gentleman of considerable native intelligence. Most definitely you should not compete with the fresh-faced ingenues. You must exercise a unique style of your own. It is fortunate that you are so lovely and are now a young woman of substance. My advice would be to—"

"Enough, ma'am!" exclaimed Lucinda. She wagged her finger at her companion. "I warn you, Tibby, if I catch you scheming on my behalf, I shall at once quit London and carry us both off to Carbarry!"

"Very well, my dear, since you are so set against it," said Miss Blythe. "I shall let you go your own obstinate way."

"I am not obstinate."

Miss Blythe sternly overrode the affronted rejoinder. "However, I do feel strongly that I must point out that the duty of any conscientious chaperone is to put her charge in the way of every eligible gentleman possible. It will be a struggle to reconcile the violation of my duty with my conscience."

Lucinda would have retorted with some spirit, but she checked herself as the door opened. She turned her head. "Yes, Church?"

The butler bowed. "Mr. Stassart, my lady."

Lucinda made an exclamation of mingled dismay and resignation. "Oh, bother!"

"Precisely," remarked Miss Blythe. Her voice had turned markedly acid.

## Chapter Six

Mr. Ferdie Stassart came into the drawing room with the confident air of one who knows himself to be welcome. He was a rather willowy gentleman who sported dandified tastes. Lucinda was taken aback at sight of him, for his attire was even more exaggerated than she recalled.

His coat was padded through the shoulders and cut so tightly to his thin form that it was obvious that he had to be wrestled into it by his valet. The starched shirtpoints that brushed his pale cheekbones were so obstructive that it was impossible for him to turn his head without moving his entire body. His smallclothes were exquisitely worked, and his waistcoat, from which dangled various fobs and an ornate eyeglass, was of a sharp yellow shade that made the ladies stare. His pantaloons fit without a crease into shining tassled topboots.

Mr. Stassart met Lucinda's startled gaze and preened himself, taking her look to be one of admiration. A raffish smile lit his boyishly handsome countenance, and he greeted her in warm accents. "Cousin!"

As he started toward her, he espied Miss Blythe, and he checked in midstride. His countenance altered ludicrously, for he had anticipated finding his fair cousin alone. He had inquired of the butler whether Lady Mays was entertaining any other callers, but he had not thought to ask about the possible existence of a chaperone.

"Why, Miss Blythe! This is something of an astonishment, ma'am. I never expected to see you here. It has been quite some time, I believe, since we last met," he said.

"Mr. Stassart," acknowledged Miss Blythe coolly. "I am pleased that you recall me. I, too, remember you. Quite well."

Mr. Stassart regarded the former governess for a thoughtful moment before he regained his smile. "I could never forget one who figured so closely with my uncle's household."

He turned his attention back to Lucinda. "I see that you have retained the services of a formidable chaperone, cousin. However, I do not think that our Miss Blythe need put herself out over such a close member of the family!"

Lucinda held out her hand to him, a polite smile upon her face. "Hello, Ferdie."

Mr. Stassart shook his head. There was a glint of amusement in his rather hard blue eyes. "Come, cousin! I shall not stand on ceremony with you. Why, we have known one another since our cradles!" He had taken hold of her hand and now, holding her captive, bent forward to place a kiss.

Lucinda turned her head so that his salute fell upon her cheek rather than her lips. She freed her hand and retreated to sit down in a wing chair rather than returning to her former place on the settee, to which she gestured. "Won't you sit down, Ferdie? I should have known that you would come to see me."

"So you should," he agreed easily, taking his seat. "When I heard that my fair cousin Lady Mays had returned to London, I set out at once to wait upon you. I have always held you in the highest regard, Lucinda, as you well know."

"Do I, indeed," said Lucinda on a dry note. "I thought it was my father whom you held in high regard. At least, you have said so whenever you have required someone to bail you out of your latest indiscretions."

Mr. Stassart pressed a well-groomed hand to his coat front in the vague vicinity of his heart. "You cut me to the quick, Lucinda. Am I truly perceived with such coldness, such unfairness, such ignorance? Alas, I can see that I am. I make bold to tell you, fair cousin, that such sentiments do not do you credit. No, indeed! In fact, I find myself to be insulted. I am not some man-milliner that you may use with impunity. I am the Honorable Ferdie Stassart, your estimable father's heir and your own adoring cousin!"

"Oh, give over, Ferdie, do!" said Lucinda, smiling. "You have never cared one whit about me, nor I for you! Why, you were always shockingly rude to all of us. My sisters and I considered you to be the merest scrub of a boy."

Mr. Stassart preferred to let pass the last part of her observation. "On the contrary! I care for you a great deal, Lucinda, very possibly more than you could know at this juncture. When I heard that you had wed Lord Mays and then that you had been banished to the country to live in virtual penury—! Why, my heart positively bled for you." Ferdie shook his head disapprovingly. "It was a disgraceful piece of work that you were forced to wed a man so unsuited to you. I was never more revolted when I heard what was in the wind."

"It is a pity, then, that you did not voice your feelings to Sir Thomas, Mr. Stassart. Perhaps he might have listened to his heir," said Miss Blythe, embroidering for all she was worth.

Mr. Stassart cast a glance of dislike in the companion's direction. He chose to ignore the lady's interpolation. "My dear Lucinda, you must believe me. Truly I have never held you in anything but the utmost regard."

"Why, Ferdie! I am overcome. But if these were your true feelings, whyever did you not visit me at Carbarry? Surely in my exile I must have welcomed such expressions of affection," said Lucinda.

He grimaced. "You must understand, Lucinda. It would not have done to cross Lord Mays. He was a rather intolerant sort of fellow. No, no! My hands were tied. I could do nothing for you." Ferdie spread his fingers in an expression of abject regret.

"What you actually mean is that you feared to anger the one who had cancelled all of your debts and secured your inheritance for you," said Lucinda with brutal frankness. She regarded her cousin's stiffening countenance with a quizzical gaze. "I am rather curious, though. Tell me, Ferdie, did you try to put the touch to Lord Mays later? And were you successful? I would scarcely think so. His lordship was no pigeon for your clumsy plucking."

"My dear Lucinda!" Mr. Stassart drew himself up, the very picture of dignity and outrage. "I shall not deign to descend to such levels as you seem to want to haunt. I had no notion that your unfortunate experiences had created such a poisonous tongue. And let me tell you, my girl, that it is vastly unbecoming! If you do not take care, you will become known as an archwife, and I do not think you would like that!"

"I really care little what society thinks of me, Ferdie. And despite your warning, I do not believe that I will be shunned. I am a widow of some substance and still of marriageable age, after all. I imagine that my credit will withstand a great deal of backbiting," said Lucinda calmly.

Ferdie took a fresh assessment of her and altered his tack. He smoothed his sleeve. "Yes, perhaps you are right. There are many hypocrites in society, dear cousin. You surely know the kind. Those who will pretend friendship when all they really wish is for your kind bounty to be bestowed upon them."

Miss Blythe yanked so hard on her thread that it snapped.

She began searching for her scissors. All the while, her piercing eyes were fixed upon the foppish gentleman who was seated across from her. He was smiling at his fair cousin in a way that made her palm itch to connect with his bloodless cheek.

"Oh, indeed," said Lucinda, almost fascinated to hear next what her cousin might utter.

Ferdie leaned forward with an earnest expression, his hands resting lightly upon his elegantly attired knees. "Dear, dear Lucinda, allow me to protect you from such beings. You can have no notion how others will attempt to take advantage of your largesse. Believe me, I have been long enough in society to know just how to steer you clear of such personages. I would be most happy to establish myself as your gallant."

"I am not some young untried miss that you may pull the wool so easily over my eyes, Ferdie," said Lucinda dryly.

"Why, I do not know what you mean," said Mr. Stassart, straightening, and a slightly wary expression coming into his eyes.

Lucinda smiled and shook her head. "Oh, Ferdie, how many years have I heard you pitch your gammon? Why, your own father refused long since to have anything to do with your excesses, while mine handed over huge sums into your hands only because you were his heir. You would have had to enter the army or flee to the colonies long since to escape your creditors if that had not been so."

"You were a child, Lucinda. You do not know of what you speak," said Ferdie loftily.

"Don't I just?" retorted Lucinda. "My unfortunate marriage was made in part to fish you out of the deep waters that you had leaped into."

He waved his hand dismissively. "While it is true that I benefited from your marriage, Lucinda, I utterly deny that you were made a sacrifice for any troubles of mine. Lord Mays was incredibly generous in the settlements. It quite moves me to recall how his lordship provided for us all. And you did not precisely go begging, Lucinda! Why, I've heard that Carbarry is a tidy little estate. Indeed, you may count yourself fortunate that you did so well for yourself."

"Ferdie, you may make all the denials you will, but you and I both know every word I've spoken is true. I am astonished that you come to me protesting an affection that you have never felt," said Lucinda. "Why, if there were an ounce of truth in it, you would have made some push to see me at Carbarry."

"I could not very well stare down Lord Mays and make unsanctioned visits to his wife. Pray be reasonable, Lucinda," said Ferdie, his mouth curling in tolerant amusement.

"You did not visit me at Carbarry not out of respect for Lord Mays, but because you assumed that I was kept on a pittance and that you would gain nothing out of the connection," said Lucinda roundly. She shook her head. "Cousin, you are precisely one of those people you have just been warning me against! Why, I would not trust you within an inch of my purse."

"These are hard words, indeed, Lucinda!" said Mr. Stassart. He showed a wounded countenance to her. "I have come today out of the purest motives of affection and this is how I am repaid. You have wounded me deeply, cousin, very deeply." He flung out a hand as though to stop her from speaking. "However, I am a resilient fellow. I hope that I am also a forgiving sort, so I shall not hold any of it against you."

"Thank heaven for that," murmured Miss Blythe sotto voce.

Ferdie pretended not to hear the sarcastic aside. He rose to his feet and struck a dramatic pose, pressing his manicured hand to his breast. "I shall take my leave of you now, dear cousin. I hope that you will reflect how basely you have used me and when next I see you, I trust that your manner will have softened toward me."

Lucinda laughed. She rose, too, and held out her hand. "For all that you are a worthless fellow, Ferdie, you are strangely amusing as well. I suppose that peculiar brand of charm is essential when one is such a desperate cardplayer. One must have something to fall back upon when one loses so consistently as you have always seemed to do."

Stung at last, Ferdie was on the point of a hasty retort. He was a gamester through and through, and he prided himself upon his expertise. But when he met his cousin's quizzical, knowing gaze, he swallowed whatever he had been about to say. It was not his object to set up her back. Instead, he took her hand and made a flourishing bow. "I shall count the days until we meet again, cousin."

"And I, too, cousin," said Lucinda with a touch of irony.

He retained her hand when she would have withdrawn it and, with a soulful glance, said ingenuously, "By the by, I met Wilfred Mays coming out of your house when I arrived. He mentioned a dinner party or something of the sort that you are planning. I do hope that I am invited?"

"To be sure, Ferdie! You see, I mean to invite all of London," said Lucinda gently.

Mr. Stassart smiled with difficulty through his anger. She had so neatly pricked all of his attempts to cozen her. He let go of her hand. "You are gracious," he said, his teeth still bared in an insincere smile.

He did not delay any longer in taking his leave. With a stiff parting nod in Miss Blythe's direction, he left the ladies to the amusement of what he felt could only be their own dull company.

When the door shut behind him, Miss Blythe jabbed her needle into her piecework and rolled it up. "Well! I must say that was as good as a play."

Lucinda laughed. "Wasn't it? Poor Ferdie! He tried so hard to play off his tricks." She glanced speculatively at the closed door. "I wonder how much he wanted. I almost asked him."

"You will never open your pockets to that one!" exclaimed Miss Blythe sharply.

"Never fear, Tibby. I have my cousin Ferdie's measure. He will make up to me as long as he believes that I will someday allow him to dip into my purse," said Lucinda. She wandered over to the mantle and idly fingered a priceless figurine. "And for the moment, it amuses me to see how long his hope will carry him."

Miss Blythe eyed her askance. "That does not sound very nice, my dear."

"It doesn't, does it? I am constantly amazed at my own cynicism these days."

Lucinda turned to smile at her companion, somewhat wistfully. "But perhaps if Ferdie tries to hang from my sleeve, he will not apply to my father. You have not seen my parents this last twelvemonth, Tibby. I doubt not that you would be shocked. My father is not so vigorous as he once was, nor is my mother. I would like them not to be made anxious for anything. Is it so wrong of me to wish that, Tibby?"

"No, Lucinda, of course it is not wrong," said Miss Blythe gently. She rose and went to the bellpull. "Shall I ring for tea? I believe it to be almost time in any event."

"Yes, do. And when Church comes in, I shall tell him that we are no longer home to callers. Does that suit you, Tibby?"

"Perfectly," said Miss Blythe. "Such a visit as we have just sustained begs time for recovery."

Lucinda laughed. "Just so!"

Lucinda and Miss Blythe spent what remained of the afternoon in a quiet fashion. They took dinner at home as had been their usual custom since coming to London. They planned to attend the theater that evening, however, and went upstairs an hour beforehand to dress.

## Chapter Seven

As promised, some of the gowns that Lucinda had commissioned were delivered. One was a lavishly trimmed evening gown for Miss Blythe. The severely cut cream silk gown bestowed elegance upon its wearer, and she smoothed its skirt with both trepidation and pleasure. Never in her life had she owned such a beautiful garment.

During the shopping trip, Miss Blythe's humble conscience had continued to prick her, and she had objected again to purchases that Lucinda had insisted upon making for her. "Lucinda, pray do not! With the excessive salary that you are giving me as your companion, I am well able to purchase my own stockings and gloves!"

"Tibby, is it not true that a companion's wardrobe and her food and her lodging are generally considered to be part of her salary?" asked Lucinda.

"Of course, but that has nothing to do with this!" exclaimed Miss Blythe.

"It has everything to do with it. I would be the most monstrous mistress alive if I did not provide the expected considerations of your position," said Lucinda firmly.

"Oh, my dear!" Miss Blythe had said, caught between laughter and tears. In the end, she had acquiesced because she had seen that there was nothing she could say that would persuade Lucinda from pouring such bounty upon her person. Therefore she had shrugged and allowed herself to accept without guilt all the benefits of her new station in life. Very much the realist, Miss Blythe knew that there would inevitably come a day when this fantastic turn in her existence would be done. Then she would recall it all as a pleasant memory. She might as well live it to the hilt while she may.

Something of this running through her mind, Miss Blythe went to her jewel box and took out the pearl drops and strand of pearls that she had treasured through the years, but had never had an opportunity to wear. A governess did not adorn herself or otherwise bring attention to her person. But tonight she was not a governess. Miss Blythe fixed the drops in her ears and clasped the pearls about her throat, her fingers a little clumsy from their trembling.

Lucinda had lent a maid to Miss Blythe as her dresser. Now the woman persuaded Miss Blythe to be allowed to arrange her hair. The result was a less restrained style that softened Miss Blythe's features and, to her astonishment, caused her to appear ten years younger. "I scarcely recognize myself," she murmured, made uncertain by the incredible change wrought in her appearance this night.

"You look a proper treat, ma'am," said the maid admiringly.

Miss Blythe drew herself up in front of the cheval glass. A smile touched her lips. "Thank you." Taking up a cloak and folding it over her arm, she returned downstairs, holding herself proudly.

When Miss Blythe entered the drawing room, Lucinda was already before her. "Forgive me, Lucinda. I did not mean to keep you waiting."

Lucinda turned and instantly applauded her companion's appearance. "Oh, Tibby! You look positively magnificent. It becomes you so very well."

Miss Blythe flushed slightly. "You are too kind, Lucinda. But I can scarcely hold a candle to you."

Lucinda glanced almost indifferently into the gilt mirror above the mantel. She was wearing a sea green gown with an overskirt of silver gauze. Diamonds glinted at her ears and collared her throat. Her hair was arranged in a cascade of dark curls that enhanced the brilliancy of her eyes. "I am well enough."

"My dear!" Miss Blythe was astounded at Lucinda's lack of vanity. "You are lovelier even than you were as a girl. You have gained a maturity, a presence, an air that is unmistakable. I would not be at all surprised if every gentleman in the theater does not stare in admiration."

"What pleasant rot you speak, Tibby," said Lucinda easily. "When I know very well that it will be the two of us appearing together that will stop hearts and stir up comment."

"Now it is you who is speaking rot," said Miss Blythe. She allowed a footman to place her cloak about her shoulders. Her gray eyes sparkled behind her spectacles. "I feel every bit the same trepidation that I did as a young girl when I was to go to my first party. It is quite a treat to be able to attend the theater."

Lucinda hugged her companion. "My dearest Tibby. You shall go to the theater as often as you wish and attend as many parties as you can possibly bear!"

Lucinda and Miss Blythe left the town house and stepped up into Lucinda's private carriage to travel to the theater. Their destination was not a great distance from Mays House, but nevertheless the ride took several minutes due to the traffic. The streets were crowded with other vehicles, both of the fashionable and the more humble sort. The noise of clattering wheels and horse's hooves and raucous voices filled the damp night air. The metropolis never truly slept.

Lucinda had rented a box for the Season, and she and Miss Blythe settled themselves happily into their chairs. They had arrived a few minutes before the rise of the curtain, and a number of acquaintances chose to recognize their presence with a civil bow or nod or wave, which Lucinda and Miss Blythe returned. Several well-dressed gentlemen in the pit, whose custom it was to ogle the attractive women present, raised their eyeglasses to stare at Lady Mays and her companion.

Miss Blythe thought the gentlemen's behavior to be outrageous, but not worthy of notice. Instead, she gazed about her with appreciation. "How nice this is, to be sure."

"Yes, isn't it? I have always enjoyed the theater. I know that you will recall that I adored our studies in Shakespeare," said Lucinda.

"Of course I do, my dear. And this is quite one of my own favorites," said Miss Blythe. "How delicious!"

"Oh, the curtain is about to be raised!" exclaimed Lucinda, leaning forward in anticipation.

Lucinda and Miss Blythe scarcely exchanged a word once the play began. Both sat enthralled at the performance of one of Shakespeare's most popular tragedies. They drew a collective breath when the curtain fell for intermission, and they blinked, reluctant to be brought back to their surroundings.

However, the ladies had little choice when there fell a knock on the door of the box, which was followed by a regular stream of visitors. Ladies came in to renew their acquaintance with Lady Mays and her companion, or to introduce various gentlemen who had persuaded them to perform the office.

It was the general consensus that Lady Mays was still a beauty of astonishing degree. Her gown, her jewels, the style of her wavy hair, were all remarked upon. Lucinda received the compliments graciously, knowing how little it all actually meant, but willing to play the game as long as it suited her.

Mrs. Grisham brought her daughter to be introduced to Lady Mays and Miss Blythe. She was an ambitious mother, and she was shrewd enough to know that an invitation to any address as prestigious as Mays House could not but help her daughter's consequence.

The girl was a pretty minx who was obviously more interested in fixing the interest of any gentleman that came within her range than in meeting two unattached ladies. Miss Amanda Grisham was shocked when she met Lady Mays. It had never occurred to her that a widow could be either young or beautiful. As she responded to Lucinda's greeting, there was an instant antagonism in her expressive eyes. Lucinda was a good deal astonished to realize that the girl saw her as some sort of rival.

Lady Mays's companion, Miss Blythe, was thought to look very well also. Mrs. Grisham was particularly impressed. "Such an elegant, respectable creature. She is obviously of good birth. You would do well to pattern yourself after her, Amanda," said Mrs. Grisham to her daughter as they left the box.

"Yes, Mama," said her obedient daughter, casting a languishing glance at a young gentleman just then passing them. He turned his head, startled.

It was not at all surprising that a number of gentlemen seized the opportunity to make themselves known to the beautiful widow. Many relied upon ladies of their acquaintance to perform the necessary introductions. However, it was already becoming common knowledge that Mr. Stassart was Lady Mays's cousin, and Ferdie found himself in the pleasant position of being opportuned for his good offices. He allowed himself to be persuaded when the anxious gentlemen began to offer him small considerations that were of value to him. Several of his outstanding vowels were retired upon his promise to secure for the grateful bucks special entree into Lady Mays's presence.

Thus it was that Ferdie came into the box with three gentlemen in tow. A large smile lit his pale countenance. "Cousin! I bid you a fair evening." He bowed low over Lucinda's outstretched hand.

Lucinda smiled, her eyes twinkling across his pomaded locks at Miss Blythe's arctic expression. "Hello, Ferdie. Have you come to discuss your impressions of the play with Miss Blythe and myself?"

Mr. Stassart belatedly acknowledged the older woman. "Miss Blythe, your obedient servant." He started to turn immediately back to his cousin.

"Civil of you to say so, Mr. Stassart," said Miss Blythe primly.

One of the gentlemen, who appeared considerably older than his companions, gave a rumbling laugh. Ferdie flung a flickering, annoyed smile in Miss Blythe's direction before he addressed his cousin. "Alas, I am not a learned fellow, so I shall not bore on about the merits or drawbacks of tonight's performance. I am come, however, to pay homage to the loveliest lady of my acquaintance." He regained possession of Lucinda's hand and folded it between his own. Dropping on one knee, he uttered, "Dear cousin, but smile upon me and I shall be satisfied!"

"Very nice, Ferdie," said Lucinda admiringly. When his grip slackened with surprise, she managed to free her hand. "I do believe that you could rival tonight's leading man. I had no notion that you had such a turn for the dramatic. Had you, Tibby?"

"I have always been of the opinion that Mr. Stassart exhibited a rare flare for playacting," said Miss Blythe blandly.

At a snort of appreciative laughter from the same amused gentleman, Mr. Stassart's fine nostrils flared. With smiling viciousness, he snapped, "Gentlemen, my cousin's former governess."

"And my very good friend," said Lucinda quietly. She was still smiling, but winter edged her voice. "Pray introduce us to your companions, Ferdie."

Mr. Stassart realized that his cousin had been angered, and he silently cursed the Blythe biddy. However, nothing of his inner outrage was betrayed in his manners. "Lord Levine and the Honorable Albert Pepperidge, who are particular friends of mine," he said.

The two gentlemen came forward, eager to pay their compliments to Lady Mays. She introduced them at once to Miss Blythe, and they reluctantly but politely greeted her chaperone.

Ferdie gestured to the third gentleman, a measure of annoyance entering his eyes. It had been this gentleman who had derived amusement at his expense. "And this is—"

The gentleman, who had stood back watching the vying byplay with a lift of amusement to his mobile mouth, stepped forward and smoothly presented himself. "I am Marcus Weatherby, Lady Mays. Miss Blythe, your servant. What your cousin is too nice to reveal, Lady Mays, is that I attached myself to his coattails when I overheard that he was coming to your box. I have used him abominably, for we are the merest acquaintances."

Mr. Stassart was emboldened by this confession to give voice to his hidden resentment. "Quite. I have never been on more than nodding terms with you, Weatherby."

Lucinda acknowledged Mr. Weatherby's bow with a cool smile, then turned back to her cousin. "But how well you have handled an awkward situation, Ferdie," said Lucinda, smiling at him. She really did not understand why she should set herself to soothe his feathers, but that it was advantageous to do so was immediately obvious.

Mr. Stassart was mollified, even unbending enough toward Mr. Weatherby to volunteer the information that the gentleman had just recently sold his commission in the army and that previously the gentleman had spent some years in India. "Weatherby is considerably older than I or Lord Levine or Albert here," he finished.

Mr. Weatherby smilingly agreed to it and sat himself down beside Miss Blythe. He bent his head toward the lady, the silver in his dark hair glinting in the candlelight.

Lucinda cast a swift thoughtful glance in the gentleman's direction. Mr. Weatherby was almost certainly all of forty years of age. He was an attractive man, well set up despite his obvious handicap. His left sleeve was empty and was neatly pinned up to the shoulder. His entire demeanor and dress proclaimed him to be a gentleman of quiet means. There was nothing of the fop or dandy about his person. He was as unlike her cousin and those others as a raven was to a songbird, she thought.

She wondered why Mr. Weatherby had chosen to thrust himself into her notice, for he did not in the least act like a man who was anxious to pay court to a lady that he admired. He had quite willingly left the field open to those with whom he had entered the box.

Lucinda's attention was reclaimed by Lord Levine, who offered his assessment of that evening's entertainment. "Dashed dull play, what?" he asked with a superior air. Mr. Pepperidge was quick to interject his own opinion. Lucinda smilingly allowed the two gentlemen to vye for her favor, all the while wondering what Mr. Weatherby could possibly be saying that was keeping her chaperone so riveted.

Mr. Stassart and his friends stayed a few minutes more. They left eventually, casting somewhat jealous eyes over Mr. Weatherby, for he had not yet been given a gracious cachet by Lady Mays. But they consoled themselves with the reflection that he had been relegated to talking to Miss Blythe while they had monopolized Lady Mays's attention. In any event, his age and his infirmity surely put him outside the interest of any lady. So the trio left in fairly high spirits, convinced that they had acquitted themselves well.

Mr. Weatherby looked up when the door closed and inquired, "Are those prosing pups gone at last?"

Miss Blythe chuckled while Lucinda actually laughed. "For shame, Mr. Weatherby! One must protest such incivility, however appropriate the sentiment."

"I say what I think, my lady. I am not one of your London exquisites who mouths pretty flatteries. Paugh!"

"Then what are you, Mr. Weatherby?" asked Lucinda, curious to hear what he might say.

Mr. Weatherby smiled. "I am a nabob, an old soldier, a thistle in the wind, my lady!"

"Lucinda, Mr. Weatherby has been recounting to me the most interesting tales of his travels. Only fancy, he has actually been to Greece," said Miss Blythe. "Oh, how I should like to tour the country of Homer and the Iliad!"

"It is a hot, dirty place, but nevertheless there is much of interest. But I would recommend that your travels wait until this civil war with the Turks is quite settled," said Mr. Weatherby. He rose from his chair. "I see that the curtain is about to rise. I

shall take leave of you now, my lady, Miss Blythe. Your servant."

When he had gone, Lucinda turned to Miss Blythe. "Well! I
believe that to be the most intriguing gentleman that I have yet
met in London."

"Is he, my dear? I own, I found Mr. Weatherby to be a fascinating conversationalist. But do you not think that the gentleman is a trifle old for you?" said Miss Blythe.

"Oh, I have no notions in that direction, I assure you," said
Lucinda. "However, I do like his odd manners, and he seems
to irritate my cousin. Is that reason enough to invite Mr.
Weatherby to our supper and ball, do you think?"

"Really, Lucinda!" said Miss Blythe, her lips twitching.
Though she shared her ladyship's sentiments, she would not
say so. She had never liked Mr. Stassart above half, but it
would be most improper in her to encourage such flippancy.
She determinedly turned her attention to the performance on
the stage.

# *Chapter Eight*

Lucinda and Miss Blythe left the theater. It was a very
damp night. While the ladies waited for the carriage to
come up to the curb, they hugged their cloaks close about
them against the cold. The sky had been overcast all day, and
dark had fallen early. The ladies, both pleasantly tired, reflected on the evening.

"It was a wonderful performance. I am so glad that we
came," said Miss Blythe.

"Oh, yes! And it was not only the play, Tibby. The evening
progressed in a satisfactory fashion otherwise, don't you
think?" asked Lucinda. "I anticipate that we shall see any

number of new invitations on the morrow. Why, we are becoming quite popular!"

"Yes, indeed. Everyone was most gracious," said Miss Blythe.

Suddenly the dense, threatening clouds opened up. Rain and sleet swept down, surprising all that were leaving the theater. Cries and curses alike were startled out of the theatergoers, and there was a dash for shelter.

The carriage had drawn up at that moment, and Lucinda and Miss Blythe scrambled up into it with unladylike haste. The door was slammed shut. The carriage dipped as the driver climbed back up on top. Lucinda and Miss Blythe pulled a rug over their knees and put their feet on the hot brick. Rain and sleet drummed on the carriage roof.

Water dripped from Lucinda's nose, and she brushed it away, laughing. "We must look like two drowned rats! What an end to a perfect evening. That will teach us to get so puffed up in our own estimation."

Miss Blythe sneezed. She apologized, ending with, "It is a most salutary lesson, indeed!"

As soon as they had returned to Mays House, Lucinda and Miss Blythe repaired instantly to their respective bedchambers to remove their wet cloaks and finery. Madison gave a distressed cry at sight of her mistress's wet appearance. "My lady! Oh, you must be frozen!"

"I am all right, Madison. But I fear that my slippers are ruined," said Lucinda, wiggling her toes in the sodden footgear. She dropped the heavy wet cloak over a chair.

"We shall soon have you out of these wet things and into your gown, my lady," said Madison. Her fingers flew over the many small buttons on the back of the gown. Within minutes Lucinda was cozy in a warm gown and robe.

The housekeeper had ordered up hot toddies for the ladies. Mrs. Beeseley herself performed the task of warming Lady Mays's bedsheets. As she energetically moved the warming pan back and forth between the sheets, she scolded her mistress. "Anyone could have seen that it was going to rain. You ought to be more careful, my lady. No doubt you will catch a terrible chill."

"Nonsense, I am never ill," said Lucinda. "A little wetting shan't harm me in the least." She tightened the tie on her robe and turned to the fire, spreading her chilled fingers to the warm blaze.

"Perhaps not, my lady," said Mrs. Beeseley, a note of doubt in her tone. She straightened, done at last with the warming pan. "Howsomever, I do have my doubts for poor dear Miss Blythe. Why, I left her not three minutes ago sneezing and sniffling something awful. The poor lady looked as miserable as a wet cat."

Lucinda looked around, her sympathy immediately aroused. "Poor Tibby! I shall go to her at once."

Lucinda went along the hall to her companion's bedroom. She knocked on the door, and the maid opened it to her. The woman bobbed a curtsy. "Good evening, m'lady."

Lucinda entered with a quiet word of greeting. "How is Miss Blythe?" she asked softly.

The maid shook her head. "Miss is sitting before the fire, feeling as wretched as she can be, m'lady." She closed the door as Lucinda went to see for herself.

Miss Blythe was huddled in a wing chair with a rug thrown over her knees. Her hair had been let down from its pins, and it hung in a thick screen over her shoulder. She cupped the hot toddy between her hands and carefully sipped at the hot brew. Her eyes were watery, her nose was red, and when she greeted Lucinda, her voice came out in a rasping croak.

Lucinda was shocked and concerned. "Tibby, you must instantly get into bed."

"It is only a small chill. You must not be anxious on my account," said Miss Blythe hoarsely.

The maid leaned quietly toward Lucinda. "Miss refuses to get into bed, my lady, and here I've warmed it up proper for her. Miss says that she don't mean to coddle herself and won't go to bed earlier than her usual."

"Tibby, how can you be so nonsensical? Of course you should go to bed," said Lucinda.

"I shan't coddle myself. It is a very bad habit in which to fall," said Miss Blythe. Her stern declaration lost most of its effect when she dissolved into a fit of sneezing.

"Well, *I* shall coddle you! Here, I shall help you into bed." Lucinda took the cup from Miss Blythe's hands and gave it to the maid.

"But I do not believe in coddling one's self," protested Miss Blythe, sniffling.

"Of course you do not. I am a great bully, however, and I insist that you get into bed. You will be much more comfortable," said Lucinda. Ruthlessly, she threw the rug off Miss Blythe's knees. She put her hand under Miss Blythe's elbow and levered her up out of the chair. "Come along, Tibby. I will not be denied."

Miss Blythe gave a dry laugh. "Very well. I see that you are determined to coerce me."

With Lucinda's arm firm about her shoulders, she allowed herself to be guided across the bedroom. She gratefully climbed into the waiting bed. The maid firmly tucked the coverlets over her. From the pillows, Miss Blythe said, "I shall be perfectly all right in the morning."

"So I should hope," said Lucinda. "I shall inquire after you in the morning, Tibby. Good night."

Miss Blythe murmured a drowsy reply. The hot toddy had been liberally laced with rum, and it was already beginning to do its work.

The following morning Lucinda asked about Miss Blythe. She was told that the lady was still abed. Concerned, Lucinda went at once to her companion's room. She could not recall a single instance when her former governess had not risen with the dawn.

Lucinda found Miss Blythe heavy-eyed and feverish. The lady was obviously suffering from a headache caused by a stuffy nose. "You must remain in bed and rest today, Tibby."

"But I must get up, Lucinda. What will you do without me to chaperone you when gentlemen callers come to visit? There are the errands that I wished to run, too." Miss Blythe fretfully picked at her coverlet. "I wished to return the books that I had taken from the Lending Library and to buy a length of ribbon and some new embroidery yarns, too."

Sitting down on the side of the bed, Lucinda took hold of the older woman's agitated hands. "Dear Tibby. It is all very easily answered. I shall manage very well, I promise you! I shall not receive anyone whom I know you will not approve. As for these errands, I can very well do them for you. Only, you must give me a sample of the color yarn that you require so that I may match it perfectly."

"It is not proper that you should discharge my paltry commissions," said Miss Blythe, sniffling morosely.

"I hope that I am not so high in the instep as that! Besides, it will do me a world of good to get out of this house for a while," said Lucinda. "I will not have you stepping a foot out of doors until you are over this chill, or we will have you taking ill."

Miss Blythe agreed to the wisdom in that, but she still protested that Lucinda should not be bothered with her errands. "I do not wish you to put yourself out on my account."

"I have a few errands of my own, too, so I shall be going out in any event. Where have you put the books to be exchanged and the yarns?" asked Lucinda, smiling. As Miss Blythe began to form another objection, she threw up her hand. "Now give over, do, Tibby. I shall not take no for an answer."

Miss Blythe smiled at last. "Are you still playing the bully, my lady?"

"I rather enjoy the role," said Lucinda.

A watery laugh was raised from Miss Blythe that ended in a coughing spell. She directed the maid to the books and the yarns, and when they had been given into Lucinda's hands, she said hoarsely, "I do thank you, my dear. I am just sorry that you are putting yourself to so much trouble."

"Nonsense. You know that I am entertained by a good novel as well as the next person. I have no doubt whatever that I shall enjoy perusing the shelves. As for these other items, I shall merely add them to my own list. Now I shall leave you to rest, Tibby," said Lucinda cheerfully, moving away from the bed and carrying the books and the sample of embroidery yarn.

The maid opened the bedroom door. Lucinda paused before exiting, saying quietly, "I wish to be informed at once if she takes a turn for the worse."

"Yes, m'lady. I shall watch her very close," promised the maid.

Lucinda went on to her own room, intending to change into attire more appropriate to a shopping trip. Her fine brows were drawn in a slight frown. She had never known her former governess to be taken ill, and it came as a surprise to discover that Miss Blythe was not the invulnerable personage that she had always thought her.

For the first time Lucinda realized that her dear Miss Blythe was becoming older. What did a woman who had been a governess all of her life do once she became too old or too infirm to hold a position? More to the point, what would she do once she no longer needed Miss Blythe as her chaperone and companion? Certainly Lucinda did not want to thrust Miss Blythe into the awkward situation of having to find another post.

Miss Blythe was enjoying everything about living in London so much. It seemed cruel to think of letting her go back to her former occupation when it offered so few of the amenities of life. There must be some way of providing indefinitely for Miss Blythe. However, Lucinda had the good sense to know that that lady would reject outright charity. There seemed no perfect or easy solution. It was something to keep at the back of her mind and puzzle over until she could come up with a satisfactory answer.

Lucinda went into her bedroom. When her dresser learned that Lucinda was intending to go out, she instantly offered to accompany her mistress.

Lucinda declined her maid's services. "I have given you the day off, Madison. I would not dream of depriving you of it now."

"But my lady, you'll need someone to carry your parcels," said Madison as she did up the buttons of her mistress's walking dress.

"John Coachman is well able to do that, Madison, for I do not anticipate many purchases. I shan't be out long, so you mustn't fret," said Lucinda, sliding her arms into the sleeves of a warm pelisse and buttoning it. She settled a velvet bonnet on her head and tied the ribbons.

"It isn't proper for you to be out alone, my lady," said Madison disapprovingly, handing a pair of soft kid gloves to her mistress.

Lucinda laughed, turning away from the mirror and pulling

on her gloves. "Now you sound like Miss Blythe. This morning I am a creature of impropriety, it seems."

"Miss Blythe is a lady of uncommon sense who knows what is due you, my lady," said Madison repressively.

"Are you saying that I want for sense, Madison?" asked Lucinda provokingly. But the dresser only sniffed, refusing to rise to the bait. Lucinda smiled as she left the bedroom.

Attired in a fashionable bonnet and pelisse, shod in half-kid boots, and carrying a warm muff and her reticule, Lucinda stepped out the front door. She had ordered the carriage brought around, and now she descended the front steps to meet it. A footman followed her, carrying the books and the yarn that she had carried out of Miss Blythe's bedroom.

The coachman stood waiting beside the door, waiting to hand her up into the carriage. Lucinda paused to give him the first destination. He nodded, then glanced up at the town house. "Shall I wait for your maid, my lady?"

Lucinda shook her head. "I will be alone today. I rely upon you to take care of me, John."

"Very good, my lady."

Lucinda got into the carriage. The footman placed the books and yarn on the opposite seat. The door was latched securely. Lucinda arranged the rug over her knees and set her feet against the hot brick. She felt the jerk of motion as her vehicle pulled away from the curb into the heavy carriage traffic.

Lucinda emerged from the portals of the Lending Library. She held two bulky parcels of books under her arm while she awkwardly attempted to untangle the strings of her reticule.

When she had left Mays House, it was with the confident opinion that she could easily dispense with the company of a maid. Her errands were none so onerous that she required anything more than her coachman to take the several small packages from her as she emerged from the shops and place them in the coach. It had been anticipation of the visit to the Lending Library that had actually persuaded her to her course. Of all things she disliked, it was to have someone waiting for her while she was perusing the library's shelves.

But now as she juggled the parcel of books that she had

chosen for Miss Blythe and the smaller parcel of her own selections, she wished that she had brought a woman with her. She cast a fleeting glance toward the street, hoping to see her carriage. Naturally the coachman had been walking the team so that the horses would not be left standing in the cold while she was inside. She did not immediately perceive her equipage, however, so she realized that her driver had probably taken the horses some distance before he turned around.

Lucinda felt one of the parcels begin to slip, and she reached up hastily to reposition it. When she did so, the strings of her reticule again twisted and bit into her wrist. "How utterly provoking!"

As Lucinda descended the library's outside steps, her entire attention was focused on the annoying reticule strings. She was completely unmindful of her surroundings. A fitful gust of cold wind caught the wide brim of her bonnet. Lucinda instinctively grabbed the brim, and when she did so, the smaller parcel of books slipped from her grasp. Lucinda uttered a cry of annoyance and stopped in her tracks, intent only on retrieving the books.

In the next instant she was rudely thrust forward from a blow to her shoulder. Everything tumbled out of her hands. Lucinda stumbled and she would have fallen except for the quick strong hand that caught her elbow and steadied her.

## *Chapter Nine*

Lucinda turned, both astonished and angered, as she pulled free her elbow. She found herself looking at a wide expanse of buttoned coat and her eyes traveled upward.

"I beg your pardon!"

The tall gentleman stared down into her indignant face. Embarrassment and contrition shaped his own expression. His voice was deep. "I am sorry, ma'am! I did not see you stop. I was admiring that team there in the street and— But allow me to help you. I have made you drop everything."

"I can manage, thank you," said Lucinda in frozen accents.

The gentleman had bent down to help gather her parcels. He cast a shrewd glance upward at her stiff expression. "You have every right to think me a clumsy rudes-body," he admitted frankly. "Pray scold me just as furiously as you wish."

Lucinda had been too angry to take proper notice of the gentleman, but now she did. His was a lean, handsome face, deeply tanned from the sun. He was regarding her with a quizzical amusement that made her uncomfortably aware of how she must appear to him. Faint color rose in her face. "I don't wish to scold you," she said.

"Of course you do. Pray do not allow the fact that we are strangers to inhibit your better instincts. Simply lay in and address me as you would your own recalcitrant brother when he has had the audacity to annoy you," invited the gentleman. "I promise you, my shoulders are broad enough to weather nearly any storm."

Lucinda saw that the gentleman had spoken but the unvarnished truth. He was indeed extremely broad-shouldered, yet it suited his well-proportioned physique. The thought crossed her mind that she had never seen anyone quite so large. She said incongruously, "I haven't a brother."

"I *am* sorry. Then you have never enjoyed that particular sisterly right," said the gentleman with ready sympathy. His gray eyes were full of a laughter that invited her to share in it.

Something within Lucinda uncoiled and responded. "But I do have a scruffy care-for-nobody cousin," she said somewhat primly. "And even he would know better than to have his eyes fixed someplace beside where his feet were leading him!"

"Come, this is much better," said the gentleman encouragingly. "You may pretend that I am this poor hapless cousin and berate me without the least cause for offense or embarrassment."

"You are a provoking creature altogether," said Lucinda, accepting her possessions from the gentleman's hands.

"So my mother has told me on more occasions than I can at this moment recall," he said.

"She is quite right to have done so," said Lucinda, preparing to go her way. She held out her hand politely. "Thank you for coming to my assistance. I must beg your pardon as well, for I did stop rather abruptly on the walkway. We would not have collided otherwise, I am persuaded."

"That would surely have been a great loss on my part," said the gentleman. He retained her hand for a moment, looking down into her smiling face. "I hope that we may meet again, though perhaps under less embarrassing circumstances. I am Hector Allanis, Lord Pembroke. You will naturally be wondering who this careless fellow is who so nearly knocked you down. Now you may tell all of your friends my name."

Lucinda laughed. "Yes, indeed! The story will be far better now that I can identify you, sir! I am Lady Lucinda Mays." She gently withdrew her hand, which he seemed to have forgotten that he was holding. "Now I really must go. Here is my coachman come to meet me."

Lord Pembroke looked round at the carriage that was pulling up to the curb. He took note of the crest and the liveried coachman. Waving the fellow back onto his seat, he said, "Permit me to perform this office, my lady. It is the least courtesy that I can extend after my clumsiness." He opened the carriage door and held out his large hand to her.

After the smallest hesitation, Lucinda allowed him to hand her up into the carriage. When she was seated and had put the parcels of books down beside her, he latched the door and stepped back. As the carriage started away, Lord Pembroke touched the brim of his beaver hat. Lucinda instinctively responded, acknowledging his salute with an uplifted hand.

As the carriage turned away from the curb, Lucinda lost sight of Lord Pembroke. She settled back against the velvet seat squabs, a half smile hovering about her mouth. The unexpected encounter with Lord Pembroke had been diverting, to say the least. The gentleman had been genuinely repentant for colliding with her. But he had not suffered long from any excess of embarrassment.

Instead, and with the greatest audacity, he had offered to

provide himself as a fitting object for the exercise of her ill-temper. As a consequence, he had completely disarmed and charmed her.

Lucinda recalled how she had had to lift her eyes to his face. Lord Pembroke was a handsome gentleman built on grand proportions. Lucinda was considered to be rather tall by fashionable standards. Rarely had she found herself to be so completely overshadowed.

It had flattered her that a gentleman of address and polish should put himself to the troublesome task of charming her out of her annoyance.

Lucinda's smile slowly dissolved. Of course, the late Lord Mays had also been a man of considerable charm and exquisite manners. It was a pity that Lord Mays had proven to be at heart quite cold and self-centered.

Lucinda shrugged aside the somber memories. Not everyone that she met in London would be like her departed husband. There were some whose outward manner was a true reflection of their genuine character. One of those was certainly Lord Wilfred Mays. He was as open as a book. Lucinda liked Lord Mays very much for his innate kindness. Another that Lucinda felt that she could trust was Lady Sefton. Her ladyship also had proven herself to be kind.

The trick was to discern those that she could confidently call her friends from those who were more interested in her position and her wealth than in herself.

Lucinda was well aware that she should be wary of those who professed their goodwill toward her in overly lavish accents. She wrinkled her nose as she thought of her cousin, Ferdie Stassart, and his foppish friends. It did not take a great deal of intelligence to recognize into which category she could place those gentlemen. Lucinda had experienced enough hypocrisy during the trial of her marriage to know that those sorts never made true friends. They dropped one from their acquaintance when it was no longer an advantage to claim one's recognition.

It was hard-won wisdom that decreed that she guard her innermost feelings and thoughts from any whom she met until she felt convinced that her trust would not be misplaced. That maxim must certainly be applied to the charming Lord Pembroke should she ever meet him again.

Lord Pembroke was the kind of gentleman who could more easily than not undermine a lady's defenses if she was not careful. He was in truth devilishly attractive, Lucinda thought, recalling his laughing eyes and imposing physique.

Lucinda wondered idly why she had not met Lord Pembroke before. Surely she would have recalled if she had ever been introduced to his lordship during the Season of her come-out or later in the months of her disastrous marriage.

But that chapter of her life had taken place the same year as Waterloo, she remembered. Perhaps it should not be so surprising that Lord Pembroke had not previously come in her way. The war with France had lasted for a long time. Despite Bonaparte's abdication in 1814, many young men of birth had remained in the army or had traveled to Vienna to attach themselves to famous personages attending the Congress of Peace.

When Napoleon Bonaparte had escaped from Elba and returned triumphantly to France to raise the standards of his army again, the forces of a dozen countries, including Britain, had removed to Brussels and the Lowlands in anticipation of a last desperate fight to wrest the control of Europe from the self-styled emperor once and for all. The *ton* had all flocked to Brussels as well, making it overnight the most glittering capital in all Europe.

The Season of Lucinda's come-out, the company in the London salons had been somewhat thin. A much more brilliant and cosmopolitan society had formed around the Congress of Peace. If her parents had had the means, Lucinda had no doubt that they would have carried her to Vienna for her debut. If she had not taken there, they would undoubtedly have followed everyone else of note to Brussels.

However, in light of the Stassarts' financial restraints and the opinion voiced by her mother that there would be no one who could possibly compete with their daughter's looks left in England, Lucinda had been brought out in London. Sir Thomas and Lady Stassart had anticipated only success for their loveliest daughter.

Despite Lucinda's obviously superior attributes, her oppor-

tunities to make a successful marriage were unfortunately and
ironically limited by that same lack of competition, for not
only the daughters of the *ton* but their sons, too, had gone to
Brussels. The number of eligible young gentlemen in residence had been negligible. Lucinda's parents had been grateful and eager to cement the attachment that Lord Mays had
apparently formed for their daughter.

It had been hoped that Lucinda's position as the wife of a
prominent peer would enable her to sponsor her sisters into society and assure them also of advantageous marriages. Perhaps
Lord Mays could even be persuaded to remove his household
to Brussels on a wedding trip, allowing Lucinda's sisters to accompany the newlywed pair so that they might be presented in
Brussels. But such grand expectations had fallen flat when Lucinda's husband had banished her from London to the country
just seven months after they were wed.

Lucinda had lived in virtual exile. She had had Carbarry and
its income, but there was not enough available to her in rents
where she could have supported the cost of a second household in London. Nor would she have really wanted to do so,
for the humiliation of her circumstances would have been too
much to have been borne.

Lucinda had maintained a correspondence with some of
those who had claimed her friendship, but inevitably the exchange of letters had dwindled. Her life was too separated from
society. Those acquaintances whom she had thought to be her
friends had for the most part gradually forgotten her existence.

Three years later, Lord Mays's totally unexpected death
while in the arms of his mistress had freed Lucinda from her
cage. Not only did she have Carbarry, but her husband's
demise had made her a rich young woman. Suddenly, the
world was open to her.

During Lucinda's exile, each of her three sisters had managed
to get herself a husband. Though a curate, a squire, and a baronet
were not the exalted personages that Sir Thomas and his wife
had envisioned for the rest of their daughters, they were able to
be content. Mere respectability, after all, had proven in each
young woman's case to provide a fuller and more satisfying marriage for her than had Lucinda's spectacular social triumph.

Lucinda sighed. She turned her eyes to the glazed window and looked out at the bustle of the street. She was no longer close to her sisters. Their comfortable lives and the growing families that they were beginning to establish had put a gentle wedge between them. On the rare occasions that she saw her sisters, there was expressed between them a fondness that had its roots in a common childhood. Perhaps if her marriage had worked out differently and she had had a child of her own, there would have been a strengthening of those old ties.

A well set-up gentleman on a showy hack passed the window. Lucinda was reminded of Lord Pembroke. As Lucinda recalled again the details of their encounter, she realized that there had been an awkwardness about how his lordship had extended her parcels with his left hand, as though the arm or shoulder was stiff.

Lucinda decided that he must have been a soldier. Lord Pembroke had not struck her as the type of man that would attach himself to a diplomat's coattails. He had probably seen action at Waterloo, she thought. So many had.

Many of the survivors of the war had retired to the country with their wives and children, having learned what was important to them and what was not. Others had simply grown indifferent to the machinations and gossip of the society that they had once been a part.

Lucinda had not been in London for much more than a fortnight before it had been brought home to her how many had taken part in the greatest and most horrific battle of the hardwon war. The fortunate ones had emerged from the carnage that was named Waterloo unscathed or with only minor wounds. Others who had survived had not been so fortunate. There were many gentlemen who had empty coat sleeves, like Mr. Weatherby, or who used crutches or canes to compensate for missing or permanently damaged limbs.

Lucinda hoped that in making her first gathering a supper and ball she would be able to entice even those who did not dance. The success of the function was extremely important to her. She hoped it would serve to reintroduce her to the society that three years before she had been compelled to forsake.

Lucinda looked forward to the evening with a mixture of

anxious anticipation. She had done her utmost to ensure a
smashing success. She had provided herself with a prominent
address and an eminently respectable chaperone. She had returned all of the polite morning calls that she had received,
and she had reestablished old ties. Lucinda could foresee no
reason why she should not shortly be able to enjoy every
amusement that was offered by the *ton*. Her supper and ball
was the first step in launching her into the desired waters.

For the hundredth time she mentally reviewed her preparations. The orchestra had been engaged. The florists had agreed
to transform the ballroom at Mays House into a blooming hot-
house wonderland. The parlor adjoining the ballroom would
make a very suitable cardroom with the addition of several
game tables, which had already been acquired. The menu had
been reviewed and revised countless times before she, the
cook, and Mrs. Beeseley had been satisfied. Lucinda's gown
and Miss Blythe's had been delivered.

Lucinda had pored over her guest list, adjusting and adding
as she thought best. At last she had been satisfied. The gilt-
edged invitations had been addressed in Miss Blythe's elegant
hand and had been sent out just the day before. Already they
had received acceptances.

Lucinda was shrewd enough to know that the function
would be well attended simply out of curiosity. After all, she
had left society under humiliating and rather mysterious circumstances. She had not been granted the opportunity to graciously cancel her engagements nor to say her good-byes. It
was therefore inevitable that she should come under close
scrutiny. It would be unpleasant, of course, but it had to be
borne. The gossip mill would tire quickly enough of her when
she was no longer a novelty.

Lucinda wanted her party to be remembered for more than
her own notoriety, and she had been painstaking in providing
all that was necessary for the enjoyment of her guests. There
would be nothing to complain of in either the entertainment
that was offered or in the refreshments, she thought.

She only hoped that Miss Blythe would be completely recovered from the unexpected chill that she had taken. Otherwise there would indeed be something for the tattle-mongers

to whisper about. A beautiful young woman could not readily hostess a social function without a relative or companion to lend her countenance.

Miss Blythe was perhaps even more cognizant of that fact than Lucinda was herself.

Lucinda knew that even if her former governess did not feel up to it, Miss Blythe would insist upon carrying out her responsibilities as chaperone and companion. For the lady's benefit even more than her own, Lucinda hoped that Miss Blythe would indeed be fully recovered. She did not want her dear Tibby to overextend herself.

However, the date of the supper and ball was yet a week away. In all likelihood there would not be the least occasion for anxiety, thought Lucinda. Miss Blythe would be standing at her side when she greeted her guests that evening.

## Chapter Ten

Lucinda's confidence was not misplaced. Miss Blythe was back to her former self fully two days before the momentous date. On the evening of the supper and ball, Miss Blythe took her place beside Lucinda at the top of the stairs and offered civil greetings to all who entered the august portals of Mays House.

Mays House had been shut up for a twelvemonth since Lord Mays's scandalous death, and so several that came to the supper and ball were as interested in what Lady Mays might have done to the interior furnishings as they were in the lady and her companion.

Apparently Lady Mays exercised some influence over her cousin-in-law to have persuaded Lord Wilfred Mays to allow her the use of the town house for the entire Season. It would be wonderful indeed if Lady Mays had not also managed to have things changed according to her tastes, for it was widely known that Lord Mays did not enter into his predecessor's prediliction for collections. In fact, Lord Mays had been heard to express the shocking opinion that his cousin's collections would make a fine bonfire.

Those of Lady Mays's guests who had expected to find changes made at Mays House were disappointed. Nothing had been reordered or removed, even down to the portrait of Lady Mays herself that was hung in the dining room.

During and after the supper, there was much comment on the portrait. Some ladies wondered that Lady Mays could have kept it on display when it must surely remind her of a painful part of her life. Others thought that she must be very arrogant to keep it up. Inevitably, though, the majority made comparisons between the portrait and the living subject. On the whole, it was generally felt that Lady Mays had preserved very well. She still looked very much like the debutante who three years before had made the marriage of the Season.

"Not a blemish or wrinkle on her," said one lady to another on an envious note. "What nonsense that she had lost her looks and Mays rid himself of her for that reason. *There* is the proof against it!" The ladies had been upstairs to refresh themselves and had passed the open door of the dining room, where they had had a good view of the portrait, before they reentered the ballroom.

"Then it could only have been over his mistress. What a little fool she was to think it mattered when she had all of this!" exclaimed another lady, looking about her at the priceless objets d'art and expensive furnishings and carpets.

"I don't know. I shouldn't have liked it if my husband had flaunted his mistress over me. I would certainly have objected," said Lady Thorpe. She was a petite redhead, known as much for her sense of fun as her absolute devotion to her husband.

Lady Thorpe's two companions tittered. One worldly matron tossed her head. "Oh *you,* Cecily! You've been wed but a sixmonth, and Gerald is besotted with you still. What would you know of the matter?"

"Nothing at all, and I hope that I never shall," said Lady Thorpe spiritedly.

The other two ladies turned their shoulders and pointedly wandered off, putting their heads together to laugh over Lady Thorpe's extraordinary naivete. A particularly condescending statement floated back to her ladyship's ears. "Give Cecily a year or two and then we shall see how high she is on that husband of hers!"

Lady Thorpe fumed at such turkish treatment. "How dare they say such things! Of me or Lady Mays!" It was simply not to be borne.

On the inspiration of her anger, Lady Thorpe looked around for her hostess. As soon as she spied Lady Mays, she approached her. Nodding to Lady Mays and another lady who had engaged her ladyship in conversation, Lady Thorpe waited until the other lady had finished and moved away.

Lady Thorpe smiled almost shyly up at her tall hostess. "Lady Mays, I wished to tell you how honored my husband, Lord Thorpe, and I are to have received your kind invitation."

"Thank you, Lady Thorpe. I hope that you continue to enjoy yourself," said Lucinda, smiling politely.

When making out her guest list, Lucinda had consulted Lord Mays as to whether there was anyone in particular he would like her to include. She had insisted upon deferring to his lordship in this small way, for she was truly grateful that he had lent her Mays House without question. Lord Mays had been gratified and had supplied her with a few names. The Thorpes had consequently received their invitation to the supper and ball because they were particular friends of Lord Mays.

Lucinda had thought the Thorpes to be a pleasant couple when she had met them and had thereafter very nearly forgotten their existence. She knew that the youthful couple were not so much her junior in years, but she felt worlds apart from them in experience. Theirs had apparently been a fairytale romance, their attachment having been formed at first sight and their marriage taking place a scarce six months later.

"Mays House is wonderfully appointed. I do not believe I have ever seen so many beautiful objects in one place in my life," said Lady Thorpe.

"Lord Mays, my late husband, was a great collector of things of beauty," said Lucinda noncommittally. Though she was still smiling at Lady Thorpe, her attention began to wander. She had heard far too often already that evening the same sort of comments.

"You are very beautiful and, yes, gracious, too. It is really unfair that you should be talked about so rudely," said Lady Thorpe.

When Lucinda's astonished gaze centered on her face, Lady Thorpe's eyes began to dance. Quite matter-of-factly, she observed, "Disagreeable old cats, don't you agree?"

Lucinda was surprised into a gurgle of laughter. She looked at the lady with blossoming curiosity. "Lady Thorpe, I suspect that you are an original."

The youthful lady's eyes twinkled. "I don't think that I should like that reputation. One would forever be trying to live up to it. And it would distress Gerald so," said Lady Thorpe. "He is the most dear thing, but terribly unimaginative."

Lucinda was set laughing again.

Lord Wilfred Mays came up at that moment. He was pleased to note that Lucinda seemed to be on good terms with Lady Cecily Thorpe. He was of the opinion that Lucinda needed to surround herself with some merry souls who would shake her out of her too-serious mien.

He addressed the two ladies with his crooked smile. His eyes were warm with approval. "I see that you two ladies are fast becoming acquainted. Nothing could be better, Lucinda, for Cecily and Gerald are solid to the bone. Their overtures of friendship are not lightly given or lightly meant."

"What a flatterer you are, Wilfred!" said Lady Thorpe, turning pink with pleasure.

"Is he not? But I think him to be kind-hearted, too," said Lucinda. She smiled at her cousin-in-law. "Indeed, I do not believe that I have met anyone kinder."

Now it was Lord Mays's turn to flush. He cleared his throat. "It is easy to be kind when one approves of someone."

"We are honored indeed, Lady Thorpe," said Lucinda, laughing.

"You will end by turning our heads, Wilfred, and then you

will see how insufferably set up in our own estimation we can be," said Lady Thorpe. She put on a haughty expression and tilted one brow in laughing challenge at her hostess. "Isn't that so, my dear Lady Mays?"

Lucinda could not resist entering into the vein of the thing. "Oh, indeed, my dear Lady Thorpe," she said. She languidly waved her fan. "*Then* we should come to look down our noses at poor Lord Mays and at best bestow only a condescending smile of recognition upon him."

"You are roasting me, the pair of you," said Lord Mays, grinning again.

Lucinda laughed. Shutting her fan, she tapped him lightly on his sleeve with it. "I at least could never look down my nose at you, Wilfred, whatever the provocation. You are too good a friend to me."

Lady Thorpe cast a swift startled glance at Lord Mays as his face settled into lines of gratification. There was a warmth in his eyes when he looked at Lady Mays that was unmistakable. Lady Thorpe was amazed by the thought that came into her head. Lady Mays was certainly an acknowledged beauty, but surely his lordship had not actually come under her spell.

The musicians at the other end of the room struck up a familiar air, diverting Lady Thorpe from her astonishing thoughts. Several couples began forming up sets. "Oh, I do adore the quadrille!" she exclaimed. "I wish Gerald was with me now, for I would at once have him take me onto the floor."

"That's right. I haven't seen Gerald of late. Where has he gotten himself off to?" asked Lord Mays, glancing about casually.

A shadow crossed Lady Thorpe's face. A measure of vivacity left her face as she replied, "Gerald wished to sit down at cards for a few moments with Mr. Stassart."

Lord Mays and Lucinda exchanged a quick look. Lucinda was horrified. Lord Thorpe was a mere babe, little older than his eighteen-year-old bride, and a thoroughly easygoing young gentleman. It appalled her that he should be in her cousin's selfish, callous hands. Something of her feelings must have expressed themselves in her expression, for Lord Mays gave a slight nod of reassurance.

"I think that I shall wander over to the cardroom and see if I can wrest Gerald free. I wished to speak to him about a hunter that I saw yesterday, for he told me a few weeks ago that he wanted to acquire one," said Lord Mays casually. After a few more departing words, he left the ladies.

Lucinda put her arm through Lady Thorpe's and in a friendly manner said, "Why don't we two go after some lemon ices? I am all of a sudden parched. The ballroom has gotten to be so warm. I have been thinking of opening a few of the windows. Do you think that anyone would have any objections?"

"Oh no, not to speak of," said Lady Thorpe, willingly entering into her hostess's concerns. She allowed herself to be borne off toward the refreshment tables, saying, "Some of the more rigid might talk of the evils of the night air, but for my part I would far rather risk a putrid throat than have melting candle wax drip down upon my head!"

"So should I," said Lucinda, chuckling. "Very well, then! Upon the approval of the very original Lady Thorpe, I shall give the orders to scandalize the rigid." They had reached the refreshment table, and she signaled a servant to her to give the orders for some of the windows to be opened.

"As though you needed anyone's approval, my lady," said Lady Thorpe, making brisk inroads on the lemon ice. "Why, as a widow, I suspect that you may do very nearly anything you wish and not risk censor."

Lucinda gave a half smile. She cast a glance down at her shorter companion. "But you said not a few minutes ago that I am discussed, and not at all in a friendly manner. Therefore it seems clear that I, too, must be careful of offending certain individuals' sense of propriety."

"It is all jealousy and envy," said Lady Thorpe dismissively. "None of them realize at what cost to you this came." She waved her hand, encompassing the elegant mirrored ballroom with its numerous sprays of sumptuous blooms, the branches of candles that created a blaze of light, the milling, noisy crowd.

Lucinda raised her brows, both amused and astonished by the lady's assumption of worldliness. "And you do?"

Lady Thorpe shrugged her slender shoulders. "I think that I should horsewhip any woman who dared to make sheep's eyes at my Gerald. I have heard how ill-treated you were at your husband's hands. How he could have set his mistress over you, I cannot fathom! Why, there is not a lady here tonight who can hold a candle to you. I have observed the way the gentlemen look at you and heard the flatteries. I think that his lordship was a great fool." She realized of a sudden that she was taking liberties with their short acquaintance. Lady Thorpe colored to the roots of her bright hair. "Forgive me, Lady Mays! I should not have spoken in such an intimate fashion to you."

"Pray do not apologize. I am not at all offended. In truth, I find your forthrightness rather refreshing," said Lucinda, laughing. "Though I must tell you in all honesty that mine was not a blighted love match, as you seem to think, so do put that out of your head. Lord Mays and I contracted a marriage of convenience. It did not prove satisfying to either party. There! You will understand now that you must not make me out to be some tragic heroine."

Lady Thorpe regarded her hostess for a moment, her head tilted in the manner of an inquisitive little bird. Her eyes were thoughtful and keenly observant. "I do not think that quite true, my lady," she said slowly. "I suspect that there is more of tragedy in your life than you have allowed anyone to know."

Lucinda was startled and not a little dismayed. The girl standing beside her had just displayed a discernment that was far beyond her years. Lucinda wondered uncomfortably how she could turn aside Lady Thorpe's too-close probing.

The lady herself put an end to it. "But I shall not tax you, nor shall I speculate. I am not one of those obnoxious tabbies always going about sniffing for a morsel of gossip! Your private affairs are your own, Lady Mays." Her gaze was caught by something beyond Lucinda, and her eyes lit up. "Here is Gerald now, with Lord Mays!"

The gentlemen came up, greeting the two ladies. Lord Thorpe immediately took his wife's hand, gently swinging it to and fro. "Wilfred tells me that you are pining for a quadrille," he said teasingly, looking down into her piquant face.

Lady Thorpe cast down her lashes, her mouth making a pretty moue. "Indeed, my lord, it is only the truth. But I had no one to partner me and so you discover me quite forlorn."

"What! Isn't there anyone about to dance attendance upon my pretty wife?" Lord Thorpe looked around as though in earnest search. "Do not fret, my girl. I shall at once engage the services of a suitable cicisbeo!"

"Oh, Gerald!" Lady Thorpe lightly hit her husband in the chest with her small hand. "You are a monstrous tease! As though I should like anyone half as well as you to squire me!"

"Surely Wilfred here—"

Lord Thorpe began laughing as his scowling spouse once more punched him with her dainty fist. "Yes, I tease you most abominably. Come along, then. This set is just forming up. Let us show everyone how it is done."

Lady Thorpe made a departing wave as she and her still-laughing lord hurried off.

"They are a sweet pair," murmured Lucinda. She shook herself and smiled at Lord Mays, who still stood beside her. "I think that I envy them, Wilfred. I wonder whether I was ever so carefree and happy and confident with my world?"

"I would like to see you like that, Lucinda," said Lord Mays with unexpected seriousness.

Lucinda stared at Lord Mays, quite taken aback at the tone of his voice. She was even more startled when he seized her hand in an uncomfortably tight grip.

## Chapter Eleven

"Lucinda, I have felt for some time that you are in need of the influence of good friends and merriment." Lord Mays spoke with unexpected fierceness.

"Why, that is precisely the reason I came to London, my lord," said Lucinda, trying to understand his lordship's sudden earnestness. She did not know what to make of it.

Lord Mays shook his head impatiently. "No, I do not mean this!" He swept the oblivious crowd with a dismissive glance. "I mean spending time with people who care for you and value you. Most of these here tonight see you only as Lady Mays, the beautiful and rich widow. They express their respects and make overtures of friendship, but it is scarcely the same thing."

He smiled crookedly at her. "And you know it as well as I, for I can see how guarded is the expression in your eyes. No, I want you to be able to laugh and jest and rest completely assured that you are with trusted confidantes."

"Bravo, my lord. It is just what I was myself telling my lovely cousin only a few days ago."

Lord Mays uttered something low under his breath and broke away from Lucinda. He stared at the gentleman who had come up so inopportunely, a decidedly unfriendly expression in his frowning eyes. "Stassart. How is this? I would never have guessed that any of us would see your face outside the cardroom as long as there were games of chance to be had."

Mr. Stassart smiled, but his blue eyes were suddenly very hard. He flicked an imaginary speck from his elegant sleeve. "In truth, my lord, the cards palled. Naturally I came at once to seek out my fair cousin. You must know that I have a great fondness for Lucinda."

Lord Mays gave a shout of laughter. His gold-brown eyes gleamed as though from a good joke. His good humor was inexplicably and completely restored. "Dipped already, Stassart?" He bowed to Lucinda and sauntered off, whistling.

Ferdie stared after Lord Mays. "I do not think that I care for his lordship," he said softly.

Lucinda was indifferent to his opinion. "Do you not? Whereas I count him as one of my closest friends."

"One can only decry your naivete, my dear cousin. However, I did not come up to argue the doubtful virtues of Lord Mays's character with you." Ferdie cast a soulful glance at her amused face. His entire attitude was worshipful as he carried her hand to his lips. "I can scarcely keep myself from you, Lucinda. Behold, I fly to your side like a moth to the lovely flame."

Lucinda shook her head at her cousin and forcibly withdrew her hand from his insistent clasp. "What do you want, Ferdie? Is it as Lord Mays said? Have you lost again? Do you wish me to frank you at my own card tables?"

Mr. Stassart swept his hand to the front of his frilled shirt, assuming an appalled expression. "Cousin! That the thought could even cross your mind is a dishonor. I would not dream of importuning you for such a purpose. No, I am well able to frank myself to whatever tune is required."

"My mistake, Ferdie. I do apologize," said Lucinda, not at all convinced. It was her unalterable experience that her cousin had little enough to do with any member of her family unless he wanted something. Certainly he had never been above importuning them for monies, and why he should cavil at doing the same with her was beyond her. But she had no wish to set the stage for an unpleasant scene and so she smiled on him. "Have you a complaint, perhaps? I should not wish any one of my guests to feel slighted for any reason."

"Oh, dear cousin," he sighed. "My only complaint, the only slight that I feel, is that I have had so little opportunity to persuade you of my everlasting devotion. I discover in myself a yearning to bask in the light of your beauty. I am all eagerness to win your precious favor. In short, Lucinda, I am like a desert without the gentle rain of your smiles upon me. Dare I admit to it? Dare I open myself to the possibility of your rejection?"

Lucinda stared at her cousin in complete consternation. She had had no clue that he even harbored such sentiments. "Ferdie, I—"

Ferdie threw out his beringed hands in appeal. In throbbing accents, he said, "Dance with me, cousin!"

Lucinda was made speechless. Then as the point of his extravagant periods burst upon her, she started laughing. "Oh, Ferdie, you are such a cad! Why in heaven do I like you so well?" She gave her hand into his.

Ferdie drew her onto the floor, his handsome face lit by the boyish grin that he cultivated. "You like me because we two are so much alike, cousin."

Lucinda drew back from him a little, her fine brows rising.

With a straight look, she said, "That we are not! You are a desperate gamester and an opportunist of the worst sort. Only see how you tricked me into believing, for a moment only, that you had become quite besotted with me! And all to throw me off guard and gain my hand for a set!"

Ferdie escorted her to her place in the set that was forming, turning to face her. He looked at her with a curiously sharp expression. "Am I not besotted with you, Lucinda?"

Lucinda shook her head, laughing. "Of course you are not! If you have persuaded yourself that it is so, then I suspect it is this—" She tossed an encompassing glance about the magnificent ballroom. "It is the glittering setting of Mays House that has turned your head, Ferdie, not me. Pray recall that I have no claim whatsoever on any of this magnificence, and you will swiftly come to realize that you are the victim of illusion."

"Ah, you believe that you know me so well! You have named me a gamester and an opportunist, Lucinda, and so I am! I stake all—my person, my fortune, my pride—and lay it before you." Ferdie's eyes measured the effect of his words. His lovely cousin was staring at him in patent amazement and uncertainty.

Mr. Stassart's smile widened slightly as he said in his soft voice, "But are you not cut from much the same cloth, Lucinda? You have staked yourself to this London season. You seize every opportunity granted you to cause the *ton* to take notice. The very society that shrugged its shoulders when you were thrust out of its scintillating center is now importuned to pay you court. It is your pretty revenge, is it not, Lucinda?"

The music dictating the set moved them away from one another, but not swiftly enough that Mr. Stassart missed the sparkle of anger in his cousin's narrowed glance. He smiled to himself. But when the movement of the dance placed him opposite Lucinda again, he had schooled his handsome countenance to a contrite expression.

He said quickly, anxiously, "Forgive me, cousin. I spoke out of turn. I recognize it too late, but offer my abject apology. It is only my familiarity with your character and circumstances that have led me into indiscretion."

"I do not think that I like you very well after all, Ferdie," said Lucinda distantly.

"I am undone. I am utterly cast down. My hopes are completely dashed," declared Ferdie.

Lucinda's color rose as his dramatic utterances began to draw the attention of others in the set. She said quietly, urgently, "Pray do not, Ferdie! We are attracting stares."

Ferdie's voice rose a notch more. "I cannot contain myself, cousin! I have sunk myself beyond reproach with you. Ah, but for one tiny smile! One small word of encouragement! Would not my spirit revive? Would not hope once more raise its head in my breast?"

Mr. Stassart's loud laments had captured the unriveted regard of everyone within earshot. Even those in other sets had turned around to stare. Lucinda's face burned with embarrassment. "That you could do this, Ferdie!" she choked.

It was to her unutterable relief that the music concluded at that instant. She turned on her heel and swept quickly from the floor, her head held high.

She did not recognize the gentleman until he stepped deliberately into her path, interrupting her swift flight. He hailed her affably.

"Lady Mays! It is a pleasure to thus come face-to-face with you. I had hoped to persuade you to join me in a glass of wine," said Mr. Weatherby.

Lucinda forced a smile to her face. "Mr. Weatherby, how nice to see you again. I am sorry, sir, but I—"

He took a firm hold of her elbow and began to steer her away from the dance floor, where several people were still looking after her and whispering behind their hands. Mr. Weatherby smiled down into Lucinda's startled face as she realized that she was being inexorably bent to the gentleman's will. "I apologize for the rough and ready, my lady. But I felt it imperative to see you quickly away from that crowd. Good Lord! Doesn't Stassart have any more sense than to throw a lady out of contenance in the middle of a crowded ballroom?"

He had guided her to the refreshment table. Releasing her arm, he lifted a decanter of wine. He proceeded to pour out a generous glass, saying, "Don't run off again while I am thus engaged. It would be taking unfair advantage of me, you know, since I have but one hand."

Heedless of Mr. Weatherby's words, Lucinda pressed her hands against her heated cheeks. She gave a shaky laugh. "I have made a fool of myself, have I not?"

"Not altogether," said Mr. Weatherby coolly. He offered the glass to her. "Here, drink this. It will give you time to compose yourself."

Lucinda thanked him and took the wineglass. She sipped slowly at the champagne. She could feel her nerves settling. When she had had enough, she set down the wineglass.

Lucinda directed a wavering smile up at her waiting companion. "Thank you, Mr. Weatherby. I can scarcely express my gratitude enough for your timely intervention. I believe that I might have rushed heedlessly out of my own ballroom if it had not been for you. What an abominable stir that would have caused!"

"Quite. And over little more than that mincing puppy's provocations," said Mr. Weatherby, directing his firm chin in an offhand gesture in the gentleman's direction. He offered his arm to her. "Will you do me the honor of strolling with me to the windows, Lady Mays? It has become tiresomely warm in here. I could do with a breath of cooler air."

"And I, sir," said Lucinda, placing her fingers on his elbow.

They walked slowly around the perimeter of the ballroom. Mr. Weatherby glanced down at his silent companion. "You may safely confide in me, Lady Mays. I promise that I shall not bray it from the rooftops, however titillating it may prove to be."

Lucinda laughed. She shook her head. "It was all such nonsense, scarcely deserving to be repeated now."

"Nevertheless it will be repeated, by everyone who was privileged to overhear what was said."

"Yes, I know. *That* is what is particularly galling," said Lucinda.

"You would do well to confide the whole to me, you know. I may be able to help you," said Mr. Weatherby.

Lucinda lifted her eyes to his face. Her brows were slightly drawn. "Why should you wish to help me, Mr. Weathe

We are the barest of acquaintances. I can mean nothing to you."

"On the contrary. Your welfare is of the utmost importance in my scheme of things," said Mr. Weatherby. At her startled expression, a flicker of a grin touched his mobile mouth. "I am not declaring myself to you, my lady."

A blush of color stole into Lucinda's face. "You have an unfair advantage of me, sir. You read my mind perfectly, while I find you to be a very dark horse indeed."

He laughed. When he met her questioning glance, his own gray gaze was rueful. "I fear that I cannot satisfy your curiosity at this juncture, my lady. Suffice it to believe that I mean you no harm and that I shall do whatever it is in my power to do to see you come off safely. Now tell me what that fop of a cousin of yours has done to set you all on edge."

Lucinda shrugged in capitulation. "Very well, then. If you would so have it. Mr. Stassart implied for all and sundry to overhear that he had offered his suit to me and that I had spurned him with a ruthless dispatch."

Mr. Weatherby swore softly. "A sorry trick, in truth. I do not wonder at your reaction, Lady Mays." He threw a sharp glance down at Lucinda's profile. "Has your cousin ever had occasion to think himself encouraged in that direction, my lady?"

Lucinda raised her eyes, her expression indignant. "Of course not! Why, Ferdie has been riding roughshod over my family for years. I would have been more likely to laugh at any suggestion of a match between us than encourage it!"

"Your family, my lady? What have they to do with this contretemps?" asked Mr. Weatherby. They had paused before one of the half-opened windows. He thrust up the sash a little higher.

A breath of fresh air eddied over Lucinda's face, and she sighed in appreciation. "Oh, my cousin is my father's heir and h‿s always taken monstrous advantage of the position. Ferdie ‿‿ ‿‿rever importuning my father for funds to settle his gam‿‿ ‿‿‿ and the like," she said. She summoned up a smile. ‿‿‿‿ ‿‿derstand, sir, the Stassarts were never in particu‿‿ ‿‿‿ ‿‿et. Therefore my cousin's claims were always seen by my sisters and me as a threat to the very fabric of our existence." Lucinda did not think it appropriate to reveal just how closely her own fate had been tied to the settlement of her cousin's debts.

"As bad as that," mused Mr. Weatherby. "I begin to understand the depth of your reaction to Mr. Stassart's ruse, my lady."

"His ruse? Whatever can you mean?" asked Lucinda, startled.

Mr. Weatherby smiled down at her, a rather grim light in his eyes. "I suspect that Mr. Stassart is desirous of forming just such a connection between you that you would most resist, my lady. Your cousin is a gamester with a history of being run off his legs. You are a widow amply endowed by your late lord. It is plain to me that your cousin is hanging out for a rich wife, and who better than the daughter of the gentleman whose heir he is? Everything is thus neatly tied up. Mr. Stassart has control of your assets and an easy avenue to your father's pockets, for your father will not allow his daughter ever to be thrown into the gutter for the sake of a few pounds now and again."

"No, indeed. However, there is a flaw in your logic, Mr. Weatherby. How could Ferdie ever entertain hopes of my accepting his suit, even supposing that was his game?" asked Lucinda. "He knows very well that my eyes are wide open to his gammon."

"Oh, you would come round to accepting his suit, my lady," said Mr. Weatherby coolly. "The weight of social opinion would eventually demand it of you. Or it would exact a heavy penalty for your refusal."

At Lucinda's startled stare, Mr. Weatherby arched a heavy brow. His expression exceedingly cynical, he said, "Think on it, my lady. This evening he has planted the seeds. You are a terrible flirt, my lady, one who plays fast and loose with her cousin's affections. Just let that suggestion take hold, and you will have the whole of London sympathizing with poor Mr. Stassart. Next he proves himself devoted to you, protesting his undying affection. He is prostrated by your indifference, by your blowing hot and cold upon him. Ladies who once smiled on you would begin to whisper disparagingly behind your back, holding you up to their daughters as an example of appalling disregard. Gentlemen who once paid you flattering attention would treat you to the disrespect meted out to any highborn lady who was caught out in deliberate and cruel deception."

"But it would be lies, all lies," said Lucinda, staring blindly out the window. She was appalled at the vision that her companion had conjured up. She looked round quickly, shaking her head. "No, I cannot believe it, Mr. Weatherby. My cousin could not possibly serve me such a trick."

The gentleman shrugged. "Have it your own way, my lady. But I shall lay this question before you. What possible motive could your cousin have to fly in the face of all the proprieties not a quarter hour past?"

## *Chapter Twelve*

Mr. Weatherby regarded her frowning expression for a moment before he drove home his point. "Whatever else Mr. Stassart is, he is a gentleman born. He knows what is due to the family name. He has a vested interest, after all! Is he unhinged that such things are of no moment to him?"

"No, no, of course not! Ferdie is always all that is correct. He is proud of his reputation of being considered good *ton*," said Lucinda.

She turned fully to her companion, having come to the decision to trust him. "Mr. Weatherby, though I cannot fully accept your analysis of my cousin's possible motivation, nevertheless it is quite true that Ferdie has put me squarely into the hands of the gossips. It is not my wish to figure as the latest *on dit!* Therefore I am asking for your advice. What is the best way to go about scotching any ludicrous rumors regarding myself and my cousin?"

Mr. Weatherby offered his arm to her once more. She hesitantly accepted his escort, wondering that he did not reply at once.

"I am taking you to your chaperone, Miss Blythe. My suggestion is that you stick close to that lady as nearly as possible. Never give Mr. Stassart the opportunity to either interview you in private or to importune you in public."

Lucinda cast a laughing glance up at him. "That is easier said than done, sir! I cannot avoid Ferdie entirely. He has been to call here at Mays House, and even though Miss Blythe sits with me, that will not be universally known. Nor does it end there. We are bound to run into one another at any number of functions."

"Deny the door to him here at Mays House. Make it known through the strictest confidences to friends that your cousin's excessive gaming has put him beyond the pale with you. Acknowledge him in public only with the shortest of bows," said Mr. Weatherby with overriding ruthlessness.

Lucinda dispassionately regarded the gentleman. "It occurs to me that you seem to hold my cousin in some aversion. Have you a motive of your own to accomplish, Mr. Weatherby?"

He allowed the trace of a smile to touch his lips. "You are a sharp-witted young woman, Lady Mays. But in this instance you have quite mistaken the matter. Here is Miss Blythe." He greeted the older woman with the easy friendliness of one of comparable age and station.

Then Mr. Weatherby turned to Lucinda and carried her hand to his lips. His gray eyes were filled with an amusement that was disturbing to Lucinda. "I shall wait on you one day this week, Lady Mays. But I think that I shall take my leave of you, and the esteemable Miss Blythe, for this evening."

"Very well, sir. I trust that you enjoyed the entertainment that was offered this evening," said Lucinda politely. She could have cut out her tongue when the amusement in the gentleman's eyes leaped into open laughter.

"I did indeed, my lady," said Mr. Weatherby suavely. He

bowed to Miss Blythe, exchanging a few cordial words, and then left the ladies.

Lucinda watched Mr. Weatherby's tall upright figure as he made his leisurely way out of the ballroom. "What a very strange man he is!" she exclaimed.

"Do you think so, my dear? For my part, I think Mr. Weatherby to be a gentleman of exceptional qualities," said Miss Blythe, still smiling. Turning her head to regard Lucinda with a measure of curiosity, she said briskly, "What is this I have just heard? That you rebuffed Mr. Stassart on the dance floor?"

"Oh, was there anything more vexing!" exclaimed Lucinda. She was at once reminded of her annoyance. "Ferdie had the audacity to play off his abominable tricks while I was standing up with him. You know his dramatic way of expressing himself, Tibby. He said something that I took offense to and instead of simply apologizing and letting it go, my cousin treated me to a Cheltenham tragedy in the midst of the set! I was never more mortified or angered. I fear that I rushed off the floor like the veriest goose. If it had not been for Mr. Weatherby's timely intervention, I believe that I might have quit the ballroom altogether."

"I wonder that I did not see any of this. Of course, I have been engaged in conversation nearly the whole evening," said Miss Blythe. She was dismayed at her own dereliction of duty. "I hold myself entirely responsible for the resulting gossip, Lucinda, for I should have kept a closer watch out for you."

Lucinda reached out quickly to squeeze her companion's hand. "Nonsense, Tibby! You are not at fault. I have only myself to blame. I should not have let Ferdie put me in such a flame."

"Mr. Stassart has obviously behaved very badly. I am surprised in him, I must admit. It is a pity that I cannot call him to book," said Miss Blythe, her thin lips tightening as her gaze fell on that oblivious gentleman.

"Mr. Weatherby had some rather blunt advice to give me in how to repair my cousin's unfortunate lapse in good manners," said Lucinda. "I rather think that I might entertain at least a portion of it. Tibby, give me the benefit of your opinion, I pray." She proceeded to reveal to Miss Blythe Mr. Weatherby's advice, ending with, "I rely on you to steer me in the right direction, Tibby. Should I do as Mr. Weatherby has said?"

Miss Blythe was frowning. "There is much merit in Mr. Weatherby's suggestions. However, I do not believe that you can in all conscience simply cut Mr. Stassart's acquaintance altogether. That would be thought very odd when he is known to be Sir Thomas's heir."

"That is what I thought, too. It seems such an extreme length to go, despite Mr. Weatherby's contention that Ferdie deliberately set that little scene for the benefit of the gossips," said Lucinda.

"How is this, Lucinda?" asked Miss Blythe, surprised.

Lucinda shrugged and smiled a little ruefully. "Why, Mr. Weatherby is of the opinion that Ferdie has taken it into his head to make me his wife and, knowing that I would have nothing to do with him, he has chosen to force my hand by holding me up to critics and gossip. Of course I denied that Ferdie could plan a thing so underhanded or, indeed, so dishonorable. Why, it is utterly inconceivable!"

Miss Blythe had listened to Lucinda's explanation with an increasingly arrested expression. She said at last, very quietly, "My dear. So much is at last explained." She took hold of her former pupil's hands in an unexpectedly firm grasp. "My very dear Lucinda, I have the most lowering feeling that Mr. Weatherby could very well be correct. I have thought for some time that Mr. Stassart's effusive expressions— In short, it is certainly not a suspicion that one would ever wish to entertain, but I am struck with how neatly it explains something that has often puzzled me of late."

"Tibby! Surely you do not believe that Ferdie desires to take me to wife? And to accomplish it in such a manner. It is preposterous!" exclaimed Lucinda.

Miss Blythe let go of Lucinda's hands. She shrugged, a perturbed expression on her face. "Mr. Stassart is a gamester and not a very successful one, my dear. Wedding a wealthy young woman has certainly always been one way for a gentleman in deep financial straits to right himself. As for the means employed, you have said yourself that you would never entertain an honorable suit from Mr. Stassart."

Lucinda's thoughts had taken a related tack. "Ferdie is not precisely the catch of the Season in the eyes of those with marriageable daughters, is he?" she asked slowly.

"My dear! Emphatically not! I have heard from more than one lady that Mr. Stassart is actively discouraged from hanging out after their daughters. No fond mother wishes her dear daughter to wed a gentleman who is certain to run through every pound that he may put his hand on," said Miss Blythe. She smiled suddenly, though without amusement. "Unless, of course, the gentleman in question has a very distinguished title."

"Oh, dear." Lucinda looked across the ballroom and caught a glimpse of her cousin. Mr. Stassart was doing the pretty over the hand of a simpering matron. His appearance was as usual impeccable, though of an extravagant fashion not to her taste. A thread of pity for him formed within her. "Poor Ferdie. I wonder whether he is quite run off his legs again." The thought dispersed the unaccustomed pity. She turned to Miss Blythe, exclaiming, "Tibby, he must not apply to my father. I won't have it."

"There is little you can do in that direction, Lucinda. But in light of what we suspect, I think you may rest assured, at least for a time, that Mr. Stassart will remain in London. He is, after all, the complete social creature," said Miss Blythe.

Lucinda chuckled suddenly. "Quite true! Ferdie positively despises the country. He will stay in town until his straits become quite, quite desperate. And if Mr. Weatherby's assumption proves correct, he will stay as long as he has hopes of pushing me to the altar. I believe—yes, I do believe that I can throw him a crumb or two to encourage him to think that his wiles are bearing fruit."

"I hope that you are not planning to encourage the creature, Lucinda," said Miss Blythe sharply, staring at her over the rims of her spectacles.

"Of course not. Nevertheless, Ferdie will feel himself encouraged. It is the nature of the gamester to harbor hope even when all points to the contrary, is it not?"

"Lucinda." Miss Blythe regarded her with misgiving. "Lucinda, just what exactly do you mean to do?"

"Nothing the least out of the ordinary, I assure you. Ferdie will make up one of the company whenever I hold a function such as this. I will greet him cordially whenever we should meet elsewhere. But at no time shall my cousin be granted a private word, nor shall I expose myself to his sole attentions," said Lucinda coolly. She flashed a sudden smile at her companion. "Ferdie fancies himself to be an excellent dancer. It is a pity that in future I must confine myself to less expert partners!"

Miss Blythe was reassured. She, too, smiled. "For my part, I shall do all within my power to fend off the gentleman," she said. "Mr. Stassart will find me to be the strictest and most suspicious of chaperones, I fear. I shall not allow you to receive him unless there is at least one other caller already present. Otherwise, dear Lucinda, I shall insist that he not be allowed to come up."

Lucinda laughed. "I am trusting you to do just that, Tibby! Oh, dear, how very much Ferdie is going to dislike you!"

"I positively relish the thought, my dear," Miss Blythe assured her.

Lord Mays came up at that moment. He bowed to the ladies, then smiled at Lucinda. "I have hopes of persuading Miss Blythe into granting her permission for me to solicit your hand for this waltz, my lady."

"I do not know, my lord. She has just assured me that she means to be ever so much stricter with me," said Lucinda, also smiling. She turned to her companion. "What is your verdict, Tibby? May I be trusted with this gentleman at least?"

"What do you say, Miss Blythe? I perceive that I am at your complete mercy," said Lord Mays.

Miss Blythe chuckled. "I have every confidence in you, Lord Mays."

Lord Mays meekly thanked Miss Blythe for her faith in him before he swept Lucinda off onto the floor. While he whirled Lucinda around to the stately music, he said, "I think that your supper and ball is a pretty success, Lucinda. I have heard nothing but good reports all evening."

"I am glad, for truthfully I was a bit anxious. I did so want it to go over well," said Lucinda. She was enjoying being partnered by Lord Mays. He was a very smooth dancer and guided her expertly. His hand on hers and his arm about her waist were warm and reassuring.

"There is no question of that," said Lord Mays. "What was it you and Miss Blythe were joking about? Is there someone whom she frowns upon?"

"Oh, we were talking about my cousin, Mr. Stassart," said Lucinda. She was surprised when Lord Mays's fingers tightened on hers. "Wilfred!"

"Has that fellow overstepped himself, Lucinda?" Lord Mays asked sharply. "I had heard some folderol a few minutes ago that I discounted as so much nonsense, but—"

"Oh, bother! The truth of the matter is that Mr. Stassart overplayed his protestations of cousinly devotion, and it was misunderstood by some who do not know the looseness of the connection between us," said Lucinda. "I was rather incensed at him for making us the center of vulgar curiosity in such an idiotic fashion, while dear Tibby was positively up in arms over it. I suspect if she could have done so, she would have raked my cousin over the coals in rattling fashion."

"Rightfully so! The effrontery of the fellow!" Catching sight of Mr. Stassart, Lord Mays's frown deepened. "Cousin that he is to you or not, Lucinda, I cannot like Stassart. That posturing and those ridiculous airs leave one positively bilious."

Lucinda laughed, her face clearing. "Pray do not allow yourself to be made ill-tempered by my cousin on my account, Wilfred. I do not regard him and so you should not."

"Yes, but it is not just you, Lucinda. There is young Thorpe, too. I never would have believed Gerald to be such a gudgeon as to fall into that cardsharp's clutches," said Lord Mays, perhaps with a lamentable lack of discretion.

Lucinda looked up in quick dismay. "What do you mean, Wilfred? Has Ferdie lured Lord Thorpe into gaming more than he should? Oh, I would not have that for worlds! Lord and Lady Thorpe are such innocents. They could not even conceive what disaster could befall them if they were ever to become addicted to that sort of life."

"That's just the thing, Lucinda," said Lord Mays, appreciating her excellent grasp of his own concerns. "I feel myself somewhat responsible for Gerald. He was in my regiment at Waterloo, and never was there a better fellow in a tight place. But he is so trusting and . . . and . . ."

"It would never cross his mind that anyone could take a frightful advantage of him," said Lucinda as with a sinking feeling she recalled Lady Thorpe's frank description of her lord.

"That is it precisely!" exclaimed Lord Mays in astonishment. "How did you know?"

"Lady Thorpe let drop something to the purpose," said Lucinda. "What will you do, Wilfred?"

"I don't know. I suppose all I can do is try to keep Gerald's energies turned in a different direction until the Season is over. I have no authority over Gerald anymore. We are friends now, rather than superior officer and subordinate. Otherwise I could drop a close word in his ear and be assured of being attended," said Lord Mays. "As it is, I don't wish to push our friendship so far that I trample on his pride."

"Oh, was there anything more vexatious! I declare that I could happily strangle my cousin," said Lucinda.

Lord Mays laughed. He whirled her a little closer. "Never mind. I doubt that Mr. Stassart shall need to be dealt with in such a violent way. I daresay the thing shall come off in a satisfactory manner in the end."

"I, for one, do not intend to spare another thought to my despicable cousin for the remainder of the evening," said Lucinda breathlessly, becoming aware of how closely his lordship was holding her.

"Then perhaps I may persuade you to give thought instead to bestowing another dance on me, my lady?" asked Lord Mays, his warm eyes glinting.

"My lord! How you do put me to the blush," said Lucinda. She laughed, saying very cordially, "You may squire me at any time, Lord Mays, for I have discovered you to be an exceptional partner."

"I shall take you up on that invitation, Lucinda," said Lord Mays.

She smiled at him. "So I should hope."

They finished the waltz in fine style to a smattering of admiring applause. Lord Mays returned Lucinda to her chaperone's side and formally bowed to both ladies. Then he remained beside them for several minutes and engaged in friendly conversation.

Lucinda's hand was solicited by many other gentlemen during the course of the ball, but she enjoyed nothing so much as she had the waltz with Lord Mays, and later, a quadrille.

The guests at the supper and ball dissipated themselves until the small hours of the morning. The last guest finally departed. Miss Blythe and Lucinda exchanged tired good nights before retiring to their separate bedchambers.

Lucinda's last thought as her head nestled into the pillow was that her supper and ball had indeed been a smashing success. Her return to the inner circles of society was on the way to being assured.

## Chapter Thirteen

A s was the butler's invariable custom, he brought a silver salver holding the morning's invitations and letters into the ladies' private sitting room. "My lady," said Church, bowing, as he set the salver down on the occasional table beside her ladyship's chair.

"Thank you, Church. That will be all for the moment."

The butler left the sitting room while Lucinda began to sort out the disorganized stack. She handed to Miss Blythe several letters before picking up her own. Her glance fell upon a familiar script, and she smiled as she said, "I have received another letter from my mother."

"Lady Stassart is a formidable correspondent," observed Miss Blythe.

That made Lucinda laugh, for not a week had passed since she had taken up residence in London that she had not gotten a letter from her fond parent.

The series of letters had been equally divided into reproaches for going up to London at all and sage tidbits of advice on how best to make her way in society. There had also been numerous fond allusions to Lord Potherby, Lucinda's neighbor and persistent admirer. It seemed that Lady Stassart was in regular correspondence with the gentleman. Her ladyship liked Lord Potherby very well. His was a sensible mind, and he could be counted upon to take heed for a lady's least comfort.

Lucinda took great care in all of her replies not to encourage by any word of hers these patent hints and comments. She had not mentioned how high Lord Potherby was in her parent's estimation, or indeed his very existence, to Miss Blythe. She knew the lady's romantic disposition too well. Miss Blythe would at once see in Lord Potherby just the sort of steady gentleman that Lucinda should wed to make her quite comfortable.

"And I certainly do not need to draw double fire," she murmured as she perused her mother's latest offering.

"What was that, my dear?"

Lucinda looked up quickly, realizing at once that she had spoken some of her thoughts aloud. "Oh, I was thinking of something that my mother says in her letter. Mama does have a way of crossing her lines and her topics," she said.

Lucinda proceeded to read out loud Lady Stassart's latest advice, which was an encouraging word on how to use fresh crushed strawberries to whiten one's complexion. She looked up to say humorously, "I trust that my mirror did not deceive me this morning, Tibby. Have I become the least brown or freckled since last I looked?"

"Oh, I think not," said Miss Blythe, chuckling. "However, one must not lay aside Lady Stassart's admonition so lightly,

Lucinda. One never knows when one might not become burned brown by the positive blaze of candles at all of these functions that we have been attending!"

"I shall be certain to keep her recipe close beside me," promised Lucinda, laughing. She glanced at her other correspondence. There was one letter addressed to her whose legend caused her to draw her fine brows together. She took the letter knife and slit the missive open at once. Spreading the thin sheet, she started to read. At length she exclaimed in surprise.

Miss Blythe looked up from her own correspondence to direct an inquisitive glance in Lucinda's direction. "Have you had bad news, my dear?"

"Not that, no. But Tibby, I have received the most unexpected and extraordinary letter from my sister-in-law, Miss Agnes Mays," said Lucinda, looking up from the scant sheet.

"What is so extraordinary about it?" asked Miss Blythe, placidly folding away her own opened letters. She retrieved her most recent embroidery project and began stitching the design for the pillow cover.

"Why, only that I have not met Miss Mays above twice in my life. She is a shrinking sort of female, rather pretty but in a mousey sort of way. Agnes was somewhat younger than her brother, Lord Mays, but she is still some years older than myself. I believe she may be all of nine-and-twenty," said Lucinda, frowning at her memories. "Upon those two occasions that I mentioned, I recall that his lordship completely ignored his sister. I am certain that she felt it."

"It is difficult when a sibling behaves so unfeelingly toward one," said Miss Blythe.

"You will understand better the rejection that she has labored under when I tell you that Miss Mays spent her life dutifully nursing first her father until his death, then her invalid mother. When I met her, she had just become the companion of an elderly aunt," said Lucinda, frowning down at the sheet in her hand.

"Poor thing. How perfectly beastly for the young woman. One must feel for her," said Miss Blythe, entering into ready sympathy. None knew better than did she the wounds and slights that could be inflicted upon one whose life was at the beck and call of others. Some of her posts had been made hideous in that respect, where she had not only been an educator of the children but she had also been treated as an unpaid menial.

"Yes, indeed," agreed Lucinda, quite unaware of her companion's depth of feeling. Her thoughts were all for the letter in her hand. "Tibby, she has written to beg me to allow her to join my household for a visit. She has heard that I have set up housekeeping in London, and having never been to town to speak of and never having been brought out into society, Miss Mays has set her heart on at least once 'tasting the forbidden fruit'!"

"Forbidden fruit!" repeated Miss Blythe. Disbelievingly, she looked over the rims of her spectacles at Lucinda. "What an odd statement!"

Lucinda shook her head, smiling suddenly. "I promise you, I do not jest, Tibby. That is precisely how she has phrased it. Listen to this now. 'And so I throw myself upon your benevolence, dear Lady Mays, even knowing nothing of your character or circumstances. I do assure you that I know how to make myself useful, and I would be most happy to fill whatever capacity that you may see fit.' "

Lucinda looked up from her letter. "Oh, Tibby! Have you ever heard anything more pitiful?"

"It is indeed a most touching plea," agreed Miss Blythe. She neatly snipped her thread. "The young woman is obviously desperate for a change in her circumstances. What shall you do?"

"Why, I shall invite her to come at once for the Season, for my heart positively goes out to her. Miss Mays sounds to me to be very much a kindred spirit," said Lucinda. "Tibby, will you mind chaperoning yet another damsel pining after frolic and fun? I should very much like to introduce Miss Mays to all of the 'forbidden fruit' that London has to offer!"

Miss Blythe smiled. Her hazel eyes twinkled when she looked up from rethreading her needle with a new shade of yarn. "My dear! Why do you ask? You know me well enough, I hope. I should enjoy it of all things. Why, it is something quite out of a fairy tale, is it not? The downtrodden heroine is rescued by a fairy godmother. All that is lacking is a convenient prince, but surely here in London there are any number of likely candidates. Therefore let us determine between us to marry off Miss Mays in the best of romantic tradition. I should like that."

Lucinda laughed. "I can scarcely figure as a fairy godmother. Nevertheless, perhaps you and I *can* make Miss Mays's visit a memorable one."

"It will be most memorable for her if we are able to bring some handsome blade up to scratch," said Miss Blythe, plying her needle again with some energy.

"You are incorrigible, Tibby," said Lucinda, laughing. She rose from her chair. "I shall go write an invitation this moment. It will be pleasant to have someone staying with us, will it not? This house is such a great echoing place."

"It will not seem so when you begin entertaining on a larger scale," said Miss Blythe.

Lucinda agreed, and on that note she withdrew from the sitting room to go to the library. Seating herself at the library desk, she drew paper and ink to her and penned a cordial reply to Miss Mays's letter.

After sanding and sealing her letter, Lucinda rang for a servant to post it. As she emerged from the library, she wondered when she could best expect her guest. It would be nice to be able to plan a few festivities in honor of Miss Mays's arrival.

Several days passed, and there was not a return post from Miss Mays advising when she would travel up to London. Lucinda began to wonder whether her own post had gone astray, for certainly the tone of Miss Mays's letter had led her to expect that lady's immediate acceptance of her invitation. She thought that if she had not heard from Miss Mays in a few more days, she would write again.

However, that expediency became unnecessary after all. The lady herself arrived one evening without warning or notice.

Lucinda and Miss Blythe had come out of the town house and descended the front steps to where their carriage awaited them. A wall sconce was blazing beside the front door, but they entered into relative shadow on the walkway as they went a few steps beyond the town house steps. The coachman had not wanted to park his carriage over a large muddy puddle, in the event that one of the ladies might not be able to easily traverse it, and so he had deferentially advised his passengers.

Lucinda and Miss Blythe were wrapped in excellent cloaks, and so they did not notice the chill as they conversed quietly and approached the carriage.

The coachman stood beside the open carriage door, ready to hand them in. Lucinda and Miss Blythe were about to step up into the vehicle when a rundown hackney drew up to the curb directly in front of Mays House. The front wheel rolled through the puddle, splashing a quantity of mud and water onto the walkway. The coachman muttered under his breath at such careless driving.

In mutual accord, Lucinda and Miss Blythe paused in their ascent. They were curious to see who had arrived, for surely the hackney had not gotten the correct address. Whomever it was would probably require direction to a neighboring house.

The jarvey jumped down from his box and pulled open the door of the hackney. In a moment a young woman descended from the vehicle, clutching a bandbox and a small portmanteau in her hands. By the lamplight, it could be discerned that the young woman was attired modestly, even severely, in a dull gray pelisse and bonnet. She traversed the edges of the puddle and stepped up onto the walkway.

The young woman peered anxiously up at the front of the town house. Then she turned to ask a timid question of the hackney driver. The man answered brusquely, scarcely pausing in his task of setting down a meager amount of baggage from the vehicle.

The young woman flushed at the driver's rudeness, but she did not rebuke him. Instead, she glanced once more, rather helplessly, up at the town house.

The jarvey quickly finished unloading the young woman's belongings. At his demand for payment, the young woman set down her bandbox and portmanteau. She fumbled for a time with the strings of her reticule before she was able to open the bag. At last she counted out the proper amount into the impatient jarvey's rough hand.

The driver pocketed the fare and climbed back up onto his box. Without a backward glance or departing word for his former passenger, he plied his whip to his horse and pulled away from the curb.

The young woman was left standing on the flagway, her few belongings scattered about her feet. She stared after the hackney as it disappeared down the street. Then she turned to gaze again at the imposing facade of the town house. Her manner was obviously forlorn.

The young woman drew the collar of her pelisse close as a chill gust stirred her skirt. It was full dark and growing colder. Obviously a decision had to be made. But still she seemed to hesitate, as though she was completely uncertain of what to do.

"Though I cannot quite make out her face, I am persuaded that this must be Miss Mays," whispered Lucinda.

"Are you quite certain?" asked Miss Blythe dubiously. "The young woman does not at all have the manner nor the dress of a noblewoman born. Even if she has been ill treated of late years, surely she would still exhibit some sign of her birth."

Lucinda gave a low, dry laugh. "Can you not conceive how that could be, Tibby? I have told you that Miss Mays was the object of her brother's scorn and rejection. I am certain that those were not the only occasions upon which she was ever made to feel his displeasure. I experienced some measure of that. It was not pleasant. However, my situation was a bit more fortunate. Whereas I suffered but a short while, I imagine that Miss Mays was made quite acutely aware of her worthlessness. She was considered to be only a useful drudge and nurse for her elderly relations. Miss Mays is accustomed to ill-usage, and it is apparent. Is it any wonder that even a lowly hackney driver treats her with disrespect?"

"I had not thought of it just like that," said Miss Blythe. "Poor child. How she must have suffered."

"Come, we shall see soon enough whether I am right."

Lucinda left the shadows thrown by her own carriage and, followed by her companion, she walked down the flagway to the solitary figure. "Miss Mays?"

The young woman gasped and whirled. She had been so intent on her study of the town house that she had not noticed that there was anyone else about. A hand crept up to her throat. "Yes. I . . . I am Agnes Mays."

Lucinda held out her hand. "I am sorry that I startled you so. I saw you arrive just now. I am your sister-in-law, Lady

Lucinda Mays. This is Miss Tibby Blythe, my companion. We were about to leave for an evening engagement when we saw the hackney set you down."

Miss Mays shook hands. Her gloved fingers trembled in Lucinda's firm grasp.

"I am so honored, my lady." Miss Mays gulped, obviously nervous. She played with the strings of her reticule. "I apologize for . . . for arriving at such an odd hour, my lady. I did not realize that . . . At least, I never thought . . ."

Miss Blythe stepped forward to rescue Miss Mays from her foundering words. She put her arm about the young woman's thin shoulders. "Pray do come inside. It is quite chilly standing about and you must be fatigued after your journey. I have always found traveling to be so tiring."

Lucinda shot her companion an amused glance, for she knew well that Miss Blythe liked nothing better than to barrel about the countryside in a well-sprung carriage. "Indeed, we must not remain on the flagway. I shall have my servants carry in your things, shall I?"

She turned and gestured to her driver. When the man had come over, she said, "Pray go up to notify Church that we shall require tea in the drawing room and that Miss Mays's baggage is to be carried inside. And we shall not need the carriage after all, John." The man nodded his understanding and raced away to do her bidding.

Miss Mays looked in consternation from Lady Mays to Miss Blythe. It was borne in upon her with sickening clarity just how inconvenient was her unheralded arrival. "Oh! But you must not alter your plans for the evening on my account. I . . . I do not wish to be a burden."

"Nonsense. How could your arrival be anything other than a delightful surprise? We have not before had the pleasure of welcoming a houseguest," said Lucinda. "Now you must come up directly and take tea."

"Indeed, we shall wish to hear all about your journey," said Miss Blythe, urging the young woman forward.

Miss Mays allowed herself to be maneuvered toward the steps of the town house. "So kind! So very kind," she said humbly. "I had no notion of finding such a welcome."

The three women went up the steps and entered the town house. The blaze of candlelight after the dark was almost blinding in its brilliance. Miss Mays blinked at such extravagance. She had never lived in a house where candles were burnt with such abandon.

"We shall be more comfortable presently," said Lucinda. She motioned the butler to her and had a short word with him. Then she turned, the candlelight striking sparks from the diamonds and amethysts she wore in her hair.

"I've asked that a room be prepared for you. But I shan't allow you to retire just yet," she said, smiling. "For naturally we should like to visit first. There is a fire already lit in the drawing room. You will be able to be comfortable and put off your things there, Miss Mays."

Miss Mays murmured something inarticulate. She looked around with huge eyes at her elegant surroundings. She had an impression of mirrors and objets d'art and a profusion of sweet-scented flowers. She stared at the number of footmen that busily attended to Lady Mays's quiet orders. Her own baggage looked battered and somehow incongruous in their competent hands. Her pale thin face grew a little pinched, and she seemed to shrink into herself. But she was not allowed time to sort out her rising fears.

# *Chapter Fourteen*

Lucinda and Miss Blythe drew their surprise guest along with them into the drawing room, all the while engaging in easy conversation. Miss Mays did not volunteer a single word to their exchange, but they assumed that she was merely shy at finding herself in the company of strangers.

Lucinda pulled off her gloves and untied the strings of her

cape. She gave them to a footman, who bowed and also received Miss Blythe's outer garment and gloves. He looked inquiringly at Miss Mays.

Upon realizing that the servant was waiting for her possessions, Miss Mays flushed to the roots of her hair. She shook her head quickly, clutching the lapel of her pelisse.

"Won't you at least lay aside your bonnet, Miss Mays?" asked Lucinda.

"Not just yet, my lady, if you please," responded Miss Mays. With a rather desperate little smile, she offered a weak explanation for her oddity. "I should not wish you to see me with my hair all ruffled and flattened from the journey."

Lucinda and Miss Blythe exchanged wondering glances. Then Lucinda nodded to the waiting footman. "Thank you. That will be all for the moment."

The footman bowed and left the drawing room. The butler came into the room with a tray of biscuits. He was followed by another footman who came in carrying the tea urn. The butler positioned the tray of biscuits and directed the placing of the tea urn. Then the servants left, the butler bowing as he closed the doors behind him.

"You must be chilled to the bone, Miss Mays. Let me serve you a cup of hot tea," said Miss Blythe, going over to the tea urn. "Do you prefer black or white? Sugar?"

"It's of no consequence. I shall take whatever is the least trouble," said Miss Mays, her brown eyes wide and apprehensive. She looked around the drawing room. She was dazzled and dazed by all the elegance and magnificence that she had already seen. This room was even more ostentatious. Gold gilt edged the ceiling and molding; silken embroidered tapestries hung on the walls; priceless figurines and vases covered the surfaces of stately furniture.

A deep oriental carpet covered the floor and muffled all footsteps. Its fantastic design was surely not actually meant to be trod upon. Miss Mays wished with all her heart that she could have removed her booted feet from its august surface.

Miss Mays's agonized gaze fell upon the lady at whose invitation she had come to London. Miss Mays was certain that she had never beheld anyone so lovely and assured as her sister-in-law. Lady Mays was attired in a becoming evening gown of warm amethyst silk that left her white shoulders bare and displayed her figure to admirable advantage. Jewels glimmered in her dark upswept curls and at her bosom and on her wrists. She appeared formidable in her beauty.

Miss Mays turned scared eyes to her ladyship's companion, Miss Blythe. This lady had spoken just as kindly as Lady Mays, but she, too, seemed the very epitome of elegance in her blue satin and pearls. She was therefore as unapproachable as Lady Mays in Miss Mays's estimation. Never in her life had Miss Mays felt more inadequate or mousey.

Lucinda was completely unaware of her sister-in-law's gathering weight of awe and dismay. She smiled and gestured graciously for Miss Mays to sit down on the settee closest to the warmth of the fire. "Pray be seated, Agnes. I hope that I may call you that?"

"Of course, my lady. I could have no possible objection," said Miss Mays. She seated herself gingerly on the edge of the satin-covered settee. She drew her booted feet close under her, hoping to thus minimize her contact with the intimidating carpet. Miss Mays started nervously when Lady Mays sat down close beside her.

Miss Blythe brought over a cup of tea on a saucer. "Here you are, my dear. I have put a bit of milk and sugar in it. If you have not yet had supper it will revive you." She urged the tea on their guest, who appeared strangely hesitant to accept it.

"Oh, I had not given a thought to supper." Lucinda smiled at Miss Mays, an inquiring lift to her fine brows. "Have you dined yet, Agnes? If you have not, I shall ring for the cook to prepare something for you."

Miss Mays burst into tears.

The young woman's hands were shaking badly. Blinded by her tears, she kept trying unsuccessfully to set her cup and saucer down on the occasional table. The tea slopped dangerously. Hastily, Miss Blythe relieved her of the cup and saucer before the hot tea was spilled over all. Miss Mays did not even notice, but at once buried her face in her gloved palms. Her quiet sobbing was heartrending.

Over Miss Mays's bowed head, Lucinda and Miss Blythe

looked at one another in astonishment and dismay. Miss Blythe nodded, encouraging Lucinda to take the lead. "I shall take away this tea and mop up a bit," she said, moving away.

Lucinda took up the role of comforter without the least notion of what she should do. "My dear Agnes, whatever is the matter?" she asked.

She could not see the young woman's face, so she untied the strings of Miss Mays's bonnet and gently laid the headgear aside. Taking her sister-in-law's nearest trembling gloved hand in her own, she said encouragingly, "Come, my dear, you have nothing to fear from us. Pray unburden yourself. What has gotten you so overwrought?"

Miss Mays replied in a muffled, suspended voice. The disjointed sentences, begun so hesitantly and only after much urging from Lucinda, eventually poured out of her.

She had written to Lady Mays out of a rare boldness borne of wistful hope. Later, she had shivered over her own impudence. She had never expected a reply, let alone one that was so graciously condescending. Lady Mays was too kind, too compassionate, toward one she did not—could not—know!

Upon receiving Lady Mays's letter she had gone at once to her aunt to share with that lady her good fortune. Her aunt had flown into a terrible fit of temper.

"She threw a clock at my head and swore at me!" sobbed Miss Mays.

The aunt declared that Miss Mays was *her* companion. She utterly forbade Miss Mays to accept Lady Mays's invitation or, indeed, to respond to her ladyship's letter.

Miss Mays had been utterly shaken and shocked. She had been thrown into flat despair. As the days slowly passed and she had obediently not set pen to paper, she grew to feel more and more burdened by guilt. The obsession took hold of her mind that she was behaving with unbearable rudeness toward kind Lady Mays.

A seed of rebellion became lodged in Miss Mays's heart and festered. It was kept watered by her aunt's constant remindings to her of her place. She was a nobody, a plain-faced mouse, a spinster at her last prayers. Her only object in life could only be to make herself useful to her betters.

Finally, Miss Mays had been unable to withstand the hateful haranguing, and she made a hasty retort.

"Oh, I should not have done it! I should not have! But I was unable to bear any more," moaned Miss Mays.

The words had poured out of her as she outlined the aunt's selfishness and meanspiritedness. Afterward, she had stood aghast at herself. Before her eyes, her aunt had turned quite purple with fury. The old woman was rendered momentarily speechless by her awful rage.

Miss Mays had begun to tremble with fear and remorse. It had not been her intention to drive her aunt into such a fit that it was likely to kill her. Miss Mays had started to utter a shivering apology, but she had been summarily cut off.

Her aunt renounced her roundly. Miss Mays was an ingrate, a viper in her bosom, a care-for-nobody, a bumbling, fumbling fool!

"I may be foolish, but I am not those other things! Truly I am not!" said Miss Mays tearfully.

The aunt had dismissed Miss Mays from her service on the spot and had ordered her things to be thrown out of the house into the yard. Miss Mays was put out with only her few possessions, without even being given the last quarter's salary owed her. She had timidly pointed out this omission, but her aunt had sworn that Miss Mays could starve and with her goodwill, for not a farthing more would she have from that lady's purse.

If it had not been for the carter who delivered the household's supply of milk and butter each week happening upon her, Miss Mays did not know what she might have done. But fortunately, the carter had taken pity on her and allowed her to ride in the back of his cart, himself placing her baggage beside her.

"Otherwise I would have had to trudge all the five miles to the village with only what I was able to carry," said Miss Mays.

When she arrived in the village, Miss Mays had purchased a ticket for the Mail Coach. She used some of the money that she had saved from the pittance that her aunt paid to her and which she had never been given the opportunity to spend.

Then once in London, she had hired a hackney to carry her to the address on dear Lady Mays's letter.

Miss Mays's faculties had been utterly suspended in her misery, and she had made her way to the only place she had known to go. But then when she had seen the imposing facade of the town house, she had realized that Lady Mays could not possibly have need of her services. Lady Mays obviously could afford any number of servants to do her pleasure. She had made a terrible error in writing to Lady Mays at all.

"It was a wicked, wicked mistake, for it was born out of my own selfishness! Now I have no place to go and no position to sustain me and I am very, very sorry to be such trouble!" A fresh bout of tears ended Miss Mays's wretched confession.

Lucinda gathered her sister-in-law into her arms for a reassuring hug. "Agnes! You must not go on so. You are not the least trouble. I am very pleased to have you here. You will be company for me and Tibby."

"But you have no place for me," cried Miss Mays, rearing away. "I cannot possibly be of service to you. Oh, what shall become of me?" She searched wildly in her pocket for a handkerchief.

Miss Blythe thoughtfully provided Miss Mays with her own daintily embroidered handkerchief. Miss Mays mopped her tear-swollen and reddened face. When she glanced down at the sodden twisted linen and saw what a work of beauty it had been before she had made such unthinking use of it, she actually groaned. "I have ruined it!"

"Of course you haven't, my dear. It will wash quite nicely," said Miss Blythe soothingly.

"I am not even fit to serve as your ladyship's lackey!" exclaimed Miss Mays despondently.

"What a funny you are, Agnes! I did not ask you to join my household as a servant!" said Lucinda on a soft laugh.

"You didn't?" Miss Mays frowned at her, sniffing still. "But then why?"

"You are my sister. I wish to bring you into your proper place. Agnes, I want to introduce you into the society in which you have always belonged."

Miss Mays stared at Lucinda, her mouth falling softly agape.

Lucinda took her sister-in-law's hand. It lay quiescent in hers. She said gently, "Agnes, you have been shamefully cheated by your family. Tibby and I shall see to it that you are restored to your rightful place."

Miss Mays stared at her with uncomprehending eyes. "I beg pardon? I . . . I do not understand.

Lucinda looked at her sister-in-law. She then glanced at Miss Blythe a bit helplessly. She did not know what else to say. She thought that she had explained the matter with perfect clarity.

Miss Blythe eased Miss Mays's hand out of Lucinda's light clasp. She drew the young woman gently to her feet. "Come, my dear. You are obviously exhausted. Nothing is making the least sense to you. I shall see that you are given a bowl of soup and some tea upstairs and then allow you to go to bed. Everything will be made much clearer to you in the morning."

Miss Mays looked at Miss Blythe. Then she turned a questioning gaze on her imposing sister-in-law, Lady Mays. Even in her shocked state, she was dumbly aware of where the authority lay.

Lucinda realized that Miss Mays was actually looking to her for her permission. She nodded encouragingly. "Go with Tibby now."

Still Miss Mays seemed to hesitate. "It is my wish," said Lucinda gently.

"Come along with me, Miss Mays," said Miss Blythe quietly.

Then Miss Mays docilely went away with Miss Blythe out of the drawing room.

Lucinda sat back against the cushions of the settee. A frown had gathered her brows. She stared into the fire, watching the yellow flames flicker.

The arrival of her sister-in-law was nothing as she had supposed it would be. For the life of her, she could not imagine that poor, wretched young woman as being able to take the *ton* by storm. She could make Miss Mays the most well-dressed and coiffed young woman in the town, but there was nothing that she could do to transform her sister-in-law's unfortunate manner.

As cruel and heedless as Lucinda knew society to be, she wondered at the wisdom of even attempting to bring Miss Mays into fashion.

Lucinda got up from the settee to pace back and forth. "She would be eaten alive," she said aloud, grimly.

Lucinda pinned her hopes on Miss Blythe. Surely if there were any worthwhile suggestions to be put forward, Miss Blythe would do so. Lucinda did not wish to put away her intention of doing what she could for Miss Mays.

## *Chapter Fifteen*

It was almost an hour later when Miss Blythe returned to the drawing room. Upon that lady's quiet entrance, Lucinda turned. "How is she?"

"She is asleep, poor child. She is burnt to the socket," said Miss Blythe. "She will be better for a night's rest."

"I have never been so filled with compassion, Tibby. That young woman has been brutally browbeaten nearly all of her life and look at what it has made of her," said Lucinda.

"Quite," agreed Miss Blythe. For a moment she watched Lucinda's restless pacing. "What shall you try to do for her?"

"Hopefully, just as I have said. I wish to see that she is restored to her proper place," said Lucinda.

Lucinda was not really surprised by her companion's suddenly thoughtful expression. Miss Blythe would naturally have thought of the same sort of reservations that she had herself.

She smiled slightly. "Why are you frowning, Tibby? Do you not agree that I should do all in my power for her?"

"Oh, most emphatically I do. However, I suspect that your object may not be so easily accomplished. As you have so correctly observed, Miss Mays has received in her life little of kindness or consideration," said Miss Blythe.

Lucinda sighed and nodded. "It is precisely that which has me in a puzzle, Tibby. Not ever having been brought out or encouraged to think of herself, Agnes will be thrown into natural confusion by pretty compliments or a gentleman's expression of interest. Nor will she know how best to deal with the snobbery that one is likely to meet among certain sets."

"Of a surety, she will not know how to respond," agreed Miss Blythe. "However, the problem runs deeper than that, Lucinda. Why, she confided to me abovestairs that she had never before set foot in this house! Her brother's house, if you please! Can you not imagine what must have been racing through her mind when we brought her into this room?"

"My word. The poor girl must have been utterly overwhelmed when she saw all of this pompous show," said Lucinda slowly. "And we two attired as we are! It is no wonder that she refused to give up her outer garments or that she burst into tears. She must have felt that at any moment she would be put out as being too unworthy of our company."

"Precisely. She felt herself quite beneath our touch. I suspect that Miss Mays would have felt more comfortable coming through the back service entrance rather than through the front door," said Miss Blythe.

She shook her head, her expression saddened. "Such a waste of that young woman's youth. It will be difficult for her to be thrust suddenly from servitude to privilege."

"Yes, I begin to understand that. Tibby, I am ashamed that I never inquired after her well-being during the time of my marriage. I knew that she was going to an elderly relation to act as a companion. I wish I had done something," said Lucinda, frowning in her turn. "But I did not know that my late lord had carried his callousness so far as to completely deny his sister a place in his life."

"But you did not know," reminded Miss Blythe gently.

"I should have suspected it, at least. He disliked to have anything about him that he did not admire for its beauty or its expense. Obviously Agnes was neither in his estimation," said Lucinda.

"You must not blame yourself, my dear. Even if you had known the extent of Miss Mays's miserable circumstances, I suspect that there would still have been little you could have done. Would Lord Mays have allowed her into his household?" asked Miss Blythe, crossing to her usual chair and sitting down. She pulled out her embroidery from its basket.

"No, I know very well that he would not have. But I could have had her with me at Carbarry. That would have been infinitely better for her, don't you agree?" Lucinda angrily slapped her palms together. "That aunt of hers! What a fiendish monster to use her so harshly!"

"There is no profit in growing hardhearted over such a one as that, Lucinda. That chapter of Miss Mays's life is thankfully at an end. It would be better now to think what is best to be done," said Miss Blythe, placing her stitches with meticulous care.

"You are right as always, Tibby," said Lucinda, a smile edging back to her lips.

Lucinda watched her companion, knowing from long association that Miss Blythe often covered her most contemplative reflections with the activity in which she was at that moment engaged.

"Very well! What shall we do with Agnes?"

Miss Blythe paused in her handiwork and looked up at Lucinda speculatively. "Why, I had thought to take her in hand a little and take up my governessing mantle again. Should you dislike it very much, my dear?"

"No, of course not. It would be the perfect thing for her!" exclaimed Lucinda. "I wonder that I did not think of it myself."

"I believe that Miss Mays needs a firm and kind guiding hand until she is able to stand on her own," explained Miss Blythe, once more plying her needle.

"You do just as you think best, Tibby. You will be the mother that she so desperately needs, whilst I shall be the elder sister," said Lucinda. "Between us, we must surely do her a world of good."

"I hope so, indeed," said Miss Blythe, smiling. "In view of what I believe, I think also that we should go about introducing her slowly to the ways of society. We should not expect her to attend anything too grand or intimidating at the first."

Lucinda sighed. "You do know what you are saying, do you not? We shall have to treat her as though she is the merest babe out of the schoolroom and she is all of nine-and-twenty! Why, I am the younger by seven years; but I feel infinitely older. How does one manage the life of one's elder without inevitably giving offense? I can foresee all sorts of complications. The very thought is already making me quake with nervousness."

Miss Blythe laughed. "I shouldn't fret too much, Lucinda. Miss Mays is quite used to having someone else order her about."

"Order her about! Why, that is the last thing I wish to do!" exclaimed Lucinda.

"Nevertheless that must be your role, at least for now. Miss Mays will scarcely know how to receive any other sort of treatment," said Miss Blythe.

"Better and better!" exclaimed Lucinda.

"I am confident that as we go on, Miss Mays will begin to try her wings a little," said Miss Blythe reassuringly. "Of course, you will need to be alert to her emerging character and adapt your manner toward her accordingly so that she will be encouraged to express her own wishes."

Lucinda regarded her companion with some dismay. "Oh, Tibby! I do not know that I am at all suited to this. When I contemplate the responsibility, I positively shudder. I am likely to make some awful blunder and then where will we be?"

Miss Blythe chuckled. "Never mind, my dear. You shall have this chick off your hands before the Season is out, I daresay. Miss Mays is just the sort of shy, retiring young female that most appeals to the chivalry in a male breast."

"A husband for Agnes." Lucinda thought about that for a long moment and hopeful vistas opened up to her imagination. She smiled slowly, almost archly. She dropped into a chair with a careless abandon. "Dear Tibby, you may play the matchmaker for Agnes to your heart's content."

"Thank you, my dear. I intend to, for I believe it to be in that young female's best interests to establish her as quickly as possible," said Miss Blythe composedly.

"You are undoubtedly right again. Agnes is not the sort of female who can ever stand completely on her own. She needs a lord's strong shoulder to lean on," said Lucinda musingly, her chin in her hand.

"And naturally you do not," said Miss Blythe, twinkling over at her.

Lucinda laughed and dropped her hand. "You well know my answer to that, Tibby."

"Oh yes, so I do," said Miss Blythe. She wisely left the subject where it lay and adroitly turned the conversation. "I suppose it is too late to meet our engagement?"

Lucinda glanced swiftly at the clock on the mantel. She was astonished at the lateness of the hour. "I had quite forgotten! I sent the carriage back, but I can as easily have it brought around again. If we rush, we may still put in a respectable appearance."

"Would it not be counted as unsufferably rude to arrive so late in the evening?" asked Miss Blythe, also glancing at the clock.

"I am persuaded that Lady Bishop would excuse our tardiness once I had explained the unexpected arrival of my sister-in-law. However, I must admit that I am not at all keen on making such an entrance," said Lucinda.

"Surely Lady Bishop would accept our excuses just as readily if we did not go at all," suggested Miss Blythe.

"Oh yes." Lucinda chuckled suddenly, her eyes dancing. "Are you gently hinting that you should like to forgo her ladyship's soiree altogether, Tibby? And what of our plans for the opera afterward?"

Miss Blythe also laughed, though somewhat shamefacedly. "Unless you particularly wish to go, Lucinda, I would prefer idling away the remainder of the evening with a good book or my embroidery," confessed that lady. "As for the opera, it is not at all as entertaining as the theater, I've found."

"I think that we have had enough of dramatics for one evening, actually," said Lucinda dryly. "I shall send round a note to Lady Bishop expressing our profuse apologies and an explanation of the circumstances. Her ladyship cannot possibly take offense, I am persuaded, for she places a high emphasis on family connections."

"Thank you, Lucinda. I did not believe you when you warned me that I might become jaded, but in truth I am not nearly so eager to go out every evening as I was," said Miss Blythe.

"Poor Tibby!" Lucinda laughed. "It will not harm me in the least to remain home at least this one evening, either. Do you know, I cannot recall the last time that I picked up a novel? Certainly not since I left Carbarry!"

"I have an excellent title that you might enjoy," offered Miss Blythe. "I shall bring it downstairs for you if you would like."

"Wonderful! Let us call for coffee here in the drawing room, shall we? But first, I want Madison to relieve me of all this finery," said Lucinda, lifting her silk skirt between her fingers.

Miss Blythe chuckled at Lucinda's expressive gesture. She neatly snipped her thread and rolled up her piecework. "We do seem to be a trifle overdressed for an evening spent in."

Agreeing to meet again in a quarter hour, the ladies went upstairs to change out of their elaborate gowns and to put on attire more appropriate to the sort of evening that they now anticipated.

When Lucinda and Miss Blythe reentered the drawing room, the coffee was served to them by the butler. Assuring himself that the ladies had no further needs, Church retired and left Lucinda and Miss Blythe to a contented perusal of their respective books.

An hour later the butler returned to the drawing room. Church apologized for disturbing the ladies. He said that Lord Mays was without in the entry hall, wishing to speak privately to Lady Mays. The butler gave a discreet cough. "And if I may say so, my lady, his lordship seems to be laboring under some agitation."

"Pray show Lord Mays in at once," said Lucinda, laying aside her book and rising.

"Shall I withdraw, my dear?" asked Miss Blythe, setting down her own novel.

"No, of course not. I am persuaded that Lord Mays was not thinking of you when he requested privacy, but of anyone else whom we might have been entertaining," said Lucinda.

"Very well. I own, I am curious," said Miss Blythe.

"Yes, and I also," said Lucinda.

The butler showed Lord Mays into the drawing room and closed the door. Lucinda saw that his lordship was attired in a plain coat and buckskins. Her brows contracted, for it was instantly clear that Lord Mays had not been to a formal gathering that evening. That in itself was unusual. "My lord, pray come in. It is only Miss Blythe and myself this evening, as you see."

Lord Mays's normally placid expression was anxious. However, despite the weight of the matter pressing on his mind, he did not forget his manners. He formally greeted Lucinda and bowed to Miss Blythe, before saying, "Forgive me for bothering you at such an hour, Lady Mays. But I have come with bad tidings of your cousin, Mr. Stassart. He has been stabbed, by a cutthroat, and he is at this very moment outside in the hackney, bleeding like a stuck pig!"

"Goodness gracious!" exclaimed Miss Blythe, her eyes widening behind her spectacles. "Was it footpads, my lord?"

Lord Mays shook his head. His expression was unhappy. It was obvious that he was reluctant to relate the tale to them.

"Come, Wilfred. You must not hide it from us," said Lucinda.

"It happened in a hell of particularly low repute. Mr. Stassart was playing at cards with several others. There was a heated argument, then a fellow leaped at Mr. Stassart with a knife," said Lord Mays briefly.

Lucinda was shocked. Little as she liked her cousin, it was still an unpleasant jolt to hear that he had been hurt. She started toward the drawing room door. "We must have him in at once."

Lord Mays caught Lucinda's elbow and stayed her. He

shook his head. "You shouldn't see him, Lucinda. Not at all the sight for a gently bred female. He should have a physician to attend him first."

Lucinda looked into his worried gold-brown eyes and realized that he wanted to spare her. She was touched by his obvious concern for her sensibilities. "If you think it best, Wilfred, then I shan't. I shall have Church get two of the footmen to carry him upstairs immediately."

Lord Mays nodded and released her. She stepped past him to open the door and call for the butler.

"I shall go find Mrs. Beeseley and have her see to a room," said Miss Blythe. Lord Mays nodded and watched as Miss Blythe made a quick exit; she murmured an apology and an explanation as she stepped past Lucinda and the butler in the doorway.

"Thank you, Tibby," said Lucinda and swiftly finished outlining the situation for the sharply attentive butler. "Have a physician sent for also, Church," she concluded. "Lord Mays informs me that it would be best."

"At once, my lady!" The butler raced away. He could be heard calling for his subordinates and issuing swift orders.

Shutting the door, Lucinda turned once more to Lord Mays. She noted the pallor of his complexion, and immediately her concern was aroused. "Are you perfectly all right, Wilfred? Shall I pour you some coffee? But it may be a bit tepid. Perhaps a glass of brandy?" As she had spoken, she had crossed over to the sideboard to lay hand on a decanter of wine.

Lord Mays ran a slightly shaking hand over his sandy hair. "I shall have the brandy, I think. Peculiar, I had thought the memories safely shut away, but I fear I have been caught off guard by this thing."

He laughed half ashamedly at himself, watching her pour the wine. "Having survived Waterloo, it is odd that I could become so rattled at the sight of a bit of blood. But I had not thought to see such stuff again. Stupid of me, I know."

"Not at all," said Lucinda warmly. She pressed a glass into his hand. "I think it speaks quite highly of your sensitivity. I honor you for it, my lord."

He flushed. Without responding, he tossed back a measure

of the brandy. When he had set down the glass, he said, "I would have taken Mr. Stassart to my own lodgings, but I am in such cramped quarters that there would be no doing anything for him there."

"Your lodgings!"

# Chapter Sixteen

Startled, Lucinda realized that Mays House had not been the closest place of succor. If Lord Mays had bypassed his own lodgings to bring her cousin to her, then he had also passed her cousin's lodgings as well, for the two gentlemen resided within a mere block of one another.

"But whyever did you not take him to his own lodgings, pray?"

Lord Mays coughed delicately behind his hand. "Fellow told me that his pockets are all to let and that the tipsters are looking for him. He daren't return to his own lodgings until he brings himself about."

"That sounds very like Ferdie," said Lucinda. The thought came to her suddenly. She cast a sharp glance at Lord Mays. "At whose suggestion was it decided to bring my cousin here?"

"Why, I suppose Mr. Stassart voiced it. Of course, I saw at once it was just the thing to do since he is your father's heir as well as your cousin," said Lord Mays.

Lucinda gave a laugh. "Did he assure you that he was my father's heir even as he lay bleeding all over the hackney seat? That does indeed sound just like Ferdie!"

Lord Mays began to look slightly anxious. "Have I not done as I should, then? Should I not have brought your cousin here?"

Lucinda made haste to reassure him. "No, you did just right,

Wilfred. It is just that I am rather suspicious of anything that my cousin has managed to turn to his own benefit. Ferdie has a habit of taking advantage of one's good nature and compassion. If he was not so seriously wounded as you seem to think, I would be tempted to send him straight back to his lodgings to face the consequences of his folly. He is something of a wastrel, as you know. I have regretted for many years that he is my father's heir, for he has abused the position any number of times."

"I see," said Lord Mays slowly. He shot a keen look at Lucinda's face. A frown gathered in his own eyes. "If the fellow gives you trouble, Lucinda, you have only to apply to me. I am responsible, after all, for bringing Stassart to your house."

Lucinda placed her hand on his lordship's arm. "You are very good, Wilfred. I do most highly value your friendship. Be assured, I will not hesitate to call upon you if I should ever find myself in difficulties."

Lord Mays grinned in his crooked, attractive fashion. He was relieved that she was not annoyed with him for his unwitting blunder. He reached over to catch hold of her hand and lifted her fingers briefly to his lips. "I shall leave you to it, then. After bringing such unexpected trouble to you, I daren't take the chance that I shall somehow offend you further!"

Lucinda smiled. "I can't think how you could possibly offend me, sir. But nevertheless I shall not hold you with me any longer. No doubt I shall be called upon before many more minutes to go up to my cousin."

At that instant the door was impetuously thrown open.

Miss Mays stood framed on the threshold. She was clutching an embroidered robe tight to her throat. Her hair was tumbled down over her shoulders and her brown eyes were wide and luminous. Altogether she presented quite a different picture from the shivering, mousey-looking female who had arrived not two hours before.

Lucinda stared, amazed. She glanced at Lord Mays and she saw that he, also, was staring at the young woman.

There was a look of astonishment and appreciation in his eyes.

Lucinda was startled by the little leap of envy within her.

Surely she was not so self-centered that she could not bear for her friend to regard another female with approbation.

"Lady Mays!" Miss Mays uttered. "Lady Mays, there is a wounded man in the bedchamber opposite mine and—"

It was then that Miss Mays saw that Lucinda was not alone. Color surged into her face under the gentleman's interested gaze. She looked prepared either to flee or to faint, if she could but make up her mind which was the more appropriate.

Lucinda took the decision out of her hands. "Pray come in, Agnes," she said calmly.

Miss Mays gasped and shrank back. "Oh no, no!"

Lucinda walked over and grasped the young woman's limp wrist. Without apology she drew Miss Mays into the room. "Do not be afraid. It is only your cousin, Lord Wilfred Mays. Lord Mays has been kind enough to bring *my* cousin, Mr. Stassart, here after he was hurt. My lord, naturally you will recall my sister-in-law, Miss Agnes Mays?"

"Of course I do, though it has been years. Good evening, Cousin Agnes."

Lord Mays made his bow over Miss Mays's trembling hand. He smiled at her and commented with unthinking appreciation, "Pretty wrapper, that. It becomes you."

"Oh!" Miss Mays flushed brighter. "I should not have . . . oh, I am so mortified! Pray . . . pray excuse me!" She snatched her hand from Lord Mays and fled.

Lord Mays gazed after her in the liveliest dismay. "I say, I never meant to put her out of countenance like that. I only meant to compliment her."

"It is perfectly all right. Agnes is exceedingly retiring and shy. I imagine it was quite disconcerting to her to be seen abroad with her hair down and *en dishabille* by her manly cousin," said Lucinda, chuckling.

Lord Mays was much struck. It was his turn to flush. "Quite right, too! Not at all the thing. It is not like we have lived in one another's pockets all of our lives. I avoided Mays like the plague when I was on the town, and I never saw his sister, either. Pray convey my apologies, Lucinda. I shall not be able to look her in the face, even though she is my cousin!"

"I shall do so, of course. However, you shall have to face

Agnes again sometime, for I am hoping to bring her out this Season," said Lucinda.

Lord Mays looked at her fixedly. "You are? Whatever for? Why, she must surely be past the age of making her bows."

"Agnes is nine-and-twenty, and the poor girl has never been presented. Perhaps you do not know, since you were not intimate with that branch of the family, and then later during the war were abroad," said Lucinda. "Agnes was kept close at home to nurse each of her parents through their last lingering illnesses and no one made the least push to do anything for her on her own account."

Lucinda forebore to mention the most glaring omission in Miss Mays's history, but it was an unnecessary discretion. Her companion was not a fool.

"Her brother would not have bothered with her, of course, for she isn't a raving beauty," said Lord Mays, unerringly cutting to the truth.

Lucinda shrugged. It would be useless to try to wrap it up in pretty words. "Precisely. Since her parents died, Agnes was employed as companion to an elderly aunt." She turned out her hands. "So you see—"

"My Aunt Sophronia, do you mean?" exclaimed Lord Mays in tones of liveliest horror. "What a hellish thing!"

"Oh, do you know the lady?" asked Lucinda with not a little curiosity. "I do not believe that I ever met her."

"You would recall the incident if you had! There never lived such an out-and-out tartar! A tongue that cut like a razor and a meanness that oozed out of her fingertips," he exclaimed.

"That sounds quite an accurate description if I may believe all that Agnes related to us," said Lucinda.

"She was all that and more," Lord Mays assured her. "My mother used to take me to see her. I was never more glad in my life when I attained my majority and I was able to tell my mother that I didn't care whether the old witch left me anything or not, I had seen the last of her!"

"Your cousin's experience of the lady was by far the worse," said Lucinda. She proceeded to tell to him all that Miss Mays had been led to confide to her and Miss Blythe.

Lord Mays shook his head, glancing again at the door through which Miss Mays had fled so precipitously. "Poor Cousin Agnes! She has led a dog's life! I feel for her, let me tell you!"

"Indeed she has, and that is precisely the reason that I have decided to do my best on her behalf," said Lucinda.

"That is deuced decent of you, Lucinda," said Lord Mays with warm approval. "The poor girl needs a bit of sympathy and support."

"Yes, indeed." Lucinda was struck with an inspired thought. It was not at all out of the realm of possibility that Lord Mays could turn out to be the prince that Miss Blythe pronounced to be necessary for Miss Mays's happiness. The two were not first cousins, and it was not unknown for a contract to be gotten up between such parties. Certainly it would not hurt to nudge things in that direction, Lucinda thought, for his lordship's sympathies had already been aroused.

"Your cousin has been employed as the family's nurse since she was a girl, and so she has not the least notion in how to go on," said Lucinda. "In all honesty I am a little anxious in how she will be received. I hope that you at least will be kind to her, Wilfred, and help her to avoid any major social embarrassment."

"You may depend upon it! The poor girl. We must all do our best for her," said Lord Mays, his kind heart stirred to its depths.

Miss Blythe came back to the drawing room to inform Lucinda and Lord Mays that the physician had arrived. "The man has assured me that Mr. Stassart does not appear at first glance to be in alarming straits. He says that Mr. Stassart's color is actually quite good given the circumstances," she said.

"That is good news, Miss Blythe." Lord Mays turned to Lucinda, saying cheerfully, "Perhaps the fellow will not be the burden that you were dreading he would be, after all, Lady Mays. A bandage or two and you may send your cousin on his way."

"That would be wonderful, indeed!" agreed Lucinda.

She met Miss Blythe's thoughtful gaze and realized that her companion was also thinking of Mr. Weatherby's warning. If

Ferdie was indeed plotting to force her into wedlock through gossip and scandal, this situation was ready-made to his hand. It would behoove her to see that her cousin was out of her house as quickly as possible.

"I should like to see Ferdie back on his feet in the shortest amount of time," said Lucinda.

"Hear, hear," murmured Miss Blythe.

"Oh, Stassart will be up and about before you know it. I've seen fellows worse off, having lost arms or legs, who made absolutely amazing recoveries," said Lord Mays, anxious to reassure.

Lucinda laughed. Her blue eyes were dancing as she replied, "Thank you, sir! I am glad to hear that I need have nothing to worry about since my cousin is sound of limb!"

Lord Mays saw that she had fallen into a teasing mood. "You are roasting me. Well, I do not mind it. I like to see you laughing."

Lucinda could feel her color unaccountably rise. "It is just that I am so easy with you that you dare to be so familiar, sir!"

"Yes, and I like that, too," said Lord Mays with what she considered to be an outrageous wink.

On that salutatory note, Lord Mays decided that it was as good a time as any to take his leave. He bowed and said good night to Miss Blythe. He was gratified when the stern-faced companion nodded to him in a friendly manner. He was beginning to recognize that the older lady was not half as formidable as he had once thought.

Lucinda saw his lordship out with unimpaired composure. Upon his reiteration that he had not meant to bring trouble to her in the person of Mr. Stassart, Lucinda again set his anxiety to rest.

"Ferdie is my cousin, after all. I could not have turned him away from my door. Not, at any rate, when he is wounded," she said, smiling.

Lord Mays grinned crookedly. "No, you could not have done it. Your heart is too sympathetic for that. However, take heed of what I say, Lucinda. I shall be over in a trice to deal with Stassart if he sets himself up to be a burden to you."

"I shall not forget, Wilfred."

Lucinda stood up on her toes to brush a light salute against his lean cheek. She smiled at his startled, reddening face. "My best of friends. I know that I may rely upon you."

"And so you may," said Lord Mays gruffly. He turned and went swiftly out the door and down the steps.

When the porter closed the door behind his lordship, Lucinda's smile swiftly began to fade. She walked back to the drawing room and paused on the threshold. She had left Miss Blythe sitting on the settee, and now she stood in the open doorway and looked across the room at her companion. "Lord Mays is gone. Now I must go up to see about Ferdie."

"I shall come with you, my dear," said Miss Blythe, rising at once.

"I had rather hoped that you would," said Lucinda.

## Chapter Seventeen

In the back bedchamber allotted to Mr. Stassart there had gathered a rather large company. The butler and two stalwart footmen had carried Mr. Stassart up to the bedroom. Mrs. Beeseley had freshly warmed the bed and then with the warming pan still firmly grasped in one competent hand, she had supervised the careful deposit of Mr. Stassart's lanky form on top of the sheets. The butler and the footmen had lingered to discuss the best way to divest the wounded man of his clothing. An occasional word was put in by Mrs. Beeseley who had her own opinion to offer.

A wide-eyed maid listened agog to it all while she poured water into the washing bowl. Unfortunately for the satisfaction of her curiosity, she sloshed the last of the water.

Mrs. Beeseley spoke sharply to the girl for her carelessness, and she sent her off to get the lint bandages out of the medicine cabinet.

"And mind that you do not dally about it!"

Lucinda and Miss Blythe entered the bedroom in time to hear the strict admonition. The maid dipped a hurried bob to the ladies before she rushed out.

Bunches of candles had been set close about the bed and burned so bright that the remainder of the bedchamber was thrown into dramatic shadow. Lucinda and Miss Blythe crossed the dim quarter of the room into the light. Their appearance was deferentially acknowledged by the servants, but was not of sufficient moment to deter the ongoing discussion.

"It be my opinion, Mr. Church, that 'is boots should be cut off," said one of the footmen with a zealot's relish. His peer nodded in agreement.

"It is my shoulder that has been wounded, you fool, not my legs," came an acid rejoinder from the bed.

Lucinda was amused. Her cousin was not only conscious, but he was fully aware of what was being argued over his supine body. She was inordinately reassured that there was nothing too wrong with him if he could so strongly object to the proposed ravagings of his elegant topboots.

"Don't you worry, young sir. I shan't let these great loobies lay a finger to your boots," said Church soothingly. The butler then cast a sulfurous look over his subordinates. The footmen were duly cowed.

"Thank God! A voice of reason." Mr. Stassart fell back on the pillow, seemingly too weak to rouse himself to further effort.

Lucinda moved to the head of the bed and looked down at her cousin's flushed, sweating face. She said softly, "Well, Ferdie! What manner of coil have you managed to embroil yourself in this time?"

Mr. Stassart was breathing rather shallowly. At the sound of her voice his eyelids flickered, then opened. His eyes were surprisingly bright. Perhaps with fever, thought Lucinda. "Fair cousin. I bid you good evening," he said hoarsely. "As for my situation, you may judge for yourself." He made a listless gesture toward his left shoulder.

Lucinda glanced before she thought. She saw that blood garishly stained his coat. A clumsy pad had been thrust inside the shoulder of the coat, presumably by Lord Mays, but it had not served to stop the seepage onto the front of his green-striped waistcoat. Lucinda swallowed at the shocking sight. It was more blood than she had ever seen.

As butterflies churned in her stomach, she decided that Lord Mays had been perfectly correct in urging her not to oversee the entrance of her cousin as he was carried into the house. She wished now that she had taken even greater heed to his lordship's warning and had waited to see her cousin until he had already been cared for properly.

However, Lucinda was made of stern stuff. She was determined that she would not give in to any weakness. Her reply as a consequence was somewhat cooler than it might have been. "Yes, you have bled, haven't you? You appear to be in a rather bad way, Ferdie."

Mr. Stassart's half-hooded eyes widened. Indignation swelled his narrow chest. "Gad, you're a cold creature. An expression of horror and compassion would not be out of place, cousin!"

Lucinda realized that her cousin was not suffering near as badly as he would have her believe. He was still attempting to gain whatever advantage there could possibly be in the situation. It was second nature to him, she thought resignedly. She would not give him the satisfaction of knowing that he had managed to overset her even for a moment.

Lucinda smiled at her cousin. "I assure you, Ferdie, my withers are quite wrung with pity."

Ferdie threw his uninjured forearm over his eyes, making a grunt of disgust. "I lie at death's door and not a tear to be shed. I thank you, cousin!"

"I am not precisely an hysterical sort of female," said Lucinda, half apologetically.

"*That* is apparent, at least!" was Mr. Stassart's bitter rejoinder.

"My lady, here is the physician. He wishes a word with you," said Church.

Lucinda turned away from the bed. The physician had just

finished washing and drying his hands, she saw. She wondered at that. As yet the man had not had opportunity to soil his hands, for he had yet to examine her cousin except by sight.

"I only wished to reassure your ladyship. Judging from the young sir's display of spirit, I do not expect to find a great deal to fuss over," said the physician.

"Quack!" uttered Ferdie. He flung aside his arm so that he could glare at the surprised physician. He was incensed by the seemingly casual statement. "Much you know about it! Why, I could still bleed to death lying here whilst you dance attendance upon her ladyship!"

Lucinda laughed, the situation suddenly striking her as ridiculous.

Ferdie swore awfully.

"Sir!" protested Mrs. Beeseley, scandalized. "There's ladies present."

"Never mind, Mrs. Beeseley. I readily understand Mr. Stassart's feelings of frustration. It was ignoble of me, indeed, to find humor at such a time," said Lucinda. She turned once more to the physician. "I shall leave him in your capable hands, sir."

"Good. We shall have to have him out of that coat and his boots for him to be comfortable, as these good people have already observed." The physician dubiously eyed the tight-fitting garment on his patient. "It will not be an easy task to remove that coat. The struggle may well encourage the bleeding."

"Aye, 'e'll likely bloody the whole bed before we can properly wrestle him out of that rig," muttered one of the footmen.

The butler rebuked his subservient for speaking so plain in front of their mistress. "Her ladyship is undoubtedly already highly concerned for Mr. Stassart, considering that the gentleman is her cousin. She'll not be needing your mouth adding to it, saucebox."

"Not her! She'll likely look on cool as you please and remark at the end that lilies would be a nice touch at the wake," said Ferdie in a self-pitying voice. He cast a glance of loathing at those standing round the bed. "Ghouls! The whole lot of you!"

Lucinda thought that there had been quite enough said. "Church, you and the footmen will assist the good doctor in undressing Mr. Stassart. Cut that coat off so that he will be spared some pain."

"A practical and compassionate suggestion," approved the physician.

"You know nothing of the matter!" snapped Ferdie, suddenly roused to animation. He raised himself as far as he was able and pointed a quivering forefinger. "I forbid any one of you to touch one thread of this coat!"

"Pray be reasonable, Ferdie. The coat cannot possibly be cleaned to its original state. It is already quite ruined," said Lucinda.

"My man will know what to do. He will, I tell you!"

"But your man is not here now, and you must be tended to properly," said the physician. "The coat must come off now."

"I shall defend myself, I warn you!" Ferdie snapped, the color hectic in his cheeks.

The butler looked at the doctor questioningly. The physician nodded. Church took out a pocket knife and bent to begin the task of slitting the sleeves of Mr. Stassart's ruined coat.

Mr. Stassart swung a wild fist. Church ducked even as Mrs. Beeseley shrieked a shrill warning. The closer of the footmen caught the patient's arm and bore it down. He then held the thrashing man down against the pillows. His fellow, with the greatest presence of mind, sat on Mr. Stassart's legs.

"You must calm yourself, Mr. Stassart. I do not wish to hurt you," reproved Church as he carefully slit open the coat. There was the loud sound of ripping cloth.

"Yes, do try to contain yourself, Ferdie, and allow yourself to be tended," said Lucinda.

Ferdie did not appear to be listening. He cast rolling whitened eyes at what the butler was doing. "My coat! My new coat! It is utterly destroyed!" There was the hint of tears in the afflicted man's voice. It cut him to the depths of his shallow dandy's soul to witness the destruction of the exquisite garment.

There was a quiver in Lucinda's voice that she could not

disguise as she said soothingly, "I shall buy you another coat, Ferdie."

Mr. Stassart's starting eyes fixed balefully upon his cousin's face. He panted, "This is your doing! Jade!"

"Sir!" The physician was shocked. "I beseech you, moderate your language. It is most unbecoming."

Mr. Stassart took no notice of the physician's disapproval. "Malicious witch! You have me at your mercy now, but I swear that I shall be revenged!" He gave a screech as Church tugged free the tattered remains of what had once been a fine coat. "It's a *rag*. My beautiful coat is a rag!"

Miss Blythe laid her hand lightly on Lucinda's arm. "My dear, Mr. Stassart has become suspiciously hysterical." She gestured suggestively toward the bedroom door.

Lucinda nodded agreement. She glanced down at her cousin's flushed countenance. "I shall leave you now, Ferdie. My presence does not appear to be in the least reassuring to you."

Ferdie swore again, drawing another scandalized protest from the housekeeper. Unheeding of anyone else, he snarled at his cousin. "Good riddance, I say! I would as lief have a rabid dog attending me!"

Lucinda retreated across the bedroom. Just as she reached the door, she heard her cousin's horrified uplifted accents. "Argh! No, no! *Not* the waistcoat, too! Have you no sense of decency, man?"

Lucinda was laughing as she stepped into the hallway. Miss Blythe followed her out of the room, as did the housekeeper.

Mrs. Beeseley shut the door with the suggestion of a slam. She clicked her tongue in shocked disapproval. "Such an awful young man!"

"Mr. Stassart is overwrought," said Miss Blythe mildly.

The housekeeper sniffed. "One can tell quality from dross, Miss Blythe!" She bustled off down the hallway.

Lucinda laughed again. "Poor Ferdie! He has fallen short of Mrs. Beeseley's expectations of a gentleman. Not that he would care one whit how a mere housekeeper views him, of course. However, he does think rather high of himself. I suspect that he *would* feel the slight if he were to hear himself referred to as dross."

"Yes, undoubtedly he would," agreed Miss Blythe.

The door opposite cracked open, and a single rounded orb peered out at them.

"Good evening, Agnes," said Lucinda affably. "It is only Miss Blythe and myself."

The door opened wide and Miss Mays poked out her head. Her face was anxious. "Lady Mays! Miss Blythe! What is happening? That man—he appeared to be in terrible pain! I was wakened by his awful groanings when he was carried past my door earlier. I have not been able to return to bed or still my fearful imaginations."

"You are not to fret, Agnes," said Lucinda. "That was my cousin, Mr. Ferdie Stassart. We have a physician with him now, who has assured us that he is not in immediate danger."

Miss Mays emerged round the corner of her door, emboldened by Lady Mays's mild tone. Lucinda was interested to note that she was still attired in the dressing gown but that her hair was now sedately confined by a prim sleeping cap.

"But whatever happened to him—your cousin, I mean—my lady? Did he perhaps run foul of footpads?"

"Oh no. Nothing so pedantic," said Lucinda, smiling. Miss Blythe chuckled, appreciating the play on words. But Miss Mays merely looked puzzled.

Lucinda sighed. It was becoming more and more apparent to her that her sister-in-law was not in the least needle-witted. She would have to restrict herself to the black-and-white with Miss Mays.

"I do not like to cast aspersions, but I must confess that my cousin is a very foolish gentleman," said Lucinda. "He was playing cards in a place where he should not have been. A low hell, in fact. There was a dispute of some sort and he was attacked."

"How shocking!" breathed Miss Mays, her eyes widening in fascinated horror. "Was Mr. Stassart dreadfully wounded?"

"No . . . yes. I really don't know! Lord Mays, who brought him to us so that a physician could be got to him, seemed to think that my cousin was in some danger. However, Ferdie was quite coherent when I spoke to him. In fact, I must say that he was quite lively in the face of his hurt," said Lucinda.

"An understatement, my dear," said Miss Blythe in her driest tone.

"Yes, well, perhaps it was," said Lucinda, laughing.

Once more, Miss Mays frowned at something that she had not understood. There was the hint of reproach in her expressive eyes as she gazed at Lucinda and Miss Blythe. Timidly, she asked, "Surely you should not make such game when Mr. Stassart lies wounded and in pain?"

Lucinda made haste to school her own expression to an appropriate soberness. "You are perfectly right, Agnes. Perhaps the shock has unbecomingly overset us. We must all await the physician's verdict, but I am positive that Mr. Stassart will recover."

"Oh, I do hope so," said Miss Mays fervently.

Lucinda addressed an aside to Miss Blythe. "Until we know better what to do, I suppose that we shall have to house Ferdie here since he told Lord Mays that he cannot return to his own lodgings."

"Whyever not?" asked Miss Blythe. Almost at once, however, her penetrating mind was quick to devolve upon the most logical explanation. "Is Mr. Stassart perhaps hiding from his creditors?"

Lucinda grimaced. "Exactly so. At least, that is the understanding that he gave to Lord Mays. I am inclined to believe it is the truth, what's more."

"A pity, for his presence could place you in a rather awkward position," observed Miss Blythe.

"I hope it does not! However, I shan't discount the possibility," said Lucinda. She slapped her hands together in an expression of annoyance. "Regardless, it is just like Ferdie to make a nuisance of himself. Whatever shall we do with him until he has recovered? For I tell you, I am of no mind to dance to any tune of his making!"

"Indeed not, my dear. Mr. Stassart is a rather selfish individual. He would run you into the ground with his demands within a week," said Miss Blythe. "I suggest that he be left to his own devices. You certainly cannot be expected to entertain him, and he must accept that."

Miss Mays had listened respectfully to the exchange, but with little comprehension of all that was said. However, Miss Blythe's statement served to prick up her ears. A tiny burgeoning hope began to unfurl inside her. Perhaps there was a service that she could perform for dear Lady Mays, after all.

"Is Mr. Stassart a testy patient?" she asked hopefully.

Lucinda turned again to her sister-in-law, stifling a sigh. "I have every expectation of his being exactly that. My cousin is indeed a very selfish individual, as Tibby has observed. He sees the world only as it pertains to the acquisition of his own desires. He has already made the most shocking scene about his coat. It was the most nonsensical thing, too, when he had to be removed from it so that the physician could examine him. I dread to think what else he may complain about!"

"Oh." Miss Mays appeared a little confused, but she was perfectly willing to enter into her ladyship's feelings. Something else had been puzzling her about the business for some minutes and she asked, "How did Lord Mays come to rescue Mr. Stassart? Was he, too, at this disreputable place?"

Lucinda and Miss Blythe glanced at one another, equally surprised.

Miss Blythe's brows arched. "My dear?"

Lucinda shook her head. "I do not know. Lord Mays did not relate how he came to be involved."

"How very odd," said Miss Blythe.

"Yes, it is. I must be certain to ask Wilfred about it when next I see him," said Lucinda.

"Would that be wise, my dear? As I understand it, gentlemen do not care to divulge the details of their activities to females," said Miss Blythe.

"I cannot see how that relates to Lord Mays and myself, Tibby, for we are the greatest of friends," said Lucinda. "What has me in a puzzle is how Wilfred came to be mixed up at all with the sort of company that Ferdie keeps. Lord Mays does not strike me as having the instincts or the propensities of the gamester."

"I am persuaded that there is a logical explanation," said

Miss Blythe. She kept to herself the astonishment she had felt at Lucinda's casual manner in referring to her relationship to Lord Mays. Miss Blythe had observed that there was a good deal of liking between them, and certainly their manner together was easy, but she had had no notion that Lucinda thought so extremely well of Lord Mays. It was something to file away and reflect on later.

"Well, at any rate I am glad to know that your cousin is not badly hurt, my lady," said Miss Mays. She offered a shy smile. "Good night."

"Good night, Agnes," said Lucinda.

The door closed softly, leaving Lucinda and Miss Blythe to continue on their way down the hallway.

## *Chapter Eighteen*

Mr. Weatherby came to call the following morning. He was fortunate enough to find the ladies still at home. Mr. Weatherby was shown at once into the drawing room, where he received a warm welcome from Lady Mays and Miss Blythe.

"Mr. Weatherby, how nice to see you again," said Lucinda, giving her hand to the gentleman. "I begin to count you as one of my friends, sir."

"You are kind, my lady," said Mr. Weatherby, bowing over her fingers. He turned then to Miss Blythe and smiled at her with a glinting expression in his frosty eyes. He shook her hand. "Miss Blythe. You are elegant as always."

"Thank you, Mr. Weatherby," said Miss Blythe, very much on her dignity. She had let her embroidery fall to her lap in order to offer her hand, but now she picked it back up. "We are naturally gratified that you have honored us today with a visit. I trust that you are well?"

"I am in rare form, ma'am. The signs of spring can be spotted if one looks closely enough, and it is a time of year in England that I always particularly enjoyed," said Mr. Weatherby. His smile widened. "Spring is the time of new beginnings, Miss Blythe."

"Yes, indeed. However, I believe that winter still has us in its grip," said Miss Blythe quietly. She placed a careful stitch.

Mr. Weatherby laughed then. His eyes had come alight with unexplained devilment. "One might say so, Miss Blythe, but pray recall that winter inevitably gives way to spring."

Miss Blythe's eyes rose swiftly and, for a second, her unfathomable glance clashed with Mr. Weatherby's gray gaze. "Indeed, sir?" she replied.

Lucinda judged from her former governess's determinedly polite expression that Mr. Weatherby was belaboring the point. She tactfully attracted the gentleman's attention. "Mr. Weatherby, I should like you to meet my sister-in-law, Miss Agnes Mays. Miss Mays arrived yesterday evening in order to spend some time with me this Season."

Miss Mays had been sitting very unobtrusively to one side of the other two ladies. At Lucinda's civil introduction, she gave a start and looked as though she could scarcely believe what she had heard. "Mr. Weatherby," she stammered.

Mr. Weatherby honored the lady with a polite bow. Miss Mays was thrown into blushing confusion by this unprecedented distinction. Mr. Weatherby, rightly discerning that any further distinctions would completely overwhelm that backward damsel, turned his attention to the other ladies.

In the course of the conversation a passing reference was made to the unusual events of the night before.

"What is this about your cousin, Lady Mays?" asked Mr. Weatherby with a sharpened glance.

Lucinda was already regretting the slip of tongue that had set Mr. Weatherby to questioning her. Her mind worked quickly as to how she could best smooth over the mistake. The matter was not really any of the gentleman's business, nor anyone else's, after all. The least said the better, for she hoped to be quickly done with her cousin. "Why, there is little enough to tell."

Miss Mays had sat quite still through several minutes of Mr. Weatherby's visit, being completely intimidated by that gentleman's presence. But at mention of what had been for her a terribly exciting experience, she could not contain herself. "Mr. Stassart sustained a horrible wound, and he is at this moment lying upstairs in a most grievous state," she blurted.

Lucinda's glance was reproachful. "Thank you, Agnes," she said quietly. "I could not have put it more succinctly myself."

Miss Mays positively quailed. Her fears instantly rose up to swamp her with the conclusion that she would be summarily dismissed as soon as Mr. Weatherby had left. She subsided in an agony of suspense.

There was nothing for it but to divulge the whole truth then, which Lucinda told concisely and without elaboration. At least there were no other visitors present to hear, she thought.

"And there you have it, Mr. Weatherby. I had no choice but to give what aid I could to my cousin, however foolishly he had acted."

Mr. Weatherby stared from under frowning brows at his hostess. "Indeed, my lady? May I take leave to tell you that I believe sheltering him in this house to be rather unwise in light of our previous discussion?"

"I know that you think so, sir. But pray reflect a moment. What else was I to do in the circumstances? It was the middle of the night, and he was bleeding from his wound," said Lucinda.

"You should have left him to the gutter," said Mr. Weatherby bluntly.

His callous words were not well received. Miss Blythe frowned and shook her head. Miss Mays so far forgot herself as to give a little squeak of protest.

"I think not, Mr. Weatherby," said Lucinda gently, coolly. "I would have succored anyone who was in such straits, let alone one who is my cousin."

"You are too soft, my lady. But it is done now," said Mr. Weatherby, shrugging. "Be rid of the puppy as soon as you can."

Lord Mays was shown into the drawing room on the tail of this rider. He greeted the ladies and exchanged cordial words with Mr. Weatherby, before saying, "Were you discussing Stassart? I wish that I had not brought him here. I don't care for the fellow."

Mr. Weatherby gave a short bark of laughter. "Nor do I, my lord. I have seen his sort too often. He is an encroaching puppy. Since you were responsible for persuading your cousin, Lady Mays, to give Stassart the shelter of her roof, perhaps you may be equally persuasive in seeing that she is rid of him."

"You trespass, Mr. Weatherby," said Lucinda quietly.

Miss Blythe stared over her spectacles at Mr. Weatherby. Twin spots of color had risen in her cheeks. "Indeed, sir, I think that you have said enough."

"Have I?" Mr. Weatherby's mobile mouth twisted a little. He looked into Miss Blythe's eyes a moment more, then turned away. "Perhaps I have, at that. Forgive me, Lady Mays. I spoke only from the purest of motives."

"I am certain of that, Mr. Weatherby," said Lucinda, accepting the gentleman's apology with a gracious nod.

Lord Mays realized that he had walked into a difficult moment. He exerted himself to smooth over the obvious tension, introducing the latest *on dits*. The talk remained impersonal for the next several moments until Mr. Weatherby had taken his leave.

When the door had closed behind the gentleman, Lord Mays remarked, "A strange fellow, that, but he has a good head on his shoulders."

"A strange man, indeed. But let us leave Mr. Weatherby, my lord. I have been all curiosity since Agnes raised the question to me last night," said Lucinda. "However did you come to be at hand when my cousin found himself in such dire straits?"

Lord Mays threw a glance at Miss Blythe and Miss Mays. "It is not something that I care to bruit about, my lady."

"Come, Wilfred! It is surely not as bad as all that. You may trust Tibby and Agnes, I assure you," said Lucinda.

"Perhaps Lord Mays would feel more comfortable if Miss Mays and I were to leave you alone, my dear," said Miss Blythe, rising. She had been rather quieter than was her usual for some seconds, and she actually seemed glad of the excuse to leave the drawing room. She gestured at Miss Mays. "Will you not accompany me, Miss Mays? I have a new direction for a silver net reticule up in my room that I am persuaded you might like."

Miss Mays instantly rose to her feet. Her thoughts were so disordered after displeasing Lady Mays that she hardly knew what she was saying. "Yes, yes! I should like to view it very much."

The two ladies quietly exited while Lord Mays was still attempting to think of a polite way to extricate himself from what he perceived to be a difficult position. He had not wanted to divulge anything at all about the previous night, but his reluctance over that had been superseded by the astonishing defection of Miss Blythe from her clear duty.

When the door had closed, Lucinda turned to his lordship. She smiled at him. "Now you may be perfectly comfortable, my lord!"

Lord Mays shook his head, frowning. "That was not at all well done, Lucinda. Now here we are without a chaperone and likely at any moment to be interrupted by some starched-up dame coming to make her call."

"Oh, do you think that we would become grist for the gossip mill?" asked Lucinda, somewhat surprised. "The thought never entered my mind."

Lord Mays did not appear to be at all gratified. He passed a hand over his sandy hair. "No, I know it. That is what is so particularly frustrating, Lucinda."

"Come, Wilfred, pray do not be vexed with me. I promise you that I shall not be so careless again," said Lucinda. As an afterthought, she added, "Yes, and particularly with Ferdie here. You are quite right, Wilfred. I must take particular care not to give ammunition of any sort to idle tongues. I should not be out of Tibby's or Agnes's company, ever, as long as my cousin is under this roof."

Lord Mays was frowning at her now. "What has Stassart done?"

"Nothing at all. How could he when he is scarce able to raise his head? However, it would not be astonishing if something was made of the fact that my cousin is staying in my house," said Lucinda.

Lord Mays was revolted by even the possibility of such talk. "That fellow Weatherby was right! You must rid yourself of Stassart without a moment's loss."

"And so I shall. As soon as he is able," said Lucinda.

She laid her hand on his lordship's sleeve and smiled coaxingly at him. "Now tell me, Wilfred. How did you chance on Ferdie just at that particular moment? Pray do not confess to me that you frequent those sorts of places, too."

"Of course I do not! What a wild fellow you must think me," said Lord Mays. "If you must have it, I was at that hell yesterday evening to extricate Gerald Thorpe from his folly."

"That boy!" exclaimed Lucinda. "Was it Ferdie who took him there?"

"Stassart has introduced Gerald to the deepest plays in town," said Lord Mays grimly. "Cecily found out somehow where they were going and begged me to stop Gerald from floating any more of his vowels. It seems that they are running dangerously close to dun territory. I have not cared for the role of bear-leader, but that is precisely what I have become this last fortnight."

"How awful for you. Indeed, I quite see how uncomfortable it must have made you feel," said Lucinda, fully appreciating his awkward position. "I suppose that Lord Thorpe has expressed some resentment at your interference?"

Lord Mays gave a short bark of laughter. "Yes, you may so, indeed! However, all that is at an end. We are on the best of terms again. When Stassart became embroiled in that quarrel, Gerald's eyes were opened at last. He saw the folly of such a life and he has sworn that he is done with it."

"Did you believe him to be sincere?" asked Lucinda. With her cousin's example always before her, she could only wonder whether anyone who had once proven himself addicted to the game tables could simply walk away.

"Oh, yes," replied Lord Mays coolly. "One does not mouth platitudes when one is fleeing for one's life. It was Gerald who held the cutthroat at bay while I hauled Stassart up from the floor and began our retreat. There was never a better fellow in a tight corner."

Lucinda thought she had probably heard as much as she cared to about Lord Mays's adventure. She did not think that she would ever forget the sight of her cousin's bloodied coat. However, there was no getting away from some discussion of her cousin.

"Wilfred, I should like to ask you advice about Ferdie. Do you think that I should just put him out as Mr. Weatherby suggested?" she asked. At Lord Mays's frown, she shrugged. "I own, it does not sound at all the Christian thing to do when he is lying in bed weakened from his wound and from the physician's bloodletting. At the same time, Ferdie is such a weasel that I can scarcely regard him with any charity at all!"

Lord Mays took a short turn about the room, throwing over his shoulder, "I have done a bit of asking around." He turned to her again and said somberly, "Stassart was not exaggerating when he claimed that the tipsters were after him. If he should reappear at his lodgings in the state that he is in, there will be no saying but that he might at once be hauled off to debtor's prison."

"Oh, no! Though Ferdie may well deserve such a fate, I would forever have it on my conscience that it was at my hand that he was finally apprehended," said Lucinda.

Lord Mays nodded. "I thought that would be your feeling. The paltry fellow cannot run to save himself if he is laid fast by the heels in bed. Stands to reason. So I thought that I shall take him back to my lodgings. Only until he is on the mend, of course. No one would think of looking for him there, for we are mere acquaintances."

"But did you not say that you were living in such a cramped style that there was no room for him?" asked Lucinda.

"Yes, well, that was true. But that was before I thought of giving up my bed to Stassart. I could take my man's cot and he could sleep on the floor," said Lord Mays.

"I could not possibly allow you to put yourself out in such a fashion, Wilfred!" said Lucinda.

"I would as lief not," said Lord Mays frankly. "Deuced uncomfortable it would be."

"Oh, if only I knew which of Ferdie's friends I might call upon," said Lucinda, slapping her palms together. Her eyes suddenly lit up. She put her hand on his sleeve. "Lord Levine and Mr. Pepperidge! The very thing. Wilfred, could you please go to them for me and explain the circumstances? Ferdie simply must not remain here."

"Of course I shall. You may rely on me," said Lord Mays stoutly, covering her hand with his. "And if they are not prepared to shelter Stassart, then I shall suggest to them that they take him away out of London until his embarrassments are in a fair way to being forgotten."

"I do thank you, Wilfred. You do not know what a comfort you are to me just now," said Lucinda.

He took his leave of her then, promising to send word to her as soon as he was able. "For it is not likely that I shall run them to earth just at once. We do not run in the same circles," he warned.

"Oh, I am aware of that! You would no more mince about in that ludicrous fashion than I would! But I trust you to succeed where I could not," said Lucinda.

Lord Mays grinned. "You have just flattered me twice, Lucinda. If you are not careful, I will begin to suspect that you are setting your cap for me and then where would we be?"

"Where, indeed!" retorted Lucinda.

Miss Blythe came back into the drawing room. "I was just informed that Lady Thorpe has come to call, and I thought that I should return for form's sake," she said.

"Quite right. Lady Mays must not be found entertaining company alone." Lord Mays caught up the older lady's hand and saluted it with a flourish. "You are a brick, Miss Blythe."

Miss Blythe flushed. She turned to watch as Lord Mays left. His lordship was whistling. Miss Blythe looked at Lucinda, her brows raised. "Well! I have never seen Lord Mays exhibit such dashing airs. Was there something said that particularly put him into spirits?"

Lucinda brushed over the last teasing banter between herself and Lord Mays and said, "Wilfred is on his way to locate a couple of my cousin's friends. He hopes to persuade one or the other of them to shelter Ferdie."

"That is excellent news, indeed. I wish his lordship every possible success," said Miss Blythe with a smile. "Forgive me if I seem rather hard, Lucinda, but I cannot help thinking that we shall all be more at ease when Mr. Stassart is no longer on our hands."

"Oh, so do I," said Lucinda. Her eyes gleamed with humor. "And I know that it will put us back into Mr. Weatherby's good graces."

"That must naturally be a primary concern," said Miss Blythe with unexpected tartness.

"You should not be so severe, Tibby. After all, though for reasons known best to himself, Mr. Weatherby was simply looking out for my best interests," said Lucinda.

"Do you think so?" said Miss Blythe.

Lucinda looked at her companion, rather startled by the dry note in Miss Blythe's voice. But she did not have an opportunity to satisfy her mild curiosity, for the door was opened and they were no longer private.

# Chapter Nineteen

L ady Thorpe was shown in, and Lucinda stepped forward to welcome her. The lady was attired in a stunning violet pelisse that should have clashed with her coloring, but merely served to emphasize the paleness of her complexion. The bonnet on her head was trimmed with several saucy black feathers. She greeted Lucinda and Miss Blythe with a few cheerful words.

Lucinda looked at her visitor closely and thought she could detect a hint of strain about the young woman's eyes. She suspected that it was due to the uncertainties brought on by Lord Thorpe's recent digressions into gaming, and she hoped that

Lord Mays had been right when he had said that he thought
Lord Thorpe was at last done with such nonsense. However,
nothing of Lucinda's thoughts was revealed in the warmth of
her greeting. Though she genuinely liked Lady Thorpe, she
was not yet well enough acquainted with her ladyship to inquire into such a personal matter.

Once the amenities were addressed, Lady Thorpe quickly
outlined the purpose of her visit. "I have decided that a light
shopping trip is just what will enliven my spirits," she said.
"And I have come to beg you both to bear me company."

"Oh, I should like it of all things!" exclaimed Lucinda. The
prospect was attractive, and it warmed her that Lady Thorpe
should have thought to ask her. She turned to her companion.
"Tibby, what of you?"

"I have a letter that I would like to finish for today's post,
so I shall regretfully decline. But may I suggest that Miss
Mays would benefit from such an outing?" said Miss Blythe.

"Yes, of course!" Lucinda turned to Lady Thorpe, who was
listening attentively. "My sister-in-law has come to visit, and
she has not the least notion how to go on. She is in need of an
entire wardrobe for the Season. Would it be too much of an
imposition if I brought Agnes along?"

"Of course not! I adore dressing someone else," said Lady
Thorpe, her eyes sparkling.

"Then it is settled. I shall inform Agnes at once of the treat
in store," said Lucinda.

"My dear, I should perhaps warn you that Miss Mays is
feeling a bit moped," said Miss Blythe. "She was distressed
that she fell into indiscretion earlier and placed you in an awkward position. I soothed her sensibilities as best I could, of
course, but you know how she takes things to heart."

"The goose," said Lucinda without heat. She had easily read
into Miss Blythe's mild explanation the likelihood of Miss
Mays's having been thrown into complete apprehension. Certainly her sister-in-law's recent experiences did not encourage
her to think that she was indispensable.

"Is there something wrong?" asked Lady Thorpe.

Lucinda shook her head. "My sister-in-law was encouraged
all of her life to bow to the selfish whims of others and never

to consider herself. As a consequence, she is overly timid and completely unsure of herself in company. She is thrown into the hips at the least mistake. This morning we had a gentleman to call on us, and she blurted out something that I would rather she had not. It was of small moment, really, but Agnes has apparently built it into something monstrous."

"I understand perfectly," said Lady Thorpe with ready sympathy. "Well, then! What could be better than a morning spent at the shops?"

Lucinda laughed, while Miss Blythe smiled. "Yes, indeed!" said Lucinda. "I cannot think of anything more made to order to persuade Agnes that she is forgiven. Give me a few minutes to change and to inform Agnes of our plans."

"Of course. Miss Blythe and I shall get along famously," said Lady Thorpe.

Lucinda sent a message to Miss Mays calculated to shock that damsel out of her doldrums and then went along to her bedroom. She changed quickly into a walking dress and returned downstairs a quarter hour later.

When Lucinda entered the drawing room, she found that her sister-in-law had already descended. Lady Thorpe was laboring to make polite conversation with Miss Mays, but she broke off when she saw Lucinda. Rising from the settee, she said, "Here is Lady Mays now. We shall be off in a trice, I expect."

"Yes, indeed. I apologize for my tardiness," said Lucinda, smoothing on her last lavender kid glove. She was attired in a cream walking dress closed with huge pearl buttons. Her straw bonnet, accented with delicate lavender blooms, was tied with a matching satin bow, and she looked altogether smart.

"Oh," sighed Miss Mays. She had thought that Lady Thorpe was the most stylish creature that she had ever beheld, but she knew now that she had been wrong. Lady Mays was without compare. She thought humbly that it would be so nice to appear to such advantage.

Upon catching the soft sigh, Lady Thorpe glanced swiftly at Miss Mays's face. There was such a wistful expression in the young woman's eyes that she was touched to pity. She said to Lucinda, "Miss Blythe had just introduced me to Miss Mays a

few moments before you came in. Miss Mays was relating to
me that you have invited her to stay with you for the Season."

Lucinda caught the delicate question in Lady Thorpe's gambit. "Yes, Agnes wished to taste all that London has to offer.
Miss Blythe and I have taken it upon ourselves to provide
everything in our power for Agnes's enjoyment. The Season
will undoubtedly prove most educational for us all, for I have
never sponsored anyone before."

"I think it promises to be famous fun. You must let me do
my part and introduce Miss Mays around," said Lady Thorpe.
She smiled warmly at Miss Mays. "You must count me as one
of your friends whilst you are here, Miss Mays."

"Oh! You are so very kind, my lady! Indeed, I do not deserve such kindness. I . . . I am so very grateful," stammered
Miss Mays, thrown into a blushing flutter.

Lady Thorpe glanced at Lady Mays and Miss Blythe, both
of whom wore the same smiling expressions. Her ladyship
knew that there must be a story behind Miss Mays, and she
was determined to have it out of Lady Mays at the earliest opportunity.

In the meantime, Lady Thorpe was realizing that the simple
shopping trip that she had planned had taken on wonderful
proportions. Acquiring a few laces and a pair or two of silk
stockings were paltry pickings when she could encourage an
orgy of spending on such a deserving case as Miss Mays. Really, that gray pelisse was truly hideous! She could well understand why Lady Mays wished to reoutfit her sister-in-law.
Following her thoughts, she inquired, "Have you any particular notions about what you wished to purchase, Lady Mays?"

Lucinda's eyes twinkled. "A little bit of everything, I
think."

Lady Thorpe smiled. "That was what I thought. Good! I
have my carriage standing outside. If everyone is quite ready,
let us be off!"

The trio said their good-byes to Miss Blythe, who went only
so far as the drawing room door with them, and they left the
town house. The carriage was waiting at the curb. There was
at once a minor dispute over who would sit with her back to
the horses. Lady Thorpe naturally contended that since it was

her carriage and it was at her invitation that they were accompanying her, she would give the better seat to her guests.

Miss Mays displayed an unexpectedly obstinate streak and insisted that she should take the humbler seat. "I do not mind in the least, my lady," she assured.

Lady Thorpe met Lucinda's amused gaze rather helplessly. "I am sure that I do not care which of us rides facing backward."

Lucinda knew that Miss Mays's pleasure in the outing would be quite destroyed if she was not allowed to efface herself as she was undoubtedly accustomed to doing. "Then do let Agnes have it, my lady. Or otherwise she will not forgive herself for putting you out."

"That is quite true, my lady," said Miss Mays earnestly. "I would not enjoy myself in the least knowing that you were put to such disadvantage."

"Very well, then. You may have it, Miss Mays," said Lady Thorpe, graciously accepting defeat.

Miss Mays positively beamed and stepped up into the carriage. Lady Thorpe paused a moment before following her example, to murmur for Lucinda's ear alone, "What a funny she is! You must tell me all about her, for I stand all agog."

"I shall," promised Lucinda. "But for the moment indulge me and help me to bully her into accepting every small extravagance."

"Bully her!"

"It will not be an easy task, I assure you!"

Lady Thorpe bestowed an expressive glance on Lucinda before she ducked into the carriage. Lucinda followed suit, well aware that she had greatly whetted Lady Thorpe's curiosity. It promised to be a famous shopping trip.

Several hours later, the ladies returned to Mays House for tea. Exhausted but pleased, Lucinda regarded the mountain of parcels that filled the carriage. Scarcely one belonged either to herself or to Lady Thorpe.

"I have never enjoyed myself more," said Lady Thorpe, nodding her head in Miss Mays's direction.

Lucinda also looked at her sister-in-law, and she smiled.

Miss Mays appeared to be caught up in a happy daze. "Nor I," she said.

The carriage stopped. Lucinda quirked an inquiring brow at Lady Thorpe. "You will come in to take tea, won't you?"

"I would not miss it for worlds," stated Lady Thorpe positively.

Lucinda laughed, knowing that her ladyship meant to have her bursting curiosity fully satisfied at last. When she entered the town house, she gave orders that the packages be carried in from Lady Thorpe's carriage. "You may take them all up to Miss Mays's bedroom," she said, drawing off her gloves. "We shall want tea in the drawing room."

Miss Blythe had heard the return of the trio of shoppers, and she came down the stairs to greet them. When she saw the number of parcels that was carried indoors, her eyes widened. "My word!"

"Oh, Miss Blythe! They are all mine!" exclaimed Miss Mays, as though she still could not believe it. "It was a wicked extravagance, but their ladyships insisted. I could not say no!"

Miss Blythe smiled. "Why do you not show me everything, my dear? I am bursting with curiosity."

"As I am also," murmured Lady Thorpe.

Miss Blythe caught the aside and she chuckled. She put her arm companionably through Miss Mays's elbow. "Come along! We shall drink our tea above stairs so that you can satisfy my curiosity."

Miss Mays was nothing loathe. She had never been blessed by such generosity in her life, and she could scarcely contain her eagerness to share her excitement with someone.

Lucinda and Lady Thorpe went into the drawing room. The tea had already been taken in and served. The butler closed the doors, and on the same instant Lady Thorpe rounded on her hostess.

"Now you must tell me everything," exclaimed Lady Thorpe. "I know that there is something odd about Miss Mays. Why, I have just spent hours in the woman's company, and she was a constant amazement. She is the humblest, most effacing creature that I have ever met."

"Quite. And you will understand why, once I have explained it all to you," said Lucinda. She told her sister-in-law's story matter-of-factly and without added pathos.

At the end, Lady Thorpe shook her head in near disbelief. "It is all like something out of a lurid novel. I am so thankful that I have never experienced such cruelty and neglect. I wonder that Miss Mays is so unaffected as she is, for I suspect that I would have grown to be quite bitter."

"It is curious, is it not? But I think that Agnes is of such a sweet, giving temperament that she is quite incapable of the meaner emotions," said Lucinda. "Tibby contends that she needs a kind husband, and I agree with her. Agnes is not the sort who could survive without someone who is willing to pick up the cudgels on her behalf."

"Yes, I quite see that. Then we shall simply have to find her a suitable mate," said Lady Thorpe. She laughed. "I have never been a matchmaker before. You have opened up wonderful new vistas for me, Lady Mays. I am truly in your debt."

"If you can discover a husband for Agnes, it is I who shall be forever in your debt, Lady Thorpe," said Lucinda.

Lady Thorpe finished her tea and set down the cup. "I must run now, but we shall get together again soon. Very soon! For I do not wish to miss one moment of this unfolding saga!"

Lucinda laughed and rose to her feet as her guest stood up. "I am glad that you suggested this outing," she said.

"Oh, so am I. I was feeling a bit low, you know, but it is amazing what a little time spent with a friend in the shops can do for one," said Lady Thorpe.

Lucinda once again experienced the warm feeling that Lady Thorpe had engendered in her. She caught up the other woman's hand and briefly squeezed her gloved fingers. "I am so very glad to have made your acquaintance. Do, pray, call me Lucinda."

"And you must call me Cecily. I should like that," said Lady Thorpe with a quick smile. "Now I really must run or Gerald will be wondering what has become of me. He has promised to take me to the theater tonight, if I shall first ride with him in his new phaeton in the park. I don't much care for high-perch phaetons as they are so high off the ground. But it will give Gerald pleasure to puff off his new equipage to me."

"At least it is your approval that he wishes to hear," said Lucinda.

Lady Thorpe laughed and nodded. "Yes, I am very fortunate," she said happily.

Lucinda saw Lady Thorpe out the front door to her carriage. As she reentered the town house and traversed the entry hall toward the stairs, the butler stopped her and handed her a twist of paper.

"Lord Mays stopped by earlier, my lady. His lordship was sorry to find you out, and he asked that I give you this when you came in," said Church. He lingered while Lady Mays straightened out the twist and unfolded the note to read it. At her sudden frown, he inquired, "I hope that it is not bad news, my lady?"

Lucinda looked up. "No; merely a temporary disappointment." She folded the note. "What is the report on Mr. Stassart today, Church?"

"Mr. Stassart is known to be resting well, my lady. The physician returned as he promised, and it was my understanding that he was very pleased with Mr. Stassart's progress," said Church.

"I suppose that he did not mention when my cousin would be able to leave his bed?" asked Lucinda.

"I regret, no, my lady."

"Thank you, Church. I shall not be in to callers for the remainder of the day," said Lucinda, moving once more toward the stairs.

"Of course, my lady," said the butler.

Lucinda paused as her foot touched the first step to look back at the butler. "Unless it is Lord Mays, Church. Send up word at once if his lordship should stop in."

"I shall do so, my lady." As he watched her ladyship move lightly up the stairs, Church could not but wonder what had been in the note from Lord Mays.

After Lady Thorpe had left, Lucinda went up to discover what Miss Blythe thought about the purchases that she had made for Miss Mays. She knocked on the door of her companion's private sitting room. At Miss Blythe's invitation to enter,

Lucinda opened the door and went in. She smiled at the older woman, who was seated before the hearth with her ever-present embroidery in hand. "Well, Tibby, how did you find Agnes?"

Miss Blythe chuckled. "Miss Mays was beside herself, just as one might expect! The attention showered on her by you and Lady Thorpe has helped her more than anything else, I suspect."

Lucinda sat down in an opposite chair. She lay her head back against the cushions. "It was a treat for Lady Thorpe and myself to see someone begin to blossom like that. Where is Agnes now?"

"I suggested that she might lie down before dinner. It has been a very exciting and fatiguing day for her," said Miss Blythe.

"Yes, indeed. I don't know that I could survive too many of like nature. We argued and pleaded and bullied over nearly every scrap of ribbon and glove and gown. But I knew it would be just like that, and so I had warned Lady Thorpe. Lady Thorpe has taken a liking to Agnes, by the way. She intends to help us to find her a suitable and kind husband," said Lucinda.

"That is something indeed," said Miss Blythe. She glanced over at Lucinda, her eyes keen. "What has you in such a fret, Lucinda?"

Lucinda looked at her, smiling suddenly. "Am I so obvious, then?"

"Only to me, I think. But then, I know you fairly well," said Miss Blythe, pulling up her thread. "Is it Mr. Stassart?"

"Yes. At least, not Ferdie himself. I have not seen him today, but Church tells me that the physician was in and pronounced himself satisfied with Ferdie's progress," said Lucinda. She rose from the chair and went to the mantel to fiddle with a small vase. "Lord Mays left a note for me while I was out. He says that he hasn't been able to speak to Ferdie's particular friends, having learned that Lord Levine and Mr. Pepperidge have both gone out of London to attend a cockfight. They are not expected to return for a few days."

"That is disappointing, of course. However, I think that you can trust Lord Mays to persist in his quest. He will eventually run these gentlemen to ground," said Miss Blythe.

"Yes, I know that I may depend upon Wilfred to do just as

he says that he will." Lucinda turned to her companion and said idly, "Lord Mays is one of the few people that I do trust, Tibby. There is not a shade of subterfuge about him. He says just what is on his mind and he is kind to boot. In fact, I do not think that I have ever met a more kindhearted person."

"Perhaps he is the very one to take on Miss Mays," suggested Miss Blythe.

Lucinda frowned. "I admit that I had thought of that very thing. But I am not certain that it will do, after all. Wilfred is not at all slow, whereas it must be admitted that poor Agnes is not in the least needlewitted. I do not think that they would suit."

"A valid observation," said Miss Blythe. "However, I believe that many connections are formed between personages of unequal intelligence, and they go along very well. Therefore we should not count Lord Mays out as a possible *parti*, wouldn't you agree?"

"We shall see how things go along," said Lucinda. She was strangely reluctant to commit herself to promoting a match between Lord Mays and her sister-in-law. She shrugged and covered a sudden yawn behind one hand. "Pray excuse me, Tibby. I did not realize that I was so wearied by the outing with Agnes and Lady Thorpe. I believe that I shall also lie down for a few minutes."

"Very well, my dear," said Miss Blythe, smiling to herself.

Lucinda left her companion and entered her bedroom. She lay down on her bed, intending to close her eyes for just a few moments. An hour and a half later, she wakened. She did not feel in the least refreshed, for there was a slight pounding in her head.

It was the evening of Lady Sefton's soiree. Lucinda would far rather have stayed at home, in the event that Lord Mays chose to call on her, but that was not an option open to her.

She had written to Lady Sefton to ask her ladyship's indulgence in bringing along her sister-in-law, Miss Agnes Mays. Her ladyship's reply had been most gracious. It would be churlish indeed to turn about at the last minute and not attend the soiree. She would simply have to forget about Lord Mays and her feeling of physical malaise and go to the soiree.

Miss Mays, also, would have preferred to remain at Mays House for the evening. Though she had yearned after the en-

tertainments of society, she was at the same time petrified at
the thought of mixing with such august company as was certainly to be present at Lady Sefton's soiree. However, putting
on a new gown of a pale peach tied with gold ribbons and having her hair done in a daring cascade of curls went far in miti-
gating her fears. She was in a flutter of excitement when she
joined Lucinda and Miss Blythe downstairs.

Lucinda thought that her sister-in-law looked much like any
other young lady might who was about to go to her first important party. Miss Mays appeared surprisingly attractive with
the high color in her cheeks and the bright light in her brown
eyes. In fact, she actually looked some years younger than her
nine-and-twenty.

Lucinda hoped that Miss Mays's excitement would carry
her through the evening. It would be lovely if she and Miss
Blythe did not have to shepherd their timid lamb too closely.

## *Chapter Twenty*

Lady Sefton's small soiree proved to be a gathering of upward of thirty couples and several unattached ladies bal-
anced by an equal number of gentlemen. Upon the arrival of
the ladies from Mays House, Lady Sefton at once came forward to welcome them.

Lucinda made known her sister-in-law. Miss Mays was at-
tractively flushed with excitement and trepidation. Her response to Lady Sefton's greeting was somewhat inarticulate,
but Lady Sefton smiled kindly on her. "You must allow me to
make you known to everyone, dear Miss Mays."

Miss Mays endured this extended introduction with more
aplomb than Lucinda had expected of her. Behind her hand,

Lucinda murmured to Miss Blythe, "I am very well pleased with her, Tibby."

"Yes, indeed. She will do very nicely," said Miss Blythe quietly.

Miss Mays effaced herself as soon as she possibly could, however, and thereafter she responded only when she was addressed and then in trembling syllables.

Lady Sefton drew Lucinda aside for a moment. "My dear Lucinda, I have noticed that Miss Mays is an extremely reserved young woman for her years. Of course I knew that there was a daughter of the family, but I do not recall ever having met her before. Surely she has been out on the town for some time?"

"You would think so, indeed. But that has not at all been the case," said Lucinda. She gave her ladyship a brief history of Miss Mays's life up to that point. "So you see, Lady Sefton, why I begged your indulgence in allowing me to bring Agnes tonight. I wished to show her every possible consideration while she is with me."

Lady Sefton nodded, her gaze resting thoughtfully on Miss Mays. The young woman was sitting as far in a corner of the large drawing room as possible, obviously hoping to be inconspicuous. "I quite understand. And you wish to introduce her into society now?"

"Yes, my lady. I pity her so exceedingly, you see, and I have hopes that she will take." Lucinda also looked over at Miss Mays, and she stifled a sigh. "As you may imagine, it appears to be a formidable task. However, Miss Blythe agrees that we must make a push at it and perhaps even secure an eligible match for her."

Lady Sefton smiled. "You have a kind heart, Lady Mays. Not many in your place would bother to take on such a formidable responsibility."

"It does appear that I have my work cut out for me," agreed Lucinda. She and Lady Sefton both watched as Miss Mays positively shrank when a gentleman approached and addressed her.

"I shall sponsor her to Almack's. That will be just the place for Miss Mays to try her wings," said Lady Sefton.

"Thank you, Lady Sefton. I am indeed grateful," said Lucinda. She had had hopes of just this very outcome, and she was extremely pleased that her main object in bringing Miss Mays to Lady Sefton's notice had been achieved.

Lady Sefton nodded acknowledgement. "I shall provide her with the mildest of dinner partners this evening. She will feel herself more at ease then, I think."

Again, Lucinda thanked her ladyship for her consideration.

"Think nothing of it, my dear Lucinda. I am happy to do it," said Lady Sefton, before moving off to speak to another guest.

When dinner was announced, Miss Blythe was claimed by an escort from among the lesser personages of the gathering, as was Miss Mays. But Lady Sefton paired Lucinda with Hector Allanis, Earl of Pembroke.

Lucinda was pleased to discover that his lordship was to be her dinner partner. She had not forgotten their meeting in any of its details. "Lord Pembroke." She offered her hand to him.

"Lady Mays! This is indeed a welcome surprise. My spirits have definitely taken a turn for the better," said Lord Pembroke, shaking her hand.

"Oh, do you two know one another?" asked Lady Sefton, glancing curiously from one to the other.

"I met Lady Mays on the steps of the Lending Library. I was so clumsy as to knock her parcels out of her hands," said Lord Pembroke, smiling. "It was not possible to remain mere strangers after that. We were forced to exchange names."

"I see. Then I know that I shall not be needed to encourage conversation," said Lady Sefton, amused.

Her ladyship moved away to see that the rest of her guests were suitably partnered. Even though their hostess was already well out of earshot, Lord Pembroke lowered his voice. "I had dreaded a dull evening, my lady. I am glad to discover that my assumption was incorrect."

"If that is so, why did you come?" asked Lucinda, ignoring the last of his statement. She acknowledged compliments as infrequently as she possibly could without giving offense. She had learned to her regret that her beauty would always garner her pretty words, but often those words had little of substance behind them. She would not allow her head to be turned by flattery.

The signal was given that dinner was served, and Lady Sefton's guests began moving toward the dining room. Lucinda allowed Lord Pembroke to escort her in and to seat her at the table.

His lordship did not reply to her question until he had taken his own chair beside her. "My mother is a close friend of the Seftons. I was coerced into accompanying her tonight as her escort," he said. "I was never more glad of anything when she fell into a group of her own cronies and Lady Sefton was forced to look around for another dinner partner for me."

Lucinda looked Lord Pembroke over in a considering way. She could not imagine that his lordship could be coerced into doing anything that he disliked. "That I cannot believe, my lord. You do not appear to me to be a gentleman who is easily driven."

"Alas, it is too true. I may be a large fellow, but at heart I am the most placid of bovines," drawled Lord Pembroke, smiling at her.

Under his warm gaze, Lucinda felt her heart flutter. Hoping to divert him, she asked, "Which is the countess, pray? I should like to ogle with the proper awe the formidable lady who was so brave as to introduce a great bovine into Lady Sefton's elegant dining room."

Lord Pembroke grinned. He gave a nod toward the end of the lengthy table. "The lady sporting the terrifying bunch of feathers is my countess mother."

Lucinda looked curiously down the table. She was certain that she must have had the Countess of Pembroke pointed out to her at some point during her marriage, but it had been a number of years since she had been the least knowledgeable about society's noted denizens. Certainly the countess had never graced Mays House while Lord Mays had been alive. No doubt the lady was of a generation which his lordship would not have been able to include in his circle of intimates.

The Countess of Pembroke was a small woman of patrician features. Her countenance was dominated by a large roman nose. While Lucinda studied the lady, the countess gave a quick laugh at something that was said to her, and Lucinda saw at once a resemblance to the gentleman beside her.

The headdress to which the countess's undutiful son had alluded was indeed an astonishing concoction. Lucinda wondered that her ladyship had chosen to wear something that was better suited to the theater then to this gathering.

She turned back to Lord Pembroke. "The countess is a lady of imposing presence, certainly. However, I can discern nothing that lends your contention validity, my lord! Her ladyship appears to me to be quite amiable and not the least formidable," she said, smiling.

Lord Pembroke leaned toward her with a confiding air. "It is the trick of those deuced feathers. They are quite deceiving in their apparent whimsy. My mother is in actuality a veritable tartar. I run in terror of her frowns, I assure you."

There was such a laughing twinkle in his lordship's eyes that Lucinda gave a gurgle of laughter. "You are too absurd."

"I like it when you laugh like that. Your entire countenance lights up," said Lord Pembroke approvingly.

Lucinda felt herself blush. Dropping her eyes, she replied coolly, "You flatter me, my lord." She focused her attention on the food on her plate.

"I have offended you! Pray forget that I have said anything. I am a clumsy fellow at best, whether it is with my tongue or my feet, as you certainly have cause to know," said Lord Pembroke.

Lucinda glanced up at him. He was regarding her with a sober enough expression, but there was still laughter in his eyes. She remarked, "I do not believe that you are ever serious, my lord."

Lord Pembroke flashed a grin. "As rarely as possible, my lady," he admitted. "The war gave me an appreciation of life. I think it frivolous to waste it in undue somberness of mind or concerns."

His lordship's notice was at that instant claimed by the lady on his far side, and he politely turned to her, so that Lucinda was spared thinking of a response to his surprising statement. She made a remark to her other partner at table, but the gentleman was too engrossed in his plate to utter more than a desultory sentence or two. Lucinda was glad when Lord Pembroke reclaimed her attention.

As dinner progressed, Lord Pembroke politely divided himself between the ladies on either side of him. Lucinda did not mind in the least that he did so, for she liked listening to his lordship's deep voice and the outbreak of his frequent laughter even when he was not directing his conversation to her.

Lady Sefton eventually rose, signaling to the ladies that it was time for them to withdraw and leave the gentlemen to their after-dinner wine. Lucinda went with the other ladies, but she felt almost reluctant to be drawn away from Lord Pembroke's side. She thought that she had seldom enjoyed a gentleman's company more. Lord Pembroke had made her laugh a great deal. He had not said a somber word through the entire affair.

Lady Sefton led the ladies to the drawing room. Her guests leisurely composed themselves on settees and chairs, breaking into small groups to talk. Miss Blythe was drawn swiftly into conversation, a sight that pleased Lucinda. Her former governess had a natural dignity that had enabled her to slide with ease into her function as Lucinda's chaperone and companion.

Miss Mays at once made her way to Lucinda's side. She waited until there was a pause in conversation and then asked, "Lady Mays, would it be considered proper if I sat down at the pianoforte?"

"But of course, Agnes, if that is what you wish to do," said Lucinda.

"Oh, I should like it above all else. I promise you, you shan't have cause to be embarrassed," said Miss Mays.

"I am not in the least concerned about that, Agnes," said Lucinda gently.

Miss Mays flushed. "Thank you, my lady!" She hurried away to claim the pianoforte before the notion had struck anyone else.

A moment later, music floated softly over the company. There were several smiles directed toward the young woman seated at the pianoforte, for it was instantly recognized that Miss Mays was very well trained.

Lady Bishop, who had magnanimously reassured Lucinda a number of times that she had been forgiven for not attending her ladyship's own soiree, leaned toward Lucinda. "She is quite good, isn't she?"

"Yes, indeed," said Lucinda, smiling. It was a pleasant surprise to discover that her sister-in-law possessed at least one social accomplishment to a rare degree. She decided on the

spot to encourage Miss Mays at every opportunity to display
her musical talent. That would be certain to garner her timid
sister-in-law some compliments and perhaps would serve to
build Agnes's confidence in herself.

"I am sorry that you were unable to attend my own soiree,
Lady Mays. But certainly I can understand when one has an
unexpected guest to arrive. Does Miss Mays make a long stay
with you?" asked Lady Bishop.

"I am hoping to persuade her to remain all Season. She has
lived very quietly up to now, having devoted herself to caring
for both her parents through their last illnesses," said Lucinda.

"I thought that I had not seen her about before. Well, well! I
had no notion that Miss Mays is an experienced nurse. I have
an elderly relative of my own who is in need of a companion."
Lady Bishop looked speculatively at Miss Mays, the wheels
obviously turning in her head. She smiled at Lucinda suddenly. "A filial dedication such as that is scarce these days.
Miss Mays is to be commended."

"Yes, indeed," said Lucinda, smiling. She did not point out
that Miss Mays had had very little say in the matter. There was
little point in villifying those that were dead.

"Perhaps when Miss Mays's visit to you is done, I shall
have a word with her. She will undoubtedly be looking for another post. A poor relation is in such an uncomfortable position, is she not? But I am persuaded that I may have just the
thing for her, for I trust in your recommendation of her character, Lady Mays," said Lady Bishop.

Lucinda smiled again, but inside she was seething. It had
not seemed to occur to Lady Bishop that Miss Mays had sacrificed a good portion of her youth through no desire of her
own, nor that she might not wish to be given another such position that could just as easily be filled by a paid nurse. Of
course, a professional nurse would command a considerably
greater salary than someone like Agnes, thought Lucinda, re-
flecting uncharitably on Lady Bishop's motives.

"I hope to show my sister-in-law the rewards of her sacrifice to family duty by sponsoring her this Season," said Lucinda quietly. "She has never been brought out, you see. Lady

Sefton has already been kind enough to offer her vouchers to Almack's. I was most gratified, as you may imagine."

"Indeed!" Lady Bishop was doing a rapid recalculation of Miss Mays's position in the scheme of things. Her ladyship had a brother who had never married. It would be gratifying indeed if Lady Mays should bestow her hand upon the gentleman, for Lady Mays was wealthy and commanded an estate of her own. These were commodities that her brother did not at present possess. Of course, Lady Mays had not yet met her ladyship's brother, and she obviously had many admirers. It was not at all a certain thing that Lady Mays would wed an obscure gentleman when there was such competition for her favor.

Miss Mays might be another thing altogether. Lady Mays was obviously fond of the young woman, and perhaps she could be counted upon to settle a nice tidy dowry on Miss Mays upon the announcement of her engagement. Certainly the diffident Miss Mays would be easier to mold into the epitome of what Lady Bishop considered to be the proper wife. Lady Mays displayed a lamentable lack of malleability. Lady Bishop had not missed that flash of temper in her ladyship's eyes when she had merely remarked that she could possibly offer Miss Mays a place. She must tread carefully with Lady Mays, for she did not wish to put her ladyship's back up. Not when there was a possibility of snaring a suitably dowered wife for her unfortunate brother.

Lady Bishop's plump face became wreathed in smiles. "You must include Miss Mays in any invitation of mine to you and your companion. In fact, pray do bring her to my little ball next week. I shall exert myself to see to her enjoyment."

"That is most gracious of you, my lady," said Lucinda, resisting the temptation to grimace. Really, the woman was patently false in her assurances of friendly concern.

The lady nodded grandly and passed on to speak to another acquaintance.

Lady Sefton came up and claimed Lucinda's attention. "Whyever did you not tell me how beautifully that child played?"

"I did not know it until this evening," Lucinda confessed.

"Such exquisite ability goes far in redeeming her lamenta-

ble lack of conversation. But you and Miss Blythe shall do
something about that, I know," said Lady Sefton.

"We hope to, my lady," said Lucinda.

Lady Sefton nodded, satisfied. "Now come. I wish to take
you around in the event there are some who do not precisely
recall who you are. You were on the town such a short time
and people quickly forget."

"That is true," said Lucinda, smiling. She allowed herself to
be gently squired by her hostess round the gathering. Though
there were some curious glances at her face and attire, there were
none who did not prove themselves gracious in their words.

One of those that Lady Sefton introduced Lucinda to was
the Countess of Pembroke. "This is one of my dearest of
friends, Lady Pembroke. You may perhaps recall Lady Mays,
my dear. She came out four years ago, the same year that Waterloo was fought."

The Countess of Pembroke looked keenly at Lucinda as she
gave the younger woman her hand. "Yes, I recall you. The
child bride of that impossible rake, Mays. I felt for you, my
dear. But one must not pass judgement upon the dead, must
one? Come, sit beside me. I would like to talk with you." Per-
ceiving that Lucinda had fallen into good hands, Lady Sefton
moved away to her other guests.

## Chapter Twenty-one

Lucinda thanked the countess and seated herself beside her
on the settee. She awaited the countess's pleasure.

The Countess of Pembroke regarded Lucinda with a quizzical smile. "I noticed that you enjoyed talking with my son at
dinner."

"Yes, I did, my lady. Lord Pembroke is an amusing table partner," said Lucinda.

The countess gave the quick laugh that Lucinda had already recognized as characteristic of both her and her son. "I'll warrant that he is. I know Hector very well. As usual, he has got up a flirtation with the loveliest young woman in attendance this evening."

"Thank you for the compliment, my lady," said Lucinda. She smiled even though she disliked the moniker. After the disillusionment of her marriage, she had a positive aversion to being reminded of her looks. "I have not minded Lord Pembroke's attention in the least. I find him easy to converse with."

The Countess of Pembroke nodded as though she found nothing unusual in that. She looked curiously at Lucinda. "You wasted little time in returning to London after your bereavement, Lady Mays. However, I suppose that is scarcely surprising in itself. I did not like Mays."

"Lord Mays unfortunately did not enjoy a reputation for geniality," said Lucinda quietly.

The countess smiled, her eyes taking on a knowing expression. "You probably did not care for him either."

"My lady!" Lucinda was shocked by the lady's forthrightness. Though there had been various anglings from others about this very thing, none had made so bold as to state it so baldly.

The countess raised her thin brows. "I am correct, am I not?"

Lucinda was silent for a moment as she regarded the other's lined face. There was nothing of the inquisitive air of the gossip about the countess's expression. The answer to her question was merely something of interest to the lady herself.

Lucinda decided that she could dare a measure of honesty with this formidable woman. She shrugged. "Lord Mays worshipped beauty. He was never in love with me. Nor, I suspect, with any other woman. We live, we breathe, we only look our best straight out of the hands of our dressers."

"Ah." The Countess of Pembroke nodded. "A pretty disillusionment for a young, ignorant girl. And now you have returned to London, only a little older but quite a bit wiser. To what purpose, my lady? Have you in mind to wed again?"

"I wish to entertain and to be entertained, ma'am. That is why I have returned to London," said Lucinda with a polite but cool smile.

"Perfectly understandable. Your exile was long and undoubtedly dull," said the countess. She smiled at Lucinda, giving her a gentle tap with her fan. "And you much resent a perfect stranger prying into your affairs. Very proper, I assure you."

"It was not my intent to offend you, my lady," said Lucinda, her manner a little stiff.

The Countess of Pembroke gave her quick laugh. "No offense has been taken, my dear. On the contrary, I like you the better for that standoffish air of yours. However, you must not think that I am making idle conversation with these rather pointed observations. No, I do have a purpose behind my questions. As you have seen, my son is an amusing fellow. He is quite willing to embark upon any number of flirtations, but his heart is never engaged. Does this disappoint you?"

"Not in the least," said Lucinda, smiling. "I like his lordship better for it. I, too, am heart-free, and I am determined to remain so. As I have already told you, ma'am, I did not return to London to snare myself another husband. I am well situated and content with my lot. If Lord Pembroke wishes to engage me in a friendly flirtation, why, I can have no possible objection."

"I find that I quite like you, Lady Mays. You are exceptionally frank and without pretension." The countess raised her brows in inquiry. "I suspect that you are also as honest with yourself, so that if your feelings underwent a change toward any particular gentleman, you would certainly be aware of it?"

"So I should hope, my lady!" said Lucinda, laughing.

The Countess of Pembroke nodded. Fiddling with the sticks of her fan, she said slowly, "What I have seen of you, Lady Mays, I approve. I think that given time we could become friends."

Lucinda wondered what purpose this extremely odd conversation could possibly have. "Thank you, my lady. Your expression of approval is naturally flattering."

"I should like to have grandchildren before I am too old to enjoy them, and so I have told my undutiful son." The countess looked up to fix a surprisingly bright gaze on the startled younger woman. "Lady Mays, if you should begin to contemplate remarriage, pray do not allow any scruples to hinder you where my son is concerned. You may set your cap at him with my goodwill. It would do Hector a world of good to be the object of a determined, honest woman's affection."

Lucinda stared for a long moment at the countess. She was absolutely stunned by that lady's calm and extraordinary statements. At last she found her voice. "I do appreciate your favor, my lady. I shall remember what you have said, believe me."

"That is all one can ask," interjected the countess quickly.

Lucinda smiled. "However, I must tell you once more that I do not intend to wed again, for I, too, enjoy the same light flirtations as Lord Pembroke."

"What a pity. You and Hector would have made such a handsome pair," said the countess in a suddenly indifferent voice. She appeared to lose complete interest in the topic and introduced a subject of quite generic proportions.

Lucinda responded suitably to the countess's gambit, relieved that the personal nature of their conversation was apparently at an end. But she could not completely put out of her head the extraordinary nature of their discourse, and she was glad when another lady claimed the Countess of Pembroke's attention. Lucinda excused herself gracefully and moved away to mingle with some of the other ladies.

Not many more minutes passed before the gentlemen entered the drawing room. The remainder of the evening passed in a pleasant fashion, and when at last Lucinda and her companions returned to Mays House, it was quite late.

Miss Mays expressed herself to be overwhelmed by the experience. "I was never more nervous in my life. All of those people and how they stared at one!" Miss Mays realized that she had not sounded appreciative of the treat. Anxious that she should not be thought ungrateful, she said hurriedly, "But it was lovely just the same, my lady. Thank you so much for taking me."

"I am glad that you enjoyed it, Agnes. Now do go up to bed, for you are practically asleep on your feet," said Lucinda. Her sister-in-law agreed that she was very tired, and she went away upstairs at once to bed.

Lucinda and Miss Blythe retired to the drawing room to take tea and to talk over the soiree. Inevitably, much of their discussion centered on Miss Mays.

"I was never more surprised than when Miss Mays sat down at the pianoforte and played as well as she did," said Miss Blythe. "I heard a number of compliments, even some of the gentlemen going so far as to express themselves pleased. We really must do something to encourage Miss Mays with her music."

"Quite. It is virtually the only thing at which Agnes shines," said Lucinda. "But she did look surprisingly well tonight, don't you think?"

"Yes, most becoming. However, it must be admitted that Miss Mays's appearance is not going to do the trick. She hasn't the vivacity nor is she in the admired style of beauty. I was thinking that we should hold a musicale, Lucinda. That at least will highlight her major accomplishment," said Miss Blythe.

"The very thing, Tibby. We shall certainly do so," said Lucinda.

"It will be a start in the right direction, in any event," said Miss Blythe on a sigh.

"Oh, we shall do better than that for her, I assure you! Lady Sefton was quite taken with Agnes's story. What do you think? She has promised to send her vouchers for Almack's," said Lucinda triumphantly.

Miss Blythe smiled. Her eyes gleamed with appreciation. "Oh, my dear! Nothing could be better. Almack's is just in the sedate style that will most suit Miss Mays."

"That is what Lady Sefton said," said Lucinda.

"Lady Sefton is a wise woman. Now, what of you, Lucinda? I noticed that the Countess of Pembroke kept you beside her for some minutes. I am curious to hear what you found to discuss with her ladyship," said Miss Blythe.

"Oh, the entire evening was the most extraordinary thing, Tibby!" exclaimed Lucinda. "Do you recall when I told you how Lord Pembroke had nearly knocked me down in front of the Lending Library? His lordship was bold enough to claim my acquaintance on that account alone. I could see that Lady Sefton thought it all rather shocking but somewhat amusing, too."

"That was bold, indeed," said Miss Blythe. "It must have been very pleasant for you to have such a gallant gentleman for your dinner partner."

"I enjoyed it hugely. Lord Pembroke had me laughing a number of times. He is such a jokester that one can never take anything he says in a serious vein," said Lucinda. "But that was not the singular experience of the evening."

"Wasn't it, my dear? I had rather thought it was," said Miss Blythe, sounding almost disappointed.

"But just listen, Tibby. Lady Pembroke has taken a fancy to me. Moreover, she told me that I could 'set my cap' at Lord Pembroke with her goodwill!" said Lucinda. "What do you think of that?"

"It would never do," said Miss Blythe decisively.

"That is just what I thought. I gently let the countess know, in the politest fashion that I possibly could, of course, that I really was not interested in wedding again," said Lucinda.

Miss Blythe was exhibiting a flattering attention to every word. "And how did her ladyship take that?"

Lucinda turned out her hands in an expressive gesture. "She suggested that I might one day tire of the sort of light flirtations that Lord Pembroke regularly engages in and that I might wish to make a determined push for her son. She told me also, quite bluntly, that she desires grandchildren and that his lordship and I would make a handsome pair! Tibby, I scarcely knew where to look or what to say. I was never more glad than when Mrs. Connagher claimed her attention and I could slip away."

"I can readily believe it," said Miss Blythe. "How very disconcerting, to be sure. But I am certain that you will be able to put it out of your head, for I doubt that Lady Pembroke will importune you again in such a way. She did not strike me as an empty-headed sort that will keep striking the same discordant note."

"No, indeed! Quite the contrary, in fact," agreed Lucinda. "She is as put together as she can be. There is not the least hint of flightiness about her, whatever odd conversations she may take it into her head to indulge."

It struck Lucinda suddenly that her companion did not seem the least bit disappointed that she had turned down Lady Pembroke's proposal so flatly. "Tibby, you have surprised me. I quite thought that you would be excited that Lady Pembroke had distinguished me with such flattering attention, and appalled that I had responded as I did. I know what a romantic you are! You still harbor hopes of my being swept off my feet by some well-born gentleman."

Miss Blythe chuckled. "My dear, do grant me some understanding. It is well known that a courtship prospers best when there is some resistance to it. The very fact that Lady Pembroke made such a suggestion to you quite effectively quashes any possible attachment between you and Lord Pembroke! It would be foolish of me to fly in the face of an established principle."

Lucinda looked at her companion for a long moment. She shook her head. "I do not know whether I should thank you or scold you. How can you say that I should not ever attach Lord Pembroke simply because his mother approves of me? I have never heard anything so nonsensical in my life."

"It is quite true, I assure you. Only recall Romeo and Juliet," said Miss Blythe composedly. "Regretfully, we must cross Lord Pembroke off the list of eligibles for you. It is a pity, but there it is."

"What list?" asked Lucinda, looking hard at her companion.

Miss Blythe's suddenly guilty expression made Lucinda exclaim. Half laughing, half exasperated, she said, "Tibby! Pray do not tell me that you have actually got up a list of eligibles!"

"It is not that, precisely," said Miss Blythe.

"Why, how perfectly monstrous of you, Tibby, especially when I told you that I did not want your matchmaking schemes woven about me! It is all right for Agnes, but certainly not for me!" said Lucinda.

"I have not woven any schemes, Lucinda. The very idea that I should go against your express wishes! My dear! I hope that you may trust me better than that," exclaimed Miss Blythe indignantly. Two bright spots of color had risen into her face.

Lucinda saw that she had truly offended her old preceptress. "I am sorry, Tibby. I did not mean to insult you. But if you are not thinking up schemes to get me married off, what is this nonsense about a list of eligibles?"

Miss Blythe's indignation became tinged by the guilty look. "I was making up a list of possibles for Miss Mays, which is perfectly in agreement with what we had spoken about earlier, if you will recall."

"Yes, of course. But what has that to do with me?" asked Lucinda.

Miss Blythe sighed. "Forgive me, my dear. Engaged in such an exercise, my thoughts quite naturally turned to you. So I jotted down a few names for you, as well."

At Lucinda's groan, Miss Blythe made haste to reassure. "It is nothing for you to be upset over, Lucinda. It was simply for my own private speculation and enjoyment. I have no intention of actually doing anything with it. I shan't even show it to you so that you will not be made self-conscious when you should come face-to-face with one of the gentlemen."

"Oh, dear. I never thought of that," said Lucinda, appalled. "How shall I face any of the gentlemen who have made themselves known as my admirers? I shall be constantly wondering which of them has earned a place on your infamous list of eligibles!"

"Pudding-heart," said Miss Blythe bluntly. She chuckled at Lucinda's shocked and affronted expression. "Yes, I can see that you are put out with me, my dear. But really, is it so bad as all that? Will you take the knocker off of your door merely because you have discovered that I have a preference for one or other of your admirers? Come, Lucinda! I hope that I know you better than that!"

Lucinda laughed. "I think that you do, indeed, Tibby. You

are quite right. I have every intention of staying in London, list of eligibles or not."

"Good, for I have been thinking that we must make a bit of a push with Miss Mays. She is far too retiring in company," said Miss Blythe.

"Yes, it is quite noticeable," said Lucinda, frowning. "It is bad enough that she has no conversation with the ladies, but if a gentleman chances to smile in her direction, she actually gives the impression that she will transform into a bolting rabbit."

"The only way to correct that is to expose Agnes to the gentlemen," said Miss Blythe firmly. "She must learn to hold her ground and smile and speak a few proper words. Otherwise, she will not gain any notice, and we shall never get anyone to come up to scratch."

"And that is, of course, the primary objective," agreed Lucinda. "Very well, Tibby. How shall we teach Agnes that most gentlemen do not bite?"

"I think we should begin by enlisting Lord Mays's help," said Miss Blythe. "His lordship has bachelor friends. Miss Mays is his cousin, after all. It will not seem so strange for him to step in on her behalf, surely. If Lord Mays can persuade his friends to stand up with Agnes at Almack's, for instance, or take her driving or some such thing—"

Miss Blythe broke off as Lucinda leaped up from the settee. She looked after Lucinda in astonishment. "My dear, whatever have I said?"

Lucinda continued to the door of the drawing room. "I forgot to inquire of Church whether Lord Mays called. I shall be back directly, Tibby." And she disappeared out the door.

She returned almost at once. A frown was formed between her brows. Miss Blythe asked sympathetically, "There has been no word?"

Lucinda shook her head. "No, none. I know Wilfred would have sent around if there had been any further news. But that is not only what is bothering me, Tibby." She looked very levelly at her companion. "Church informs me that Agnes has been keeping company with my cousin Ferdie."

Miss Blythe stared, aghast. "My dear. When I suggested

that Agnes needed to be exposed to male company, I hardly meant Mr. Stassart's!"

"Well I know it, Tibby. What that baby means by slipping into the bedroom of one of Ferdie's stamp is more than I can fathom, but I intend to find out," said Lucinda grimly.

"Do you mean to say that she is with him now?" asked Miss Blythe, shocked.

"So I am informed. It seems that Agnes was not quite as exhausted as she led us to believe," said Lucinda, turning away toward the door.

Miss Blythe rose hastily. "I am coming with you, Lucinda. She is my charge as well. If a peal is to be rung over her head, I shall do it. I have a few more years of experience in dealing in that area than have you!"

"It is not Agnes that I am at this moment thinking of," said Lucinda, her eyes glittering in the candlelight. "I have a few choice words to say to my dear cousin. He shall not soon forget them, I promise you!"

She swept out of the drawing room with Miss Blythe in close pursuit.

## Chapter Twenty-two

Lucinda thrust open Mr. Stassart's bedroom door. It never entered her head until she had already walked inside what she might possibly find. But it was too late to put discretion into play. Her presence had already been noticed.

Two astonished faces stared at Lucinda and Miss Blythe. Mr. Stassart lay propped up against the pillows of his bed, attired in a dressing gown. His left arm was in a sling and rested lightly atop the coverlets.

Miss Mays perched in a chair near the bed. She was attired

in her evening gown, her cloak thrown over the back of the chair. Between her and Mr. Stassart was a game board lying on the bed. The miscreants were obviously playing cribbage and for points, since there was a large pile of matchsticks at Mr. Stassart's hand and a lesser number on Miss Mays's side.

Mr. Stassart was the first to recover. An amused expression crossed his face, and he settled back against the supporting pillows. "Now there is the devil to pay. We have been found out, Miss Mays!"

"Oh!" Miss Mays regarded the stunned expressions of the ladies with dawning dismay. "Have I done something that I should not?"

"I think it would be best if this was discussed elsewhere, Agnes," said Lucinda with admirable restraint.

"Of course you haven't, Miss Mays. It is I who have been amazingly at fault. Isn't that so, fair cousin?" murmured Ferdie.

"Quite." Lucinda turned to Miss Mays, who had risen from the chair and stood next to it with one hand raised to her throat. The young woman's eyes had grown large and fearful. Recognizing that her sister-in-law was fast falling into the throes of a panic, Lucinda made an effort to soften her expression and her voice. "You are to go with Miss Blythe now, Agnes. She knows just what to say to you. I will be along shortly."

"Oh, oh, oh! I am undone! I know that I am!" Miss Mays covered her face with her hands and gave a gusty sob.

Miss Blythe took hold of her elbow. "We shall have none of that, if you please. Now come along. There are a few things that I wish to say to you, Miss Mays!"

Miss Mays went docilely, already sniffling.

"The lamb being led to the slaughter," said Ferdie pityingly.

"More like to the shearer," said Lucinda tartly. The door closed firmly behind Miss Blythe and Miss Mays, and she turned a hard stare on her cousin. "What do you mean by such conduct, Ferdie? Agnes is my sister-in-law, not some trolloping housemaid! I knew you for a worthless scoundrel, but I did not know you were a blackguard to boot! How could you

place Agnes in such a damaging position? Have you no sense
of shame, no sense of decency?"

"Cousin, cousin! Why these histrionics?" Ferdie threw out
his hand at the game board. "We were playing cribbage. I
admit to cheating a trifle, but there is nothing in that, I assure
you! Miss Mays scarcely knows the difference."

"Yes, and she scarcely knows the difference between a gentleman and a bad man, either!" retorted Lucinda.

Ferdie flushed. "I am not a bad man," he stated with dignity. "I am many things, but that I am not. I do not besmirch
the good names of ladies of quality."

"Do you not, Ferdie?" asked Lucinda softly. There was a
wealth of meaning in her tone, at which he suddenly narrowed
his eyes. Lucinda did not wait for him to realize her suspicion
concerning herself, if there indeed was one, but continued,
"The servants are talking, Ferdie. Perhaps it is only cribbage
that you have been playing at, but you have done a damage to
my sister-in-law's standing in this household. I do not regard
that lightly."

"Oh, do give over, Lucinda. What is a fellow to do lying in
bed for hours at a time?" said Ferdie wearily. "I was about to
go out of my mind when in pops Miss Mays offering to divert
my thoughts."

At Lucinda's expression, he cast her an indignant glance.
"Really, Lucinda, your face is about as open as any book! Se-
duction is not the first thing that came to my mind. I am in no
condition to make the attempt, even if I was tempted, which I
was not! Miss Mays is not in my style at all. Too skittish by
half. I prefer statuesque beauties who offer a challenge. I look
for one who is a fitting mate for a gamester, who must thereafter gamble whether he will go home to a beautiful virago or
a lovely angel. Ah, Lucinda! If you could but see yourself as I
see you now. The fire in your sparkling eyes, the pout of your
lovely lips, the—"

"Stuff it, Ferdie," said Lucinda rudely. She put her hand on
the cord that kept the bed curtain tied up. "I shall expect you
downstairs in the morning for breakfast, Ferdie. As far as I am
concerned, you are recovered enough to be up on your feet
again."

Ferdie lay back against the pillows in a weak attitude. His hand went to his pallid brow. "But I am so weak still, dear cousin. I fear that I shall do permanent damage to my constitution if I am forced too soon to strenuous exercise."

"You shall get out of this bed in the morning, or I shall have my men put you out," said Lucinda quietly. "I shall not allow you to presume upon my hospitality for much longer, and so I warn you!" She jerked the heavy cord and the curtain fell down, obscuring her cousin from her sight.

"Good night, Ferdie!" Lucinda turned on her heel and marched away across the bedroom.

Behind her, Mr. Stassart thrust apart the bed curtains with his head. "You are a cold fish, cousin! A cold fish!"

As she opened the door, Lucinda turned a hard smile in her cousin's direction. "Pray do not forget to blow out the candle, Ferdie. I would not wish the light to keep you awake, for dawn is but a few hours away."

"Dawn!" gasped Ferdie. His astounded expression gave way to fully roused indignation. "I say, you don't mean to have me tumbled out of bed at some ungodly hour! I won't have it, I tell you! I shall have you know that I never rise until noon at the earliest!"

"The candle, Ferdie," said Lucinda. He swore wrathfully at her, but she paid him no heed. Lucinda stepped out and shut the bedroom door. Something crashed against the other side of the panels. Angered, she was about to go back in when she caught herself up. There was no possible victory to be gained by whirling in to scold her cousin over throwing a childish tantrum. No, she had said what she had wanted to, and she had laid down her ultimatum. Anything more would simply dilute the effects of her displeasure.

Besides, there was another matter that needed her attention. Lucinda sighed and turned toward Miss Mays's bedroom door. She saw that it was not completely shut, a crack of light showing around its edges. She crossed the hall and pushed the door fully open. Immediately she could hear wrenching sobs punctuated by an occasional word in Miss Blythe's calm voice.

"What a perfectly wretched end to a lovely evening!" she exclaimed and went in.

Miss Mays saw her at once, and her face twisted in misery. "Oh, Lady Mays! I am s . . . so sorry! Had I known that . . . but I did not! I did not! Oh, oh, oh!" She wailed loudly, "I thought you would be pleased!"

"Pleased!" Lucinda turned astonished eyes on Miss Blythe. "What the devil is she talking about? Why would I be pleased?"

Miss Blythe had risen from her place beside the weeping young woman and walked over to the water bowl to wring out a cloth with fresh water. She said gravely, "There is no need to swear, Lucinda."

Lucinda flushed, at once repentant. "Of course you are right, Tibby! I have let my temper run away with me. Forgive me, pray."

Miss Blythe nodded acknowledgement. She turned back to Miss Mays and put a hand under that young woman's chin. A reddened woebegone face was fully revealed, and Miss Blythe gently wiped away the still coursing tears with the cool cloth.

"There now, Agnes. That will make you feel more comfortable," she said soothingly, encouragingly. "You will be much better able to talk with Lady Mays now."

It was doubtful that Miss Mays agreed, for she shuddered. But she nevertheless turned to face Lucinda. There was fear in her brown sloe eyes, and Lucinda was reminded of nothing so much as a trapped rabbit.

She sat down on the bed beside her sister-in-law and took one curled hand in her own. "Agnes, why did you think that I would be pleased to find you with Mr. Stassart? Didn't you realize that it is not at all the thing to visit a gentleman in his bedchamber?"

Miss Mays shuddered again. She shook her head quickly. She refused to look at Lucinda. "Miss Blythe explained it all to me. I have been very wicked, very wicked, indeed!"

There was such abject despair in her voice that Lucinda's eyes flew to Miss Blythe's face. Miss Blythe shook her head. Lucinda correctly interpreted this as her companion's way of saying that she had done all that she could.

"I would not say that you have been wicked precisely, but certainly you have been very foolish. Now listen closely to me, Agnes. No, look at me! That's a good girl. When I invited you to stay with me for the Season, I made myself responsible for you. I cannot simply wash my hands of you now. That would be ignoble of me, indeed," said Lucinda.

Miss Mays threw her arms around Lucinda and clung, crying, "Oh, you are too good to me! I do not deserve it, truly I do not!"

Lucinda tried to extricate herself, but her sister-in-law's embrace was too tight. On a note of laughter, she exclaimed, "Agnes, you are stifling me. I shouldn't like it in the least if I was to suffocate."

At once she was released. Miss Mays stared at her anxiously. "You are not hurt, my lady? Pray say that I have not hurt you!"

"No, of course you haven't. Agnes, you are a goose."

"Yes, I know that I am very foolish. Everyone has always said so, so it must be true," said Miss Mays, sighing a little.

Lucinda was glad to see that at least the noisy part of Miss Mays's emotional outburst was done. She heard a relieved sigh from Miss Blythe's direction, and she almost laughed. But that would not have been appropriate in the circumstances. For one thing, Miss Mays would have been utterly confused by such a display, and Lucinda felt that she could not afford the least confusion to interfere in what she wanted to get across to her sister-in-law.

"Agnes, pray tell me why you thought I would be pleased that you were visiting my cousin?" she asked.

"Why, because he was certain to be such a very bad patient," said Miss Mays hesitantly. She made a little forlorn gesture. "I had hoped to make myself useful to you. I do know how to nurse someone and to keep them entertained. I am really quite good at it. It is the only thing that I am good at."

"You are a wonderful musician," said Miss Blythe firmly.

"Quite true. You are also a funny, helpless baby who looks very pretty in peach," said Lucinda.

Miss Mays blushed. She looked shyly at them both. "Oh! What nice things to say!" She didn't seem to mind in the least being described as an infant. On the contrary, she looked quite pleased. She was so used to hearing herself renounced and vil-

ified that any kind word was something to regard with gratitude.

Miss Mays smiled at Lucinda. "I shan't go to see Mr. Stassart anymore."

"Very good. My cousin will be coming downstairs tomorrow, in any event, so you must not concern yourself that he is
not making good progress," said Lucinda.

Miss Blythe raised her brows as she digested this pronouncement, but Miss Mays accepted it at its face value.
"How wonderful! I know that you will be much less anxious
now, my lady," she said happily.

"I will be even less so when my cousin is finally on his
way," said Lucinda.

"Oh, it will not be long now, now that Mr. Stassart is getting out of bed," said Miss Mays, speaking from the well of
her extensive nursing experience. "It is when a person stays
overlong in bed that he begins to lose much of his strength.
Mr. Stassart is young, besides. He will be able to go home
very soon."

"I know that you are right, Agnes. In point of fact, I was
just encouraging my cousin to that effect," said Lucinda with a
small laugh.

Miss Mays beamed at her. "There! We are all comfortable
again. Are we not, my lady?"

"Yes, Agnes, we are all comfortable again," agreed Lucinda. She rose from the bed. "I shall have your maid sent in
to undress you for bed. It is very late."

"Oh, pray do not waken her. I told her that I would do for
myself tonight," said Miss Mays, wringing her hands.

Lucinda eyed that telltale gesture. She said hastily, "It will
be just as you say, my dear. Now I really must say good night,
for my own dresser will be wondering what has become of
me."

"You must not keep her waiting on my account," agreed
Miss Mays. She saw that Miss Blythe was also leaving, and
she trailed them to the door. When Lucinda and Miss Blythe
had exited, she offered another shy smile to them. "Good
night."

"Good night, Agnes," said Lucinda.

The door shut softly. Lucinda turned her head to look at her companion. "How much I admire you, Tibby. I do not think that I could have borne to put up with a number of such charges, as you have done over the years."

Miss Blythe chuckled. "They have not all been so difficult to handle, my dear. Indeed, I can recall one who was a veritable treat to be around. She was always my favorite pupil."

Lucinda reached out her hand quickly, her eyes misting. "Oh, Tibby! Must you make me cry in the small hours of the morning?"

"Go to bed, my dear," said Miss Blythe gently.

Lucinda glanced over at Mr. Stassart's door, and her unaccustomed sentimentalism evaporated. "Oh, I shall. But first I must relay a few orders concerning my cousin, Ferdie," she said.

"Whatever do you mean?" asked Miss Blythe curiously.

"Only that my cousin is to be assured of every consideration in the breakfast room," said Lucinda blandly. They had traversed the hall and, having reached her own door, she parted from Miss Blythe with a quiet good night.

The next morning when Lucinda went down to the breakfast room, she found her cousin sprawled sulkily in a chair. "Good morning, Ferdie," she said cheerfully.

He glared at her. "Much you know about it. I was dragged from my bed and positively thrust into my clothing by those churlish bullies of yours. Look at me! My cravat is permanently creased; there are wrinkles in my coat and waistcoat. These are not the sort of garments that I am used to, by the by! You promised to replace my coat, cousin! This is hardly fair return!"

"If you are so discontented with my efforts on your behalf, Ferdie, I suggest that you return to your own lodgings and get your man to attend to you properly," said Lucinda.

As she had known he would, her cousin quit his complaints and subsided into low grumbling.

Miss Blythe and Miss Mays soon joined them at the breakfast table.

Miss Blythe nodded to Mr. Stassart. "I am glad to see that you are recovering, Mr. Stassart."

Mr. Stassart made a bow. "It was inevitable, Miss Blythe. One would not dare to malinger in this house," he said, somewhat bitterly.

Miss Blythe raised her brows a little. "Indeed!"

The company was served and the servants left. Near the conclusion of breakfast, Church came in and bent to say something quietly in Lady Mays's ear. Lucinda looked up quickly. "I shall come at once."

"Is there something untoward, my dear?" asked Miss Blythe.

"Not at all. Lord Mays has come to call," said Lucinda, rising from the table.

"What! Surely you are not going to receive his lordship without benefit of chaperone," said Ferdie maliciously.

Lucinda looked at him. "Lord Mays is a gentleman and a friend, sir. I have complete confidence in him."

"As do I," said Miss Blythe coldly, staring down Mr. Stassart's pretensions.

Ferdie shrugged, and then wished that he had not. Bad temperedly, he snapped, "I wonder that you would expose yourself to gossip, cousin. But I am aware that you think nothing of my opinion. I am merely your father's heir and will one day be head of the family. So who am I to cavil at my cousin's careless conduct? Just do not come moaning to me when word gets about that you receive gentlemen without the advantage of a chaperone!"

"And who will put word about, Ferdie? You?" asked Lucinda quietly. She saw that it had been a home shot, and her lips curled in a contemptuous smile. "Pray do not think that I am unaware of your machinations, Ferdie." She swept toward the door, her head held high.

"I have been slandered, most viciously and unfairly! What do you mean by it, Lucinda? I say, I demand an answer," exclaimed Ferdie.

"Mr. Stassart, should you be putting yourself into such a passion? It is quite unhealthy for you," said Miss Mays diffidently.

Ferdie stared at her, his mouth hanging open. He was astonished. This mouse of a female had actually dared to remonstrate with him. His rather hard blue eyes suddenly narrowed. "Miss Mays—"

"Why do you not go practice on the pianoforte, my dear? I shall walk with you to the music room since I am headed toward the library," interposed Miss Blythe, smoothly derailing whatever blistering remark that Mr. Stassart had meant to deliver.

"Oh, but what of poor Mr. Stassart?" asked Miss Mays.

"I am certain that it will do Mr. Stassart a great deal of good to have a few moments alone in which to collect himself," said Miss Blythe bitingly. Rising from the table, she firmly took Miss Mays in hand and steered her out of the breakfast room.

# Chapter Twenty-three

The butler opened the drawing room door, and Lucinda swiftly entered. Her expression lit up at sight of the gentleman standing in front of the mantel. "Wilfred! I am so glad to see you."

The butler quietly closed the door, privately determining that there would be no interruptions to this particular interview.

Lord Mays turned at Lucinda's entrance and instantly went to her, catching hold of the hands that she held out to him. "Lucinda! I came as swiftly as I could to tell you. I have just this moment returned to town."

"Yes, I can see that you have," said Lucinda, having already taken note of his attire. His lordship was wearing a driving coat, a few extra whippoints thrust through the top buttonhole, and there was a rakish windblown look about the ruddiness of his complexion and hair. She drew him over to the settee. "Tell me at once what has happened."

Lord Mays sat down, apologizing for his dirt. Lucinda assured him that it did not matter in the least, but urged him to go on with his story.

"I was able to run those idiots, Lord Levine and Mr. Pepperidge, to ground at last. They had left the cockfight and gone on to a mutual acquaintance's hunting box for a rare night of it."

"Oh, dear! How unfortunate!" exclaimed Lucinda. "They were not completely incapacitated, I hope?"

Lord Mays snorted his disgust. "Disguised to the gills, I assure you! I thought that Lord Levine would heave his freight all over the floor of my curricle any number of times. But I stopped to hold his head, and that seemed to steady things a bit. He was still a bit wobbly when I let him off at his lodgings, but at least he was upright. There was no doing anything with Pepperidge at all."

"Then you brought Lord Levine back with you? And he will take Ferdie in with him?" asked Lucinda. At his lordship's nod and grin, she threw her arms about him. "Oh, Wilfred, thank you! You have no notion how happy I am to hear it."

Lord Mays had instinctively put his arms around her, returning her embrace. There came an arrested expression into his gold-brown eyes as he looked down into her smiling face. "I was glad to be of service to you, Lucinda." He cleared his throat. "Lucinda, I . . ."

Lucinda felt of a sudden unaccountably breathless. She straightened away from his lordship, very aware that he seemed slow in releasing her. She said quickly, brightly, "Such good news, my lord! Ferdie has been such a nuisance, you have no notion. I shall be glad to be able to show him the door."

"Has the fellow shown his impertinence, Lucinda? I shall know how to deal with that," said Lord Mays, rising with a purposeful light in his eyes. His fists were bunched suggestively.

Lucinda also rose, catching at his lordship's sleeve. "Pray do not, Wilfred! It is not at all what you think. Actually, I suppose it is, though Agnes was involved and not me. Last night I discovered her in his bedroom, playing cribbage, if you please! She had not the least notion what a compromising position she had placed herself in, of course! But Ferdie most certainly did. The only excuse he tendered was that he had been so utterly bored that he could not turn away her offer to entertain him."

Lord Mays had listened to her explanation with a fixed expression. It seemed to calm him somewhat. At the end, he said frankly, "The fellow is an out-and-out bounder, Lucinda. My advice is to send him this very instant to Lord Levine's before he can get up to any further mischief. There is no knowing what he might take into his head next. The fat would be in the fire if he should try to compromise you, or Agnes, of course, and some starched-up lady come to call and chanced upon such a scene. There is no knowing what kind of talk is already running through the servants about poor Agnes."

"You are right, of course. Very well. I shall do so at once," said Lucinda. She started toward the door. "I left Ferdie in the breakfast room, but he is undoubtedly gone from there. I shall ask Church if he has seen him."

Mr. Stassart had indeed left the breakfast room. He had repaired to the billiards room to idly roll a few of the balls to and fro, but it was poor sport and he soon abandoned it. He sauntered out of the door in search of better entertainment. He was heartily weary of his own company, and he had never known a duller household in his life. There was not a game of chance to be had. The opportunity to play cribbage with Miss Mays for a penny a point had been mildly amusing, as an adult might play at a child's game for a time and find it diverting, but the thought of indulging in such tame stuff again made him shudder.

He heard the sound of music, like a rippling stream. Ferdie followed the sound. He pushed open the door to the music room and stepped inside.

Miss Mays was sitting at the pianoforte. Her fingers flew, her body swayed, with the passion of the music that she was bringing forth.

Ferdie was astonished. He could not believe that this passionate flame, this fervent muse, was the same colorless Miss Mays. The beauty of her playing held him spellbound for several minutes. It gradually occurred to him to wonder whether the ardor that she displayed at the keyboard could be unlocked through other means.

Ferdie sauntered across the carpet. Stepping up close behind Miss Mays, he bent to touch a light kiss under her ear. Miss Mays started violently, her fingers striking a monstrous discordancy. The top of her head cracked sharp against Ferdie's chin. He reared back, biting back a curse.

Miss Mays jumped to her feet and whirled. The pianoforte was close behind her, and she leaned against it. She stared at Mr. Stassart, her eyes dilated. Then her expression changed. "Oh! Mr. Stassart, are you hurt? I did not in the least mean harm to you."

Ferdie gingerly fingered his chin. "I believe that I shall live, Miss Mays. But I do urge you to not to leap up in just that dangerous way. One might take a real hurt from such a blow."

Miss Mays straightened, instantly sympathetic. Stretching out her hand to him, she said, "I am so very sorry! Does it pain you terribly? Shall I run to get a cold compress for you?"

Ferdie captured her hand with his and carried her fingers to his lips. "I require nothing, dear lady, but the honor of basking in the warm echoes of your music. You are an extraordinary musician, Miss Mays. Extraordinary! Such passion, such ardor, such delicate power! I stand in worshipful awe. I am entirely at your command." As he had spoken, he had managed to slide his good arm about her trim waist. With his body, he pinned her against the pianoforte.

Miss Mays had put up her hands between them, and she pushed ineffectively against his chest. "Sir! Mr. Stassart, you must let me go!" There was agitation in her voice and on her face.

Ferdie leaned over her, bringing his face closer to hers. "My dear, dear Miss Mays," he murmured. He sought her lips, but she turned her head swiftly. She was a squirming, trim little package pressed against him. Ferdie tightened his arm around her and bent her over the pianoforte, determined to have his way. "A kiss, sweet, dear Miss Mays," he panted.

"No! Oh, no!" cried the distressed lady, beating at him with her palms and twisting her head away. In the struggle a vase on the top of the pianoforte was knocked over onto the floor with a loud crash. The vase disintegrated into a thousand pieces.

The door of the music room was thrust open, and Lord Mays stood on the threshold. In a bare second, he had taken stock of the situation, and he leaped across the room.

Grabbing Mr. Stassart by the shoulder, he whirled the other man around. He threw a punishing right into Stassart's jaw.

Mr. Stassart went down. He yelped from shock and hurt. Dazed, he attempted to rise from where he had sprawled onto the carpet. But then he chanced to look up and saw the grim set of Lord Mays's expression. This was swiftly followed by the distinct impression of that gentleman's still bunched fists. Ferdie deemed it prudent to remain where he was. He fell back, groaning.

Miss Mays, who had been cringing against the pianoforte, now flew across the space between herself and Mr. Stassart. She threw herself down beside Mr. Stassart's inert body. "Oh, you are hurt!"

She swung her head up to stare at Lord Mays. Flags of indignation flew in her cheeks, and her brown eyes flashed. "You callous beast! How could you hit a wounded man?"

Mr. Stassart stopped groaning long enough to look up at her in astonishment. His own expression was duplicated on Lord Mays's face. Ferdie, ever quick-witted at the least sign of opportunity, commenced to groan with great fervor. He added an artistic touch by fumbling with his hand at his throbbing jaw.

"Oh, you poor man!" crooned Miss Mays, sitting down and carefully lifting Mr. Stassart's head into her soft lap.

"Here, I say!" protested Lord Mays feebly. "Not at all the thing, cousin!"

Ferdie flicked his eyelids a couple of times before apparently being able to focus upon her anxious face above him. "Where am I? Miss Mays? Can it be you? Ah, no, it is an angel!"

"Now see what you have done! He is delirious. I shouldn't wonder at it if he is not put into a raging fever after your brutal treatment, my lord!" said Miss Mays fiercely.

Lord Mays's eyes fairly started from his head. "No such thing! I just planted the fellow a facer." A sense of strong ill-usage rose up in him, and he said indignantly, "Good God, cousin, I have just saved you from this dastard's unwelcome liberties!"

Ferdie had closed his eyes, enjoying his unique position. But at his lordship's untimely reminder, he uttered another loud groan. "Oh, my head! My shoulder! Has my face begun to swell? Am I bleeding!"

"Go away! Haven't you done enough damage?"

"Miss Agnes Maria Mays!"

Miss Mays started severely at the awful pronouncement of her name. She stared up at Miss Blythe's stern visage. Abruptly, all the evils of her situation burst upon her. She had been caught once more in an unladylike pose.

She scrambled to her feet and Mr. Stassart's head dropped hard against the floor. He let loose a string of curses, but Miss Mays never heard the gentleman's shocking lack of control. It was doubtful that anyone else did either, for Miss Mays had promptly burst into noisy tears.

"What a looby!" exclaimed Lord Mays. He stretched a hand down to Stassart, who was groaning in earnest and nursing his head. "Come on, you shouldn't stay down there. She might take it into her head to stumble over you and there you would be, trapped beneath a watering pot!"

Ferdie was instantly struck with the truth of these words. He grasped his lordship's hand, and as he was pulled to his feet, he exclaimed, "Yes, by Jove! And though I do not care for this coat, it is the only one that I have at present."

Miss Blythe had put her arm around Miss Mays's shoulders. "Come, my dear. This is no place for you. I shall take you up-stairs."

As the two ladies turned to the door, Lucinda walked into the room. She stared in consternation at the weeping Miss Mays, and then her gaze swept around to her cousin, who was brushing down his coat. "What has gone on here?" she asked very quietly.

In response, Miss Mays weeped louder. Miss Blythe's lips thinned. She raised her voice. "I am taking Agnes upstairs. I shall deal with her there. I shall leave Mr. Stassart to you, Lucinda."

Lucinda waited until Miss Blythe had guided Miss Mays from the room before she rounded wrathfully upon her cousin. "How could you, Ferdie? When I expressly told you last night that Agnes was not to be treated like some light-skirt."

Ferdie threw up his hand. "I admit that I was off my head for a few moments. I was seduced by her playing of the pianoforte and—"

"What rot!" exclaimed Lucinda. "The truth is that you took advantage of an ignorant young woman, not taking a thought to anything else but your own selfish desires!"

"I knocked him down for that, Lucinda," offered Lord Mays in a conciliating way.

"Thank you, Wilfred! I wish you had milled him down a few more times for good measure!" said Lucinda.

Lord Mays coughed. "Couldn't very well do that, my dear. Miss Mays wouldn't let me."

Lucinda stared at Lord Mays, her fury momentarily suspended. "Not let you? Whatever do you mean? Why, Agnes was in hysterics just now. I would have thought she would have been egging you on to it!"

Ferdie gave a nasty laugh. "Your little sister-in-law gave me her lap and nursed my head, dear cousin. She only fell into strong hysterics at sight of Miss Blythe. I can't say that I blame her for that. That woman has always given me a strong desire to spit."

"Mind your tongue, you!" warned Lord Mays.

Mr. Stassart honored his lordship with a mocking bow. "Forgive my lapse, my lord. Behold, I am all contrition."

Lord Mays gave a snort of disgust. He turned to Lucinda. "For all that he is a dashed court-card, Stassart speaks the truth of the matter."

"Court-card! You slander me, my lord. I admit that I am

nice in my tastes and perhaps a bit finicky in my dress. But I am no court-card!"

Lord Mays ignored Mr. Stassart's indignant digression. "Once I had knocked down Stassart, Cousin Agnes flew into me with the most astounding denunciations. She accused me of practically murdering Stassart here and took his head in her lap. Lucinda, I swear to you that I was never more thrown off balance than when she turned around on me as though I were a criminal."

"I do not believe it!" exclaimed Lucinda, having difficulty reconciling this picture with what she had envisioned to have happened.

"The sooner you have this fellow out of your house, the better it will be for you," said Lord Mays.

"Yes, indeed! Ferdie, I was just coming to tell you, and now I may do so with even greater pleasure! I am throwing you out, Ferdie. Lord Mays has persuaded Lord Levine to take you in. How he protects you from the tipsters is your worry, for I wash my hands of you!" said Lucinda.

Ferdie drew himself up with an assumption of grand dignity. He adjusted his sling with a fussy air. "I shall not hold these hasty periods against you, cousin. I recognize that you are overwrought. It is only what one might expect of a high-strung beauty."

"Shall I help him along, Lucinda?" asked Lord Mays with a suggestive flexing of his hands.

"Pray do," said Lucinda cordially.

Ferdie stepped backward, putting some distance between himself and Lord Mays. "I am just going," he said hastily, defensively. "However, there is a bit of a difficulty. My pockets are to let. I haven't even the fare for a hackney. Dearest cousin, may I make so bold and request an advance of you?"

"How much do you lack, Ferdie?" asked Lucinda quietly, a strange smile touching her lips.

"A few hundred pounds. That is all that I require. I daresay that I could squeeze by on that," said Ferdie promptly.

Lucinda turned her gaze on Lord Mays. There was a mischievous light in her eyes. "What say you, my lord? Shall I frank Ferdie to the tune that he lacks?"

Lord Mays regarded her for a moment with a frown, which abruptly cleared. He gave a bark of laughter. "By all means! I have no objection, for it is a reasonable request."

Ferdie looked at Lord Mays almost with friendliness. "I say, that is deuced decent of you, Mays. I never expected you to come the pretty."

Lucinda went to the door and called for the butler. Quietly, she made a request. The butler nodded and reached into his own pocket. He withdrew a few pound notes and some coins. Lucinda scooped up what she needed, thanked the butler, and turned back to her cousin. She put out her hand, and automatically his hand rose to meet hers.

"Here you are, Ferdie—the price of a hackney fare," she said cheerfully. She dropped the meager amount into his outstretched palm.

Ferdie stared at what he held. Then he raised his head. He smiled. "Very amusing, I am sure. But let us end this game, dear cousin. Am I not to be properly provided for?"

Lucinda raised her slim brows. "Ferdie, you complained that you did not have the price of a hackney fare. I have provided it. I believe that I have fully honored your request."

Ferdie's face hardened. He would have liked to have thrown down the sum he had been given, but it was not in his nature to toss away his substance except on the game tables. "I now know what I am thought of, I see. You will rue this day, my fine lady."

"Are you threatening Lady Mays?" barked Lord Mays. He did not move, but he positively emanated a threatening presence. Very quietly, he said, "If I hear one whisper, one innuendo, I shall come after you, Stassart. Then we shall see how well you do without a female's skirts to hide behind!"

Ferdie's pale countenance lost another shade. Lord Mays's expression was smoldering, his wide stance remarkably menacing. Ferdie recalled that his lordship was accounted as quite a bruiser in the ring. Vividly he recalled the power behind the one blow that had knocked him off his feet. His instinct for survival was roused to alarm.

Ferdie began edging toward the door. "You misunderstand me, my lord. I would not dream of offering threat to my

cousin. Dear me, no! I meant merely that dear Lucinda's conscience, which has been oddly suspended throughout this unfortunate episode, shall some day smite her."

He was near enough to the door then to breathe a little freer,
and he could not resist the final word. "I shall await in confidence for that day and your certain apologies, dear cousin!"
Then he nipped through the door, slamming it shut behind
him, and was gone.

Lucinda went straight into a peal of laughter. She fell into a
wing chair, her head falling back against the cushions, still
laughing. Lord Mays rested his elbows on the back of another
chair and regarded her with a smiling face.

A few moments later, Lucinda regained some measure of
control. She shook her head at Lord Mays, still chuckling. "I
never thought to see my cousin put at such disadvantage. It
was truly a delight to behold!"

Lord Mays placed his hand over his heart and inclined his
head, taking an actor's bow. He straightened, his crooked grin
in place, saying, "I was happy to be of service once again. It is
becoming a habit with me, it seems."

Lucinda stood up and crossed to him. She took his hand and
laid the back of it against her cheek. "You are becoming a
very nice habit, Wilfred."

Her smiling gaze looked straight into his eyes. Lord Mays
sobered. He reached up his other hand and touched her face.
His fingers caressed her cheek. There came a startled expression into Lucinda's eyes. What might have been said or done
was never to be known, for at that instant the door opened.

Lucinda and Lord Mays broke apart. By the time a footman
had entered, a number of feet separated them. Lord Mays was
contemplating the view from the window, his hands clasped
tightly behind his back. Lady Mays was softly running her fingers over the keys of the pianoforte.

The footman paused, sensing something electric in the at-
mosphere. He was carrying a dustbin and broom. "Begging
your pardon, m'lady, but Mr. Church said as how he had noticed that there was a broken vase."

"Oh, yes," said Lucinda in a cool voice. "It was accidentally
toppled earlier by Mr. Stassart." She stood, intertwining her

fingers in front of her. "I should go up to see how Agnes is doing. She was not feeling well, as you know, my lord."

"Of course," said Lord Mays, picking up his cue. He strode forward and took the hand that she held out to him. He stood looking at her for a long moment, then managed to smile. "I shall wait on you another day, my lady."

Lucinda nodded, and she watched as Lord Mays turned and walked away from her.

## Chapter Twenty-four

Miss Mays had naturally been frightened that her shocking lapse with Mr. Stassart had been her ultimate undoing, for Miss Blythe had given her a thundering scold for her foolishness. But Miss Blythe had completely understood that it had not been her fault that Mr. Stassart had tried to kiss her.

"That will happen on occasion. However, Agnes, you showed ingratitude and extreme lack of judgement to then reject Lord Mays's service on your behalf," had said Miss Blythe sternly.

"But poor Mr. Stassart!"

Miss Blythe threw up her hand. "Pray do not speak to me of that deceiving creature again, Agnes. I will not hear it! You will do better not to mention his name to her ladyship, either."

Miss Mays had awaited her interview with Lady Mays with shivering trepidation, for in her mind she had acted so wickedly that she could not be pardoned. However, beyond also giving her a scold, dear kind Lady Mays had not sent her away in disgrace. Thus Miss Mays had not missed a single invitation that was subsequently delivered to Mays House.

In the weeks that followed, Lucinda and her two companions embarked on an orgy of social functions and affairs. One of the most notable was Lady Bishop's ball.

The gathering itself was a rather insipid affair, Lucinda thought, glancing about her critically at the meager company. However, Lady Bishop had treated the ladies with flattering consideration. Lucinda and Miss Blythe were assured of possible attention from their hostess. Her ladyship had also kept her word and exerted herself to be certain that Miss Mays never lacked for a partner.

Early on, Lady Bishop had introduced her brother to Miss Mays. The Honorable St. Ives Bradford bowed over Miss Mays's hand and diffidently solicited her for a waltz.

"Oh! I don't think . . ." Miss Mays threw a rather wild glance at Lucinda.

"My sister-in-law has not yet been to Almack's, and so she has not been granted permission to waltz," said Lucinda smoothly. "Perhaps a round dance instead?"

She had been rewarded with such a relieved look from Miss Mays that Lucinda had wondered at it. The Honorable Mr. Bradford had accepted the rebuff with good grace. He had stood beside them for a few minutes, making desultory conversation. His eyes rarely deviated from Miss Mays's face even when he was addressing Lady Mays. Lucinda thought this, too, was odd. There was little of vanity in her, but she was too used to admiration not to notice its absence. She noticed also her sister-in-law's nervousness.

When the gentleman at last moved off, she at once inquired, "Agnes, what is it about Mr. Bradford that has you in such a twitter?"

"He . . . he looks at me so!" Miss Mays could not articulate herself any better than that, and she cast a despairing glance at Lucinda.

Lucinda smiled and patted her hand. "You need not stand up with him if you don't wish to, Agnes. I don't expect you to like every gentleman that crosses your path."

"Thank you, Lady Mays!" said Miss Mays. "I don't know how it is, but I cannot like Mr. Bradford."

Both ladies were subsequently claimed for the next set, and it was not until some minutes later that Mr. Bradford was once more brought to Lucinda's attention. Mrs. Conagher, a sturdy lady whom she had met at Lady Sefton's soiree, recognized her with a friendly word. The lady lazily plied her fan, commenting on the dullness of the party. "I wouldn't have come except that I had already pledged my word to Lady Bishop. I knew how it would be, of course. Lady Bishop is a notorious nipcheese and always offers the most indifferent refreshments. However, one does not wish to give offense."

"No, indeed," responded Lucinda. "However, the smallness of the company probably does very well for my sister-in-law, Miss Mays. She is unused to large gatherings as yet."

"A rather tongue-tied young woman. I do not envy you the task of puffing her off, especially given her age," said Mrs. Conagher. "She will do well enough, I suppose, if you do not look very high for her. I must say that I am surprised that you would encourage St. Ives Bradford, however."

Lucinda threw a sharp glance at the lady. "What do you mean, ma'am? I was not aware that anyone was in the way of being encouraged."

"Oh?" Mrs. Conagher shrugged. "My mistake. It is common knowledge that Lady Bishop would like to see her libertine brother respectably riveted, preferably to a female of some means. Her ladyship was just confiding to me that she rather favors Miss Mays."

Lucinda took a moment to digest the several implications. She shook her head, puzzled. "But why should she settle on Agnes? My sister-in-law has not a feather to fly with."

"But you do, my dear. You have an open fondness for Miss Mays, readily apparent to everyone. It is expected that you would come down handsomely on Miss Mays's behalf should she contract a *parti*." Mrs. Conagher regarded Lady Mays with a worldly smile. "St. Ives Bradford has an unsavory reputation. Lady Bishop is determined to see him settled so that his little peccadillos will be whitewashed. Her ladyship sees Miss Mays as a very possible candidate. I shall leave you to decide how best to handle your business."

"I appreciate the information, Mrs. Conagher," said Lucinda quietly. The lady nodded and withdrew. Lucinda looked about the ballroom for her sister-in-law. The round dance that had been promised to Mr. Bradford was just forming up, but Lucinda did not see her sister-in-law on the floor.

Miss Blythe came up. "My dear, I just saw Mr. Bradford and Agnes leave the ballroom. Had you given them permission to walk in the gardens?"

"No, I did not. Tibby, I have just learned the most disquieting thing about Mr. Bradford's character." Lucinda spoke quickly as she watched a haughty gentleman approach her. "Here is Lord Sarsall come to claim his dance. I cannot get away. Tibby, will you please go after Agnes?"

"Of course!" Miss Blythe sped quickly toward the door giving onto the gardens.

Lucinda bestowed her hand on Lord Sarsall, who had at last reached her. Smiling at his lordship, Lucinda allowed herself to be led onto the dance floor. She wished very much that she could accompany Miss Blythe instead. But she had the greatest faith in her former governess. Miss Blythe would do all that was necessary.

Not many minutes later, Lucinda was relieved to see Miss Blythe and Miss Mays return to the ballroom. She finished the round dance with every appearance of enjoyment and exchanged pleasantries with Lord Sarsall as he returned her to her chair. His lordship bowed to Miss Blythe and Miss Mays before he retreated. Lucinda at once turned to her companions. "Well?"

"Mr. Bradford apparently enjoys flirting," said Miss Blythe quietly. She was holding Miss Mays's hand, and she squeezed the younger woman's fingers. "I am very proud of Agnes. She knew that she should not go out with Mr. Bradford, and she delayed their progress long enough for me to arrive on the scene."

"I tripped on my hem and tore it. Mr. Bradford was not pleased, but there was nothing that he could do but allow me to pin it up," said Miss Mays. She looked anxiously at Lucinda. "I did not wish to go with him, but he was so very insistent. He . . . he said that the moonlight was very pretty in the gardens, and he had such a hold on my arm! And he looked at me in such a way. I do not like him in the least."

"Nor do I, Agnes. Will either of you find it disagreeable c me to wish to return home early?" asked Lucinda.

"Oh, no!" said Miss Mays hopefully.

Miss Blythe chuckled. "I believe we have all had our fill c Lady Bishop's hospitality this evening."

"Or any other evening, I suspect," said Lucinda, rising. Sh led the way over to their hostess and made their excuses.

Lady Bishop was rather miffed that the ladies of May House were leaving, but she had no choice but to accept the excuses. "I shall wait upon you in the not too distant futur Lady Mays," she said. "And certainly there will be othe evenings, as well."

Lucinda expressed her pleasure, mentally making a not that she and her companions would place any invitation from Lady Bishop at the bottom of the stack.

The following Wednesday evening, Lucinda and Mis Blythe accompanied Miss Mays to Almack's. Miss Mays wa agog with nervous pleasure. She knew very well that enterin the portals of the august club was restricted to those who er joyed the sponsorship of one of the patronesses. She had al ways dreamed of making her bows at Almack's, and so sh felt far less trepidation than she did over most of their othe outings.

The evening was a resounding success. Miss Mays cam back to Mays House in a happy daze. Lucinda told Mis Blythe that it was just as Lady Sefton had said it would be The sedate pace of Almack's had been just right for Mis Mays.

"Perhaps now Agnes will begin to gain a bit more confi dence," said Lucinda.

Miss Blythe nodded, though her expression was thoughtfu "I do hope so."

Miss Mays did not really enjoy the many gatherings and en tertainments. She was too timid to ever like large crowds. Sh found herself yearning for the rare times when she and Mis Blythe walked sedately in the park. It was so very nice to b out of doors and away from all that frightened and confuse her.

However, Miss Mays knew that she should not repine. Lad

Mays was kindness itself, and her ladyship had provided all that Miss Mays could ever ask or require. It was little enough that Lady Mays expected of her in return, after all. She had only to smile and bestow her hand and enjoy herself. Miss Mays wondered why she felt so low.

Scarce was the evening that found the ladies of Mays House sitting at home. Of late they had been able to put off their heavy cloaks and drape shawls over their shoulders when they stepped out. The chill of winter had slowly given way to the soft air of spring, just as Mr. Weatherby had predicted that it would.

Lucinda wondered from time to time why she did not see that gentleman as often as previously. It was as though he had decided to avoid her. She mentioned something of the sort to Miss Blythe. "It is strange that Mr. Weatherby has not called on us lately, don't you think? I quite thought that I could count on him as one of my faithful admirers!"

"Is it strange, my dear? He is somewhat older, after all. I do not think that a gentleman of such worldly experience can be held long by a lady as youthful as yourself," said Miss Blythe, rather dauntingly.

Lucinda was almost vexed with her. "Oh, was Mr. Weatherby never on your list, Tibby? I quite thought he must meet some of your requirements."

"Not in the least. Mr. Weatherby is completely unsuitable," said Miss Blythe. "However, I have noticed that Lord Pembroke is becoming rather pointed in his attentions. Wherever we go, his lordship at once seeks you out to solicit a dance or to take you into dinner. He was somewhat taken aback at the dinner party last night, I thought, when Lord Mays claimed the right of a cousin to escort you. Are you still on terms with the countess?"

"In point of fact, I am," said Lucinda, almost defensively. "Her ladyship is very kind whenever I chance to meet her."

Miss Blythe shook her head. "A pity," she observed. "I should have liked to see you become a countess."

"You are nonsensical today, Tibby!" said Lucinda.

The conversation had taken place in the drawing room. Miss Blythe was embroidering as usual, and Lucinda was at-

tempting to knot a silver reticule according to the directions on
the settee beside her. She was on the point of giving up and
held up her efforts. "Only look at this wretched tangle! I have
made a rare mess of it, have I not?"

Miss Blythe glanced over and agreed to it. "Perhaps you
should call in Agnes. She knotted a very pretty reticule just
last week."

"Yes, I know," said Lucinda despondently. "I so admired it
that I thought that I would do one for myself."

Miss Blythe chuckled.

A moment later, Lucinda's face cleared as she laughed at
herself. "Speaking of Agnes, where is she this afternoon? I
have not seen her since we returned from Mrs. Conagher's al-
fresco luncheon."

"I heard her in the music room earlier," said Miss Blythe.
She paused in her embroidery. "I am worried about her, Lucinda. She is not happy with us."

"Is she not? I quite thought that she was adjusting very
well," said Lucinda, surprised. "Why, she has not broken
down into floods of tears since I put Ferdie out of the house. I
understand that he has taken a repairing lease, by the way."

"Not with Sir Thomas and Lady Stassart, I hope?" asked
Miss Blythe, instantly concerned.

Lucinda shook her head. "I do not believe so, for Mama has
not mentioned him in her letters to me. It is a relief to me, of
course. I was so very harsh with him, Tibby! I gave him nothing but the fare for a hackney, which I borrowed from Church!
Ferdie was highly insulted, I assure you. But I suppose that it
gave him such a disgust of me and all the rest of the family
that he has found someone else to batten off. No doubt it is
someone with whom he can riffle the cards."

"Mr. Stassart does not seem to derive enjoyment from much
of anything else," agreed Miss Blythe.

The butler came in to give Lady Mays a visitor's card. Lucinda was surprised when she read it, and she wished very
much that she had given orders that she was not in. However,
she was a fair person, and she resigned herself to the inevitable. In any event, the gentleman was a persistent individ-

ual, as she had good cause to know, and he would merely keep
returning until he had achieved his purpose.

"Pray show his lordship in, Church," she said quietly.

The butler bowed and exited.

Miss Blythe was sensitive to the nuances of her former
pupil's voice. She looked speculatively over the rim of her
spectacles. "What is it, Lucinda? You seem somewhat perturbed at the prospect of seeing this caller."

"It is Lord Potherby. His estate borders Carbarry, and he
was a frequent visitor while I was there," said Lucinda with a
notable lack of enthusiasm.

"Is Lord Potherby an impudent, importuning fellow? Shall I
send him to the rightabout?" asked Miss Blythe, at once assuming the worst.

Lucinda laughed, shaking her head at the very thought of
Lord Potherby behaving with anything but the most correct of
manners. "Oh, no, his lordship is not that sort at all. Rather, he
has been a most persistent and unencouraged admirer."

She hesitated, wondering if it was wise to put Miss Blythe
into the whole picture. There was always the possibility that
her matchmaking companion would see her parents' approval
of Lord Potherby as license to encourage the gentleman in his
suit.

Lucinda shrugged, for in the end it would scarcely matter.
She would not be swayed any more by Miss Blythe than she
had been by her parents. Never again would she enter a relationship that was not entirely of her own will. "Lord Potherby
enjoys my parents' favor. They have a strong fondness for his
lordship."

"Indeed!" said Miss Blythe, her interest now thoroughly
aroused.

Lord Potherby was ushered into the drawing room. As he
greeted Lucinda, Miss Blythe studied him curiously. Lord
Potherby appeared to be about thirty years of age. He was im-
maculately attired in riding coat, breeches, and topboots, so
obviously he had ridden to Mays House. He was of middle
height, well built but tending to a slight thickening round the
middle. His most prominent feature was a leonine head of

thick auburn hair. Miss Blythe thought that he had the look of a prosperous squire.

Lucinda had risen to extend her slim hand to her unexpected visitor. "Lord Potherby, this is a surprise. I had no notion that you were in London."

Lord Potherby bowed with punctilious care over her fingers, releasing them after a slight press. "I am not at all astonished to hear you say so, my lady. I had no notion myself that I would be coming up to town until two days ago." He laughed heartily in recalling his own astonishment at such an extraordinary deviation of character.

"I do not believe that you have met my companion, Miss Tibby Blythe," said Lucinda.

Lord Potherby bowed to Miss Blythe. They exchanged polite greetings. Miss Blythe would have risen to offer her hand, but his lordship waved her back. "No, no, pray do not stir yourself, ma'am. It is a pleasure to see a lady working her embroideries. I would not for the world disturb your efforts."

Miss Blythe smiled and graciously acknowledged his lordship's consideration. "It is a comfortable habit, my lord."

"Won't you be seated, Lord Potherby?" Lucinda suggested. She sat down herself, knowing that his lordship would not take a chair while there was a lady still standing.

Lord Potherby bowed and made himself comfortable in a wing chair. He crossed one leg over the other. Looking about critically, he said, "This is a comfortable room, though a bit rich for my taste. I suppose Lord Mays had the decorating of it?"

"Yes, Lord Mays was a great collector, as you know. He enjoyed having his possessions on display," said Lucinda. She gestured at the tea service. "May I offer you refreshment, my lord? We had the tea brought in just a few moments ago, so it should not have grown tepid."

"Don't mind if I do," said Lord Potherby, already eyeing the biscuits and heavy plum cake on the serving plate beside the tea service.

As Lucinda poured the tea, she asked his lordship how much sugar he took with it. Lord Potherby ponderously teased her for not recalling just how he liked his tea. "We have been such good friends that I am quite put out that you have forgotten. I had hoped to have made a rather deeper impression upon you, my lady."

At Lord Potherby's heavy-handed gallantry, Miss Blythe glanced quickly at Lucinda's face. His lordship's manner bespoke some familiarity, and after Lucinda's rather tepid description of Lord Potherby, Miss Blythe thought that she might be offended by the gentleman. However, there seemed nothing untoward in Lucinda's pleasant expression. Indeed, there was a smile in her eyes as though she were laughing at a private joke. Miss Blythe wondered then whether Lucinda was as indifferent toward Lord Potherby as she had indicated.

Lucinda handed his lordship's teacup and saucer to him, saying, "Why, as to that I am certain that we are such good neighbors that you will not take it amiss if I seem careless toward you, my lord! Pray try some of the plum cake. It is quite one of my cook's best efforts."

"Thank you, Lady Mays. You are gracious, indeed. It looks quite delicious," said Lord Potherby, happily commandeering a large piece. He was a man of a few simple passions, and one was a true appreciation for culinary excellencies.

Lucinda launched into a gentle discourse on various topics calculated to entertain a gentleman caller. Lord Potherby responded with flattering attention. At the end of ten minutes, when the plum cake had had significant inroads made into it and Lucinda had twice refilled Lord Potherby's teacup, she said, "Now tell me, Lord Potherby, how you come to be in town. I am quite curious, for when you last visited me at Carbarry, I seem to recall that you were quite excited by a new irrigation project on your lands."

"Indeed I was! And the irrigation is going extremely well. You are gracious to inquire, my lady. I am very pleased with the progress that is already being made," said Lord Potherby, beaming. "There is much more to be accomplished, however, if I am to turn a profit this first year."

Lucinda lightly folded her hands in her lap. "Then how could you have possibly torn yourself away, my lord?"

Miss Blythe bent her head to her embroidery, trying not to smile. Her former pupil's attitude was determinedly polite, even friendly, but Miss Blythe could read the signs well enough. Lucinda was on the fidget. She had always had that trick of intertwining her fingers when she could not keep her hands still.

"It is all due to my undying admiration of you, my lady," said Lord Potherby, bowing from the waist.

"Indeed. How flattering, my lord."

# Chapter Twenty-five

Miss Blythe looked up quickly, hearing the cooling note in Lucinda's voice.

Lord Potherby was immune to any suspicion that he might be treading on thin ice. "Nothing else could have enticed me away at just this particular juncture, but when I received your mother's kind letter, and she mentioned how much you were enjoying the Season, I felt that I had to take a jaunt to town myself. I wished to assure myself of your continued well-being, my lady, as well as to reiterate to you the depth of my devotion."

Lucinda gave a laugh. She shook her head, smiling. Gently, she chided her admirer. "Come, Lord Potherby! Well I know that the conversation of a mere female cannot possibly hold a candle to the fascination inherent in rivets and pipes! You shall surely admit to me in a moment that you are in London to inspect examples of just those things."

Lord Potherby appeared somewhat abashed. He cleared his throat. "Quite so. You know me too well, my lady." He recovered his aplomb. "However, while it is true that I have an eye on certain innovative examples, my main object in coming just at this time was to assure you of my continued admiration. I would not wish you to forget me in the frolics offered by society."

"I doubt that would be possible, my lord," said Lucinda on a tiny sigh.

Notable needlewoman that she was, Miss Blythe was so startled that she stuck her needle in her finger. She had never thought to hear her former pupil speak with such a note in her voice. It must inevitably give offense.

But Lord Potherby positively beamed at Lady Mays. He had detected nothing of the irony in her ladyship's words, but instead took them as a compliment to himself. "That is prettily said, my lady! Indeed it is. It quite raises my hopes."

Lucinda's expression registered dismay. Fortunately for her, she was saved from having to make a suitable reply when the drawing room door opened and her sister-in-law entered.

Upon seeing that Lucinda and Miss Blythe were not alone, Miss Mays hesitated to enter. "I am sorry. I did not realize . . ."

Lucinda rose, saying with relief, "Agnes, pray come in! Here is someone that I should like you to meet. Lord Potherby, this is my sister-in-law, Miss Agnes Mays. She has been staying with me these past several weeks."

Lord Potherby had immediately risen to his feet upon the advent of the lady. He smiled at her and took the hand that she held out toward him. He made a very correct bow. "Miss Mays, it is a pleasure."

"Thank you, my lord. I assure you that the sentiment is mutual," said Miss Mays with only the hint of a nervous stammer.

Lord Potherby looked at her curiously. "It is odd that I do not recall your name, for I was acquainted with your brother, Mays."

Miss Mays flushed to the roots of her hair. "My brother and I did not get along, my lord," she said in a low voice, averting her face.

Lord Potherby glanced swiftly at Lady Mays. He was dismayed that he had somehow stepped over the line and put Miss Mays out of countenance.

Lucinda quietly explained, "Agnes resided with her parents, nursing them through their last illnesses for years, and then was with an elderly aunt who lived somewhere in the country. She saw very little of her brother, for she was not a part of the social round that he frequented."

"I see. You are to be commended, Miss Mays. I doubt that there are few young ladies who would have sacrificed themselves so selflessly," said Lord Potherby.

Miss Mays's gaze rose swiftly to meet his lordship's. Her color was again heightened, but this time not from mortification. She offered a shy smile. "You are kind to say so, Lord Potherby."

Lucinda resumed her chair. "We were just taking tea, Agnes. Would you like a cup?"

"Oh, no, thank you, Lady Mays. I am perfectly fine. I came in only to discover whether we were engaged later today, for I had wanted to walk in the park. It is quite sunny and warm this afternoon," said Miss Mays. She glanced, puzzled, at Lord Potherby. He was still standing before her. She did not realize that Lord Potherby was politely waiting for her to take a seat before he, also, sat down.

"My dear, why do you not sit here beside me? I would be grateful for your help with these tangled yarns. We may then comfortably discuss this excursion to the park," said Miss Blythe.

Miss Mays's face lit up. "Oh, do you think that we can, Miss Blythe? I would like it above all things." She moved to the settee and perched beside Miss Blythe, picking up the tangled yarns.

Lord Potherby was at last free to sit back down. "Do you like to walk, Miss Mays?" he inquired politely.

"Oh, yes! I quite like to be out of doors, and it scarcely matters what the weather. But Lady Mays and Miss Blythe will not go out when it is raining or the least bit chilly, so I must wait for a clear day if I am to have their company," said Miss Mays.

"I, too, enjoy a vigorous tramp out of doors," said Lord Potherby. "I am made restive if I am inside too long, for I am always wondering what is happening in my fields or with my stock."

"Lord Potherby is a noted expert in the newest agricultural methods, Agnes. He has just been telling Tibby and me that

his latest irrigation project is shaping up to be a success," said
Lucinda.

"Oh, how wonderful for you! You must be very pleased, my
lord," said Miss Mays, glad for him.

"Indeed I am. I shall be happier still when the crops are in
the ground and I may turn my attention to my sheep. We will
be coming into lambing season soon," said Lord Potherby. "It
is an anxious time, for we sometimes lose the greater portion
of the lambs. I do not understand it, nor does anyone else. The
ewes often throw too early. Sometimes the ewes die, leaving
their offspring. But we shall do what we can and hope for the
best, as always."

"I do hope that you shall not lose a single dear little lamb
this time, my lord. How very distressing for you, to be sure! I
adore animals of all kinds, and so I can readily enter into your
feelings. One's heart must be wrung with compassion for the
dear creatures," said Miss Mays. "Do you attempt to place the
orphans with the ewes that lost their young?"

Lucinda listened to her sister-in-law with astonishment. She
had never heard Miss Mays participate in a conversation with
anyone with such animation. She looked toward Miss Blythe
and that lady raised her brows to indicate her own surprise.

Lord Potherby leaned forward, intent upon Miss Mays's in-
telligent question. "Now there you have it in a nutshell, Miss
Mays. We have tried any number of times to save the orphans
by placing them with ewes whose own lambs were stillborn.
But invariably the ewes reject the orphans."

"Perhaps it is the way the orphans smell. I have noticed that
each animal has its own peculiar odor to its coat. If there was
some way to persuade the ewe that she was smelling her own
baby . . ." Miss Mays faltered as she realized that all three of
her companions were staring at her. The color rose in her face
again. "I . . . I am sorry. I did not realize. I am rambling on so
foolishly."

"Not at all! Not at all!" exclaimed Lord Potherby. "You
have made quite a sensible observation, ma'am. I wonder that
I did not think of it myself. I most assuredly must turn this
over in my mind, Miss Mays, for I feel certain that you have
hit upon the key to the thing."

Miss Mays uttered a gratified but incoherent acknowledgement of his lordship's condescension. Fortunately for the saving of her countenance, more callers were announced and all attention was diverted from herself.

Lucinda rose to greet her new callers with some relief. For some minutes she had felt that she had strayed into some strange land, where she and Miss Blythe had somehow become totally inadequate in their conversational skills.

"Lord Pembroke! Lord and Lady Thorpe. How happy I am to see you all," said Lucinda. She shook hands, and even before she had finished making her greetings, two other gentlemen were shown in. "Lord Levine and Mr. Pepperidge. It is gracious of you both to call. I must make known to you all my friend, Lord Potherby, who has come up to visit."

Lucinda had not said so, but the implication was that Lord Potherby had come up to London to visit her. Lord Levine and Mr. Pepperidge therefore acknowledged his lordship with cold stares and the barest of bows. They made it their business to monopolize their hostess so that this Potherby fellow would see that Lady Mays did not need any other admirers coming around her.

Miss Blythe did not approve of the gentlemen's possessive manners, and she determinedly inserted herself into the conversation. She knew her duty well enough, she hoped, not to allow a couple of coxcombs to run roughshod over her dear Lucinda.

Lord Pembroke took in the situation with an amused glance. The two dandies resembled nothing so much as two small dogs tussling over a hearty bone, he thought. He was disinclined to put himself to the trouble of competing for Lady Mays's favor when it would make him look just as ridiculous, and so he applied himself to entertaining the unremarkable Miss Mays. He had a shrewd notion that he would thus earn Lady Mays's smiles and at the moment that was a pleasant objective.

Lord Pembroke was too conversant with social niceties to ignore the other people in the room, and he put forth several polite observations to the Thorpes and to Lord Potherby, as well. But he flattered Miss Mays with his attention.

However, Miss Mays did not appear at all gratified. She was reduced to blushing confusion within minutes, and it fell to Lady Thorpe to counter Lord Pembroke's quick repartee.

Lord Thorpe got into the spirit of the thing, and the three quickly formed into a merry trio.

Lord Potherby had been struck with a slight jealousy. It was obvious that Lord Levine and Mr. Pepperidge were on the most civil terms with Lady Mays. However, after a very few minutes he concluded that her ladyship could not possibly prefer those gentlemen's posturing over his own straightforward admiration, and he was able to rest a little easier.

He enjoyed the light banter between the Thorpes and Lord Pembroke, though he did not always catch the point of everything that was said. However, that was certainly to be expected since he was not familiar with half of the personages to whom they referred.

Lord Potherby noticed that Miss Mays, also, did not seem to follow the roaming conversation very well. "Miss Mays, do you find all this talk as confusing as I do?" he asked with a friendly smile. He was amazed at the expression of gratitude and relief in her soft brown eyes.

"I fear that I do, my lord. I am not at all quick, you see," she confessed.

"For my part, I prefer a female who is sensible to one whose tongue runs on fiddlesticks," said Lord Potherby, his gaze resting for a moment on the trio opposite.

Miss Mays glanced quickly at the vivacious Lady Thorpe, and she actually giggled. "Oh, but Lady Thorpe is extremely kind," she assured his lordship earnestly. "You have no notion how many times she has helped me out of a hideous moment at some function or other. She simply says something in that laughing way that she has, and whomever it was that put me out of countenance is perfectly satisfied. Then I may be comfortable again."

"Do you not care for London?" asked Lord Potherby, surprised. He had assumed that since she was a Mays that she would naturally gravitate toward the same sort of life that he had known that her brother had led. Perhaps even more so, since she had spent much of her youth caring for others.

Miss Mays shook her head, a despondency at once apparent in the slight sag of her thin shoulders. "I am afraid not. It is a terrible lack in me, for I practically begged dear Lady Mays to let me come to her so that I could experience what living in London was like. I am such a sad trial to her ladyship and Miss Blythe. You can have no notion."

Lord Potherby was astonished. "Are you hinting that Lady Mays and her companion have treated you with less than respect? I would find that very difficult to believe of her ladyship, at least."

"Oh, no!" Miss Mays was dismayed that he should place such a construction on her words. "Lady Mays and Miss Blythe have been very kind to me. You can have no notion. Why, I have a whole wardrobe of lovely gowns and drawers and drawers of gloves and lace handkerchiefs and . . . and everything that I could ever possibly need. I am taken to the best parties, and I stand up at nearly every dance. I have even been admitted to Almack's! But I have no conversation, and I am not in the least clever and I never understand what is said around me. It . . . it is so very lowering!"

The words had almost poured out of her. Miss Mays was aghast at herself to have confided so much to a perfect stranger and a gentleman at that! She flushed hotly. "Pray forgive me! I never meant to . . . that is, sometimes when I do not think beforehand, my tongue rattles away and I never know what I am going to say!"

Lord Potherby gathered her agitated hands between his wide palms. "My dear Miss Mays, I am honored at your confidence. Pray do not be embarrassed, for I have found nothing at all of the least offense in anything that you have told me. On the contrary! I thought you to be a sensible young woman when I met you. That impression has but strengthened. Pray consider me to be a friend, for I shall not betray any confidence that you may honor me with, now or in the future."

Miss Mays was reduced to blushing pleasure. "Oh, my lord! You are too kind."

At Lord Potherby's modest disclaimer, she shook her head quickly. "Oh, but indeed you are! Quite the nicest gentleman that I have up to now met. I do hope that you make a long visit to London."

Lord Potherby looked into the hopeful brown eyes that were

lifted to him and something inside him ignited. "I had not planned to do so. The lambing, you know," he said slowly.

Miss Mays averted her face, nodding. "I understand, of course. One must never neglect one's duty."

"There is so much at stake," said Lord Potherby, arguing with himself.

"Oh, yes, the little lambs cannot be let to die," said Miss Mays, looking up with a brave smile.

Lord Potherby looked down, unable to meet that valiant gaze, and he discovered that he still held both Miss Mays's hands. He was holding them rather tightly, too, for her fingers had whitened in his grip. He was covered with confusion and at once released her. "Forgive me! I have hurt you. I do not know what came over me."

"It is of no consequence," said Miss Mays. "I did not perfectly notice."

They regarded one another fixedly for a second, before Miss Mays again averted her face and took an inordinate interest in the pleating of her dainty muslin skirt.

Lord Potherby was on the point of speaking to her again when he was addressed by Lady Mays. His lordship looked up, startled, to discover that he was the last visitor remaining. He started up at once. "Lady Mays! I apologize, for I have outstayed my welcome to an outrageous degree."

"Not at all, my lord," said Lucinda cordially. She glanced from Lord Potherby to her sister-in-law. "I am glad that Agnes was able to entertain you to such good effect, for I fear that I was unable to bear my part in doing so! But my friends and admirers have all taken their leave, and now I may extend a proper invitation. I have consulted with Miss Blythe and we are agreed that we have no dinner engagement tonight. If you are not otherwise engaged, my lord, will you come to dine with us and perhaps afterward escort us to the theater?"

Lord Potherby bowed deeply. "I shall be most honored, Lady Mays. I shall repair to my lodgings at once and come back when I have returned my hired hack to stable. I drove up to town in my own curricle, of course, but that will not be appropriate for this evening."

"We have a suitable carriage, my lord, so there will be no

need for you to make other arrangements," said Lucinda. She held out her hand to his lordship. "I am glad that you have come today, my lord."

Lord Potherby bowed over her fingers. As he straightened, he said, "As am I, my lady." He politely took his leave of the other two ladies and exited.

"I must go upstairs and see what my maid has set out for me to wear this evening," said Miss Mays, rising from the settee. There was a dash of color in her face, and her eyes held a bit of sparkle.

"Of course, Agnes," said Lucinda, nodding. She waited until Miss Mays had hurried from the drawing room before turning to Miss Blythe. Raising her slender brows, she said, "Well, what do you think?"

"It would do very well," said Miss Blythe decisively.

"Are you going up straightaway to revise your list of eligibles, then?" asked Lucinda with a wry smile.

"You must see the necessity, my dear," said Miss Blythe with a chuckle. "Lord Potherby is the only gentleman that she does not appear to fear."

"Yes, I was amazed at how well they seemed to deal. Well, I have set the stage, Tibby. Lord Potherby will be sitting in our pockets all the evening. Let us do our best for Agnes, for he would make her an excellent husband."

Miss Blythe agreed. "He would take her away from London and everything that frightens her. Is he well situated, Lucinda?"

"Lord Potherby has a very snug manor house, and his lands are extensive. Agnes will be able to walk about to her heart's content, inspecting crops and irrigation systems and tending to infant lambs," said Lucinda. She shook her head. "It would not do for me, but I am a very different sort."

"I would find it a dull life, too, I fear. However, it will do very well for Agnes. She will adore it," said Miss Blythe. "I suppose that we should also go upstairs and ready ourselves. I suspect that Agnes will be back down betweentimes for fear of keeping his lordship waiting."

Lucinda walked with Miss Blythe toward the door. "I only hope that we are able to bring him up to scratch, Tibby."

"Why, my dear! I never thought that you would enter so wholeheartedly into matchmaking. After all, you have such an aversion to it!" said Miss Blythe blandly.

"It is a personal aversion only," said Lucinda, laughing.

They were ascending the stairs by then. Lucinda trailed her fingers casually along the banister. "It occurs to me that we will have unequal numbers at dinner. Perhaps I should also invite Lord Mays and another gentleman."

Miss Blythe paused at the top of the stairs. "You shall do just as you think best, my dear. However, I do feel that it will appear less obvious if there are a couple of other gentlemen at table."

Lucinda smiled. "I shall do just that, then! I shouldn't wish to put anything in the way of Agnes's chances."

Miss Blythe agreed to it, and the ladies went their separate ways.

## Chapter Twenty-six

The dinner party and theater outing was an unqualified success. Lord Mays chanced to be free that evening, and so was another gentleman of whom Miss Blythe had previously expressed her approval.

Lucinda's original thought had been to invite Mr. Weatherby to even the numbers, but in the end she decided against it. Mr. Weatherby had not called in some time, and these days whenever the ladies chanced to meet him in society, he lingered only long enough to exchange pleasantries. It was a pity, for Lucinda had liked the gentleman very much, and she had thought that her former governess had seemed to enjoy his tales of exotic places.

At the last minute Lucinda had the happy thought of sending an urgent summons to Lady Thorpe, expressing a desire

for her ladyship's assistance in promoting a match for Miss
Mays. Just as she had known it would, her message had the effect of bringing Lord and Lady Thorpe to her door.

As Lucinda greeted Lady Thorpe, that lady whispered, "I
could not resist! Gerald was rather bewildered when I suddenly changed our plans, so you must think of something to
reconcile him to not attending a masquerade."

"A masquerade! But is that not rather fast of you, Cecily?"
asked Lucinda teasingly.

Lady Thorpe twinkled up at her. "Oh yes, but it doesn't
matter if you go with one's own husband. *That* makes it very
dull and respectable!"

Lucinda laughed. "I am certain that it does! Wilfred is here,
you know."

Lord Thorpe, who had been busy handing his gloves and hat
to an attentive footman, came over in time to overhear Lucinda and his face lit up. "Just the fellow I wished to see. I
wanted to thank him for steering me to that hunter." His lordship strolled happily into the drawing room, already quite contented at the sudden turn in his evening. Lucinda and Lady
Thorpe followed, chatting amiably.

All the rest of the guests had already arrived, and dinner
was shortly served.

Since it was such an informal party where everyone else
knew each other, Lord Potherby was without doubt the honored guest. His lordship was naturally seated beside his hostess, with Miss Mays on his other side. Past Miss Mays were
seated Lord and Lady Thorpe. On Lucinda's far side was Lord
Mays, and beyond him, Miss Blythe and an Admiral Carter. It
was a sociable group, and the time passed quickly with light
conversation and an excellent repast.

Lucinda was reminded by Church of the hour, and surprise
was expressed when she announced that it was near time to
leave for the theater. There was a flurry to gather together
shawls and other such things. Then the party embarked in two
carriages for the theater.

The offering that evening was a comedy. Nothing could
have better guaranteed the complete conviviality of the gathering. When the curtain dropped for intermission, Lord Thorpe

exclaimed, "I am deuced glad that we did not go to the masquerade!"

"Yes, it has been a delightful evening," agreed Lady Thorpe. She glanced at her hostess, her eyes brimful of mischief. "I daresay we have all thoroughly enjoyed your hospitality, Lucinda." She gave the faintest of nods toward Lord Potherby and Miss Mays, who were in earnest conversation. There was a glow about Miss Mays's countenance that was unmistakable.

Lord Mays did not miss the significance of that gesture. He looked with curiosity at Lord Potherby and his cousin. Then he glanced at Lucinda. She was smiling and exchanging pleasantries with the admiral and Miss Blythe, but her eyes lifted suddenly as though she had felt his gaze. Inexplicably, a faint color came into her cheeks. Lord Mays grinned and turned to Lord Thorpe, remarking, "I much prefer these roistering fellows over the tragic figures that the ladies seem to like."

"By Jove, so do I," agreed Lord Thorpe.

The door of the box opened, and the first of a stream of visitors entered. Lucinda greeted them all civilly, even her cousin, Mr. Stassart. He was no longer wearing the sling, she noticed. As she gave her hand to him, she said, "Well, Ferdie. You appear in much better trim than when I saw you last. And you are returned to London! I had heard that you were on a repairing lease. How is that you have returned?"

Ferdie waved an airy hand. "Why, as to that, I enjoyed a rather good streak at the races, which persuaded me that my luck was in. You behold me plump in the pocket, dear cousin, and firmly established on my way to amassing a fortune."

"I am glad to hear it," said Lucinda quietly, though inside she wished that her cousin would waken from his delusions. She knew that he would merely repeat the same cycle over and over. It was a pity, in a way, for even though she did not much like her cousin, she yet cared what became of him. However, there was nothing that she could do for him but to continue to keep him in her nightly prayers.

"I know that you are acquainted with everyone else, Ferdie, but I fancy you have not yet had the opportunity to meet a friend of mine who has recently come up to London for a visit." She introduced her cousin to Lord Potherby, and the gentlemen exchanged greetings.

There was an instant antagonism between Mr. Stassart and Lord Potherby, each recognizing in the other the qualities that he most disliked.

Ferdie saw a complaisant worthiness of the sort that had always made him grit his teeth. His father was just such a one and had always sat in critical judgement of him. He assumed that Lord Potherby was already staring at him in an overbearing way.

Lord Potherby sensed a carelessness, a selfishness, about Mr. Stassart that disallowed the claims of either duty or honor. He was convinced of it as he observed in what manner Stassart pressed his acquaintance with Miss Mays. The lady was obviously uncomfortable around the raffishly handsome gentleman, and she was completely unequal to turning aside of Stassart's fulsome gallantries and his sly glances.

Lord Potherby's protective instincts rose with startling force. His color became heightened with anger. This harassing flirtation was no way in which to treat a lady. He interceded a time or two on Miss Mays's behalf, which earned him grateful looks.

Stassart's eye was caught by a lady across the way and he bowed to her, before blowing her a flourishing kiss.

Observing this, and taking note of the sort of female that Stassart was giving his attention, Lord Potherby concluded that the dandified gentleman was a regular bounder who should not be allowed anywhere near a decent woman. He was shocked that Lady Mays tolerated the fellow.

Lord Potherby's opinion was reinforced when he overheard Lord Mays's murmured exclamation. "Why, Stassart just got the nod from the widow Marie Clare. He's leaving now to go to her. What would she want with him? Everyone knows that she is a high flyer."

"Didn't you hear? Stassart is rolling in blunt just now. And he does have a hand with the ladies," responded Lord Thorpe, yawning behind his hand. He had slumped in his seat and was waiting for the curtain to be raised again. This business in the box had always been a bit tedious to him.

"Oh, don't I know it! I once caught him making up to Agnes," said Lord Mays.

Lord Thorpe sat up sharply. "No! That innocent? Well, I hope that you drew his cork for him."

"I didn't," said Lord Mays regretfully. "But I think that I very nearly broke his jaw."

Lord Potherby was denied more of what he found to be a fascinating conversation. The curtain was raised, the last of the visitors left the box, and the second half of the comedy played on. However, Lord Potherby did not find it quite as amusing as he had earlier.

A small hand was laid on his sleeve, and Miss Mays's anxious voice inquired, "Are you not enjoying the production, my lord?"

Lord Potherby shook himself free of his reflections, and he covered her hand in his. "I shall enjoy it as long as I have you to share it with me, Miss Mays."

Miss Mays blushed. She knew that she should not allow Lord Potherby to continue holding her hand, but it felt so reassuring. She stole a glance at his lordship's manly profile and sighed happily.

After the comedy, Lucinda's party returned to Mays House for coffee. It was a brief interlude due to the time, and the gathering broke up within an hour. After her guests where gone, Lucinda turned to her sister-in-law and said cheerfully, "I must say, Agnes, I don't believe that I have ever seen you display to better effect. Have you, Tibby?"

"No, indeed," said Miss Blythe, also smiling.

"Oh, it was positively the best evening of my entire life," said Miss Mays, and she drifted up to bed.

Lucinda and Miss Blythe exchanged an expressive glance.

"Let us hope that Lord Potherby felt the same way," said Lucinda.

"All we can do is wait and see," said Miss Blythe. "I think it would be a very good notion to include Lord Potherby in as many of our amusements as we can during his stay in London."

"Oh, definitely," agreed Lucinda. "In the morning I shall write to all the hostesses whose invitations we have accepted and request their permission to introduce Lord Potherby into their gatherings."

"Very good, my dear," approved Miss Blythe. "We shall

give Lord Potherby every opportunity and hope for a happy conclusion before many weeks have passed."

"I hope to bring him up to scratch before that, Tibby, or otherwise the fish will have jumped off the hook," said Lucinda, mixing her metaphors.

When her companion looked at her inquiringly, she reminded, "Do not forget the dear little lambs."

"Oh, dear," said Miss Blythe blankly.

A week later when Lord Mays came to call on Lucinda, his expression was such that she knew at once that there was something of import that he wanted to share with her. Her heart lurched, for he appeared so somber that she thought some terrible thing had taken place.

As soon as the amenities were gotten past, she asked anxiously, "What is it, Wilfred? Is there something wrong?"

"I am not sure. That is why I came at once to you, Lucinda." Lord Mays took her hands. His expression very somber, he said, "Lucinda, Lord Potherby came to see me this morning. I recalled that I had met him here at Mays House, and I saw him at once. You may imagine my shock when he told me that he had come to me because I am head of the Mays family. It was deuced odd to think of myself in those terms, let me tell you! But that is neither here nor there. Lucinda, he informed me that he has admired you for quite some time and had hoped to come to figure in your affections. His lordship was very open, very frank. He—"

"For heaven's sake, Wilfred, are you trying to tell me that Lord Potherby has made an offer for me?" exclaimed Lucinda. "Why, I have been expecting him to do so anytime these past several months."

"Not for you, no."

Lord Mays regarded her with some worry. "I hope that it is not a great disappointment to you, Lucinda, but his lordship has not offered for you at all. He has offered for my cousin, Agnes!"

"For Agnes?" said Lucinda. At his concerned expression she felt a rising irresistible urge to giggle.

Lord Mays patted her hands. "I see that it is a disappointment to you, Lucinda. His lordship thought it might be a shock since he has made no secret of his admiration for you. Believe me, there was never anything more abject than Potherby's face when he admitted to his frivolous change of allegiance. But he is staunch in his assertion that his feelings for Agnes are too strong to set aside. He assures me that he has well-grounded suspicions that she harbors the same feelings for him. I am sorry, my dear, but you have lost Lord Potherby to Agnes."

Lucinda's chest felt on the point of bursting. A laugh tore from her, then another. She laughed in earnest then. "Lost Lord Potherby! And to Agnes! Oh, how rich that is!"

Lord Mays regarded her in dismay and alarm, mistaking the throes of her laughter for strong hysterics. "Lucinda! You are beside yourself." He seized hold of her arms and shook her urgently. "Lucinda, you must not! Listen to me! Potherby is not worth this, pray believe me!"

Lucinda put both her hands up against his chest to brace herself. She shook her head, still laughing. "Oh, Wilfred! You misunderstand, truly you do! Oh, was there anything better! I must tell Tibby! We have snared Agnes her prince!"

She began to extricate herself from Lord Mays's slackened grasp, but his hands tightened on her. She looked up in surprise.

"Then you do not mind? About Potherby and Agnes, I mean?" he asked.

"Of course not! I have been holding Lord Potherby off for months. It is one reason that I came back to London. I had hoped that a few months's absence would allow him time to realize that we would not at all suit," said Lucinda. A crease was beginning to form between her brows. "Wilfred! You did not actually think that I would ever seriously entertain a suit from Lord Potherby!"

Lord Mays slowly released her. There was a gathering sheepishness about his expression. "He did seem to be an unlikely candidate for you. But then when he kept assuring me how bad he felt about turning coat so suddenly and how he knew that you had always relied upon his friendship, I began to wonder."

"It is true that Lord Potherby has always been a good and reliable neighbor. It is also true that he has been a faithful admirer, and one, moreover, who enjoyed the favor of my parents. However, I never thought for one instant of becoming his wife," said Lucinda. She balled her fist and lightly hit Lord Mays. "Really, Wilfred! I thought you knew me better!"

"Then it is all right that I gave Potherby my permission to solicit Agnes's hand," said Lord Mays, relieved.

"What an idiot you are, Wilfred," said Lucinda fondly and without the least offense meant. "Of course it is all right. Tibby and I have both wondered whether Lord Potherby might not suit Agnes. Only see how right we were! Oh, I must go up to tell Tibby! She will be delighted."

Lord Mays caught her wrist when she would have hastened away, and he gently pulled her back toward him. "I would like you to tell her something for me, also."

Lucinda looked at him, puzzled. "What is that, Wilfred?"

"This!" Lord Mays hauled her into his arms and passionately kissed her. For several long moments he thoroughly demonstrated his expertise. When at last he raised his head, his gold-brown eyes were blazing, and there was the suggestion of a curl about his lips. He said, a little hoarsely, "You enjoyed that, Lucinda."

"Oh, yes," agreed Lucinda in a dazed fashion. She appeared half asleep with her eyelids only half opened. But the glimmering of her eyes told a different story. She clung to his lapel. "How awful of you to take me unawares, Wilfred."

"Did you not guess my feelings for you?" he asked, reaching up one hand to brush her cheek. She nuzzled into his palm, and he cupped her face, once more lowering his head. He kissed her lingeringly, with a banked fire. "Well, Lucinda?" he asked softly.

"I thought that I saw something in your eyes, but as quickly as I looked, it vanished," said Lucinda. She glanced quickly at him, and as quickly away. "I . . . I was never certain that I had seen anything."

"I did not want to scare you off. You had told everyone how you did not intend to wed again. Oh, yes! I heard it from any number of people, Lucinda. It has been one of the ongoing *on dits* of the Season," said Lord Mays. He chuckled suddenly. "It was generally believed that the lady was protesting too much that she enjoyed her solitary state and that the real reason you had returned to London was to snare a second husband for yourself."

"But I didn't!" exclaimed Lucinda. "Oh, I am so mortified. I never guessed that I was the object of such rude speculation."

"You will not like it when I tell you that your cousin, Stassart, has offered odds in the clubs against your accepting anyone's suit," said Lord Wilfred.

Lucinda's eyes glittered. "Ferdie always did have the most abominable luck," she remarked.

Lord Mays gave a bark of laughter. His gold-brown eyes were alight as he gazed upon her. "I am glad in this instance."

Lucinda reached up to wind her arms about Lord Mays's neck and pressed close to him. "Wilfred, dear kind Wilfred! Pray kiss me again!"

Lord Mays was not at all loath to do so.

## Chapter Twenty-seven

The door opened quietly, but Lucinda and Lord Mays were oblivious to it. Miss Blythe stood on the threshold of the open door, stunned. Then she cleared her throat. She had to repeat herself several times before the intent couple finally realized that they were no longer alone.

Lucinda and Lord Mays turned their heads. His lordship at once released Lucinda, and she reached up in a vain attempt to smooth her hair. "T . . . Tibby! I did not realize that you had come in," she stammered.

"That is very obvious, my dear." Miss Blythe's visage was stern as she turned her gaze on the gentleman standing so awkwardly beside her blushing former pupil. "Lord Mays, what is the meaning of this?"

Lord Mays put a finger up to his cravat. It seemed to have tightened suddenly. He had come to think of Miss Blythe as a friend, and it was a distinct shock to be treated to her arctic stare. "I have asked Lady Mays to become my wife. At least, I actually haven't, but I hope that she will."

Miss Blythe turned her eyes to the younger woman. "Lucinda! Do you mean to stand there and admit that you yielded yourself to this exhibition without securing Lord Mays's declaration?"

Lucinda was fast recovering her equilibrium. Half laughing, she said, "I fear that I must, Tibby. It is shameful of me, I know."

"Do you intend to wed his lordship?" demanded Miss Blythe. There was a tremor in her voice.

Lucinda glanced at Lord Mays. He smiled crookedly at her and slipped his arm about her waist. She leaned comfortably into his embrace. "Oh, yes," she said softly, still looking into his face. "I certainly do intend to wed him."

Miss Blythe burst into tears. She fumbled for a handkerchief. "Forgive me!" she gasped. She turned and rushed out of the drawing room.

Lucinda and Lord Mays stared after her in consternation. Then they looked at one another, the same dismay reflected upon their faces.

"My word! What is that about?" exclaimed Lord Mays.

"I do not know, but I intend to find out," said Lucinda. She caught his hand. "Pray do not leave until I come back to you."

He raised her hand to his lips. His gaze was warm. "I shall ask Church to bring me something, some sandwiches and coffee. That will give me all the excuse I need to remain here kicking my heels."

"Thank you, Wilfred. I knew that I could depend upon you," said Lucinda.

"You may depend upon me for the remainder of your life," said Lord Mays simply.

Lucinda's color rose. She smiled at him before she exited the drawing room. In the entry hall, she discovered the butler to be hovering close by. Without wondering at all at the butler's convenient proximity, Lucinda said, "Church! Have you seen Miss Blythe?"

The butler bowed. "I believe that I saw Miss Blythe go into the library, my lady."

"Thank you, Church!"

"My lady, is something wrong? Miss Blythe seemed a little less than her usual composed self," said the butler.

"I trust not, Church," said Lucinda, already moving away. She bethought herself of something and paused to look back at the butler. "Lord Mays is hungry, Church."

"I shall see to it immediately, my lady," said Church.

Lucinda hurried on to the library. After a slight hesitation, she pushed open the door. She saw Miss Blythe at once. The lady was seated at the desk, penning a letter, occasionally setting her handkerchief to her nose to ward off another sniffle.

Miss Blythe had looked up when the door opened, and she smiled tearfully when she met Lucinda's anxious gaze. "Pray come in, Lucinda. I promise you that I shall not treat you to another such show."

Lucinda went over to her and knelt at her former governess's knee. Looking up into her face, she said quietly, "What is it, Tibby? Don't you wish me to wed Lord Mays?"

"My dear!" Tears came once more to Miss Blythe's eyes. She lifted her spectacles and wiped her eyes. "Drat! And I promised not to play the watering pot again. I have been too often in Agnes's company, I suspect!"

Lucinda laughed, somewhat shakily. "Yes, perhaps that sort of thing is catching. Now, Tibby, do cut line! Whyever are you so upset at the prospect of my marrying Lord Mays? Is it because he is my cousin-in-law, and that you fear I am making another hideous mistake? For I do assure you that is not the case. I care for Wilfred very much and—"

"No, no! You quite mistake the matter, Lucinda. I have nothing at all against the match. In fact, you and Lord Mays between you have made me very, very happy!" Miss Blythe's voice caught at the last. She laughed at herself and at Lucinda's expression.

"Oh, I can see that my behavior is quite inexplicable to you, Lucinda. Perhaps, if you read this letter, you will better understand." Miss Blythe offered the sheet that she had just penned to Lucinda.

Lucinda took the letter with a questioning glance at Miss Blythe, and then started to read it. She looked up quickly. "Why, it is to Mr. Weatherby! But what has he to do with my marrying Lord Mays?"

Miss Blythe gestured at the sheet. "Pray read it, Lucinda."

Lucinda shook her head, but did as she was bid. She exclaimed almost at once, but she did not look up until she had perused the last incredible line. Then she lifted her head and stared at her companion. "Tibby Blythe! Why, you sly thing! You have conducted a romance of your own all of these years and I never once guessed!"

Miss Blythe's cheeks had turned deep rose. "I suppose that it all sounds very clandestine and scandalous to you."

Lucinda rose to her feet and carefully placed the letter back onto the desk. "I frankly admit that I am confused, Tibby," she said. "But perhaps I should have realized that something was afoot when Mr. Weatherby suddenly stopped calling or making up one of my court. However, I would still never have connected that with you!"

"I had written to him to stay away, you see," said Miss Blythe. "After those terribly blunt opinions that he had uttered concerning Mr. Stassart, I knew that I could not trust him to keep my confidence. I don't mean that he would have deliberately betrayed what was between us, but that his intense desire to have the thing concluded would lead him into indiscretion. And that I could not have, for I did not wish to place any burden on you, dearest Lucinda!"

"Oh, Tibby, I still don't understand. Why would you send Mr. Weatherby away when you felt such an attachment for one another? What possible difference would it have made to me?" asked Lucinda.

"But, my dear, I could not leave you alone. I could not protect you from that first terrible marriage, but I hoped that I could help you to a better one. And so it has proven, for Lord Mays is just what I had in mind for you," said Miss Blythe.

Lucinda was touched by the depth of her companion's loyalty. She knew that it would be useless to point out to Miss

Blythe that that lady's own happiness should have taken paramount importance, so she did not even make the attempt. Instead, she asked, "Was Wilfred on your list of eligibles, Tibby?"

"Not at first, no. However, it soon became perfectly clear to me that you and his lordship were besotted with one another, but you were both too foolish to recognize it," said Miss Blythe. "And so I did my best to promote the match, quite unobtrusively, of course. That was why I accepted so easily your explanation of the friendship between you, and I did not cavil at leaving you alone with Lord Mays whenever the opportunity arose. Forgive me, Lucinda! I fear that I did scheme on your behalf, after all."

Lucinda laughed. "I shan't hold it against you, dear Tibby! It has all worked out for the best, just as you always thought it would. But now you must reveal to me how you came to love Mr. Weatherby and why you never wed the gentleman all of these years."

"That is simple enough. Marcus was already married," said Miss Blythe composedly.

There was a moment of silence. "Perhaps you should explain it all to me," said Lucinda with admirable restraint.

The story that was unfolded to Lucinda's fascinated ears was one of blighted love. Miss Blythe and Mr. Weatherby had known one another when they were young. They had fallen in love with one another, but before any declaration could be made, another woman had come between them.

"My elder sister," said Miss Blythe quietly, looking into the past. "Eliza was the beauty of the family, and Marcus had met her first. But somehow, after he had met me, he no longer had eyes for Eliza. She could not bear to lose him, especially to someone as plain as me. Eliza set about whispers that he had pledged himself to her, that there had actually been an understanding between them, and that he had cruelly renounced her. Since he had paid her court, it was all eventually believed. The storm of gossip and criticism gathered such weight that Marcus was forced to wed Eliza or risk social ostracism."

"That is why Mr. Weatherby reacted so strongly over Ferdie's public dramatics and also when I took my cousin into my

house," said Lucinda. She had sat down some minutes before
in a chair, her chin resting in her hand, as she listened.

Miss Blythe nodded. "Yes. It looked to be the same sort of
thing, and quite apart from the attachment that he knew I had
for you, Marcus wished to spare you the pain and ignominy of
such circumstances."

"The dear man. But surely, if he loved you, he might have
fought for you?"

Miss Blythe shook her head, a sad smile touching her lips.
"Marcus was a second son, and he had had to rely on benefactors to secure his first position. It would have cost him everything to have flown in the face of all that was arrayed against
him. And my father would never have consented to his suit for
my hand, not then. I begged Marcus to run away with me to
the border, but he refused. He knew that would only be the
crowning folly, and he would not condemn me to the inevitable life of penury and scandal."

"How awful. And so you could not be together." Lucinda
realized that the story was not complete. "But what happened
to your sister, his wife? And how did Mr. Weatherby find you
again after so many years, for I gathered from several things
he had said that he had spent many years abroad."

"Oh, yes, he did. Directly after they were married, Marcus
was posted to India. I suppose that his benefactors wished to
hush up the scandal as quickly as possible, and so they sent
them out of the country. Marcus did very well for himself in
India. He became quite a wealthy man," said Miss Blythe.
"But it was not a happy marriage. Eliza regretted most deeply
ever wedding Marcus, and perhaps his own bitterness at being
forced into the union had much to do with her feelings. In any
event, Marcus left the trading company and joined the army.
He was under Wellesley, the Sepoy General."

"You mean the Duke of Wellington," said Lucinda.

"His grace had not then distinguished himself to that
honor," said Miss Blythe, smiling. "When Wellington returned
to Europe to head up the British forces in the Peninsular, he
brought Marcus with him from India. Eliza was delighted, for
she thought that at last she would be going home. But by then
our father was dead, the lands had fallen into the hands of a

distant relation, and I was well embarked upon my career as governess. There was nowhere for Eliza to go. She was forced to remain with Marcus. He did the best he could for her by situating her in a large house in Lisbon and allowing her to mingle with Portuguese society to her heart's content while he was off with the rest of the troops. But it did not answer. Eliza never learned to like either foreign lands or their inhabitants."

"Tibby, surely Mr. Weatherby did not have the opportunity to tell you his entire life story," said Lucinda, awed.

Miss Blythe laughed. "That is just what he has done, my dear, as I have told him mine. We have been in correspondence for all of these years. Eliza detested it, but she could not stop it. I was always very sorry for my sister. She was completely unsuited to the man or to the life that she insisted upon taking to herself. Eliza died last year in Brussels."

"And so Mr. Weatherby came back to England for you," said Lucinda.

Miss Blythe nodded. "He knew where I would be, for I had written to him."

"That was why he practically foisted himself upon Ferdie that first evening at the theater. He did not actually wish to meet me, but he wanted an acceptable social introduction to you!" said Lucinda.

"No one remembered the old scandal anymore, but Marcus thought to simply reappear, claiming a long acquaintance with me, might resurrect it," said Miss Blythe. A tremulous smile touched her lips. "He said that he had waited too long to have all that old business dredged up to color our lives all over again."

"I have been shamefully used," said Lucinda, shaking her head. "I have been the shield for a torrid romance and not once did I suspect it. Really, Tibby, it is too bad of you not to let me in on your secret. I would have enjoyed encouraging Mr. Weatherby's attentions toward you."

"I have no doubt of that," said Miss Blythe dryly, which made Lucinda laugh.

The library door opened, and the two ladies turned inquiring faces. Lord Mays marched into the room. He took up a determined stance a few feet in front of Miss Blythe. There was a martial look in his eyes. "I have been thinking, and I have

*Gayle Buck*

come to a conclusion. Miss Blythe, I am sorry if you do not approve of my wedding Lucinda. However, I must tell you that neither your disapproval, nor anyone else's, will sway me in the least. I will still marry Lucinda."

"Wilfred, it is not at all necessary to—"

His lordship threw up his hand. "I am sorry, Lucinda, but Miss Blythe must be made to understand. I shall not give you up. That is the end of the matter."

"Bravo, my lord," said Miss Blythe approvingly. She rose from her chair and picked up her letter. "If you will excuse me, my lord, Lucinda, I have a very important letter to post." She left the library with Lord Mays looking after her in bewilderment and Lucinda laughing.

Lord Mays turned to Lucinda. "I don't understand. I thought she was set against it."

"Oh, not at all! Wilfred, it is the most famous thing!" said Lucinda. "You and I are to wed, and Agnes and Lord Potherby are to wed, and Miss Blythe and Mr. Weatherby are to wed!"

Lord Mays stared fixedly at her. "Miss Blythe and Mr. Weatherby?"

"Yes! They have loved one another for years, and now they may marry at last. Isn't it wonderful?" exclaimed Lucinda.

"As wonderful as all this might be, Lucinda, I must tell you that I will not be married in such company," stated Lord Mays unequivocally. "I have nothing against either gentlemen, nor Miss Blythe, but I won't have my cousin Agnes flooding the church with her tears. Deuced if I have ever met such an unstable female. I have just left her filling buckets in the drawing room."

"What are you talking about, Wilfred?" asked Lucinda, alarmed. "What has happened with Agnes?"

"She came into the drawing room while I was enjoying my sandwiches. I told her that I wished her well in her marriage to Lord Potherby. The next thing I knew she had thrown herself on my coat and burst into tears!" said Lord Mays. "She had such a clutch on me that I felt like a hooked fish. I was never more dismayed in my life."

"I expect that she was just expressing her happiness," said Lucinda soothingly. There was the hint of a quiver about her lips, however, for she could well imagine the scene.

"Well, she can express it all over Lord Potherby's coat front if that is what he likes," said Lord Mays wrathfully. "It quite put me off my sandwich, let me tell you. That started me thinking about Miss Blythe's dissolving into tears—who would have thought she had it in her!—and I realized just what I was up against."

"Whatever do you mean?" asked Lucinda, fascinated by his expression.

"Why, I know how tenderhearted you are. You wouldn't be able to stand for Miss Blythe to be unhappy. You would put me off, just until she got used to the idea, and then where would we be?"

Lord Mays answered his own rhetorical question. "There would be something else come up, such as your parents taking a dislike to me because of Mays, though we were never in the least alike. Or Potherby would switch his allegiance from Agnes to you again, and I couldn't have blamed him, for a sillier female I have never seen. Then there is your cousin Stassart—"

Lucinda was openly laughing by this time. "Wilfred, you dear sweet man. You are right, of course. We must not waste a moment. It will have to be a special license."

"A special license?" repeated Lord Mays. His crooked grin slowly appeared. "It will cause a flurry of gossip, Lucinda."

Lucinda walked her fingers up his damp lapel, obviously the area that had suffered the full onslaught of Agnes's happy storm. "My dear Lord Mays, I have been the center of speculation for years. It scarcely seems right to leave it all behind with a perfectly tame wedding ceremony."

Lord Mays caught her in such a tight embrace that it felt as though her ribs were cracking. But Lucinda did not care in the least. He was kissing her in a very thorough and satisfactory manner.